ffers, Alex.
u will meet a
ranger far from home :
12.
305224964852
09/20/12

you will meet a stranger far from home

WONDER STORIES

Alex Jeffers

LETHE PRESS · MAPLE SHADE, NEW JERSEY

YOU WILL MEET A STRANGER FAR FROM HOME: WONDER STORIES
Copyright © 2008, 2009, 2010, 2011, 2012 Alex Jeffers. ALL RIGHTS RE-
SERVED. No part of this work may be reproduced or utilized in any form or
by any means, electronic or mechanical, including photocopying, microfilm,
and recording, or by any information storage and retrieval system, without
permission in writing from the publisher.

Published in 2012 by Lethe Press, Inc.
118 Heritage Avenue · Maple Shade, NJ 08052-3018
www.lethepressbooks.com · lethepress@aol.com
ISBN: 1-59021-103-0
ISBN-13: 978-1-59021-103-8
e-ISBN: 978-1-59021-422-0

The stories in this volume are works of fiction. Names, characters, places, and
incidents are products of the author's imagination or are used fictitiously.

Credits for previous publication accompany each story.

Set in LTC Metropolitan and Missiva.
Cover and interior design: Alex Jeffers.
Cover images: tropicalpix (front)/Lior Filshteiner (back).

LIBRARY OF CONGRESS CATALOGING-IN-PUBLICATION DATA
Jeffers, Alex.
  You will meet a stranger far from home : wonder stories / Alex Jeffers.
     p. cm.
ISBN 978-1-59021-103-8 (pbk. : alk. paper)
I. Title.
PS3560.E33Y68 2012
813'.54--dc23
                                                    2012005440

For, what with my whole world-wide wandering,
What with my search drawn out through years, my hope
Dwindled into a ghost not fit to cope
With that obstreperous joy success would bring, -
I hardly tried now to rebuke the spring
My heart made, finding failure in its scope.

—ROBERT BROWNING: "Childe Roland to the Dark Tower Came"

Every second in a minute
that we breathe and call our lives
(you're not alone)
should be exciting as we make it

—THE YOUNG PROFESSIONALS: "Dirty Messages"

Argument

My first fiction sale, when I was sixteen, was a short story of the science-fictional far future entangled with myths of the far past. My first fiction *publication*, when I was seventeen (that first sale took two years to see print), was an even shorter story set in the mundane here-and-then and containing no elements that contradicted consensus reality.

Neither story is reprinted here. I would just as soon nobody ever read either ever again.

Still, they offer a productive exemplum: As a writer of fiction, I've always been a chimeric amphibian, unwilling to commit to a single mode or genre, scuttling from the antique, oblique, oceanic depths of myth and fantasy onto the muddy shores of the known and knowable, now and then leaping for the enigmatic stars. A very few of the very recent works in *You Will Meet a Stranger Far from Home* place themselves fairly securely in their appointed modes: realistic, fantastical, science-fictional. Most, however, are quite pleased not to be entirely one thing or another: chimerae. Amphibians.

All of them, together, are dedicated to you, O stranger I may never encounter, O amphibious reader, O Chimera!

Alex Jeffers
Pawtucket, Rhode Island
Spring 2012

Contents

Wheat, Barley, Lettuce, Fennel, Salt for Sorrow, Blood for Joy

FOR SANDRA MCDONALD, WHO WANTED A HAPPY ENDING

When Luke wakes with the dawn, he's pretty well sure where he is. Not his house in Berkeley, California—his bed at home doesn't rock except during earthquakes. He's aboard a big sailboat, the *Esin*, a Turkish gulet, which his dad chartered for a two-week cruise along the Aegean coast. But he's *not* in the bunk of his cramped little cabin that smells faintly bad, mouldy, musty—sour, as if some earlier passenger had given in to seasickness before reaching the head and residue still festers between the planks of the floor. He opens his eyes. The gulet's two masts go up and up into a cloudless sky blanching toward blue. He fell asleep on the foredeck, on one of the sunbeds. Somebody, Perla or his dad, threw a blanket over him before going below. The blanket and the bits of the sunbed that weren't covered—and his hair!—are damp with dew. The air smells so good, so salty and crisp. He inhales thirstily, pushes the blanket off, sits up.

Freezes.

Somebody lies sleeping on the other sunbed.

Not *somebody*. Levent. The deckhand. The beautiful, beautiful deckhand. Luke swallows hard. When he saw Levent the first time, boarding the *Esin*

composed 2011, Pawtucket/Providence, Rhode Island

first published in Boys of Summer, *edited by Steve Berman (Bold Strokes Books, 2012)* two days ago, he hadn't been able to think for a full thirty seconds. The thought that finally bubbled up was *Damn!* Then, *I'm going to kiss you if it's the last thing I do.* Levent was still wearing a shirt then.

Not now. Now he's pretty close to stark naked, no blanket or sheet, just the little scarlet swimtrunks he wore all day yesterday grappling the sails and whatever incomprehensible sailory duties as the *Esin* skipped down the coast, stretching and flexing so Luke hardly dared look at him or he'd start drooling.

He wants to look now—gaze, ogle, devour Levent with his eyes—but the sun coming up over the mainland hills puts Levent in shade. He's lying on his side so the light plates his upper shoulder, cocked hip, the length of one thigh in liquid gold, makes a brilliant halo of the dew clinging to his curly black hair. Shadow and his crooked arm hide the amazing belly and spectacular chest and Luke can't really make out his face. That face.

Luke's dreaming, soppy romantic dreams, swimming together through languid warm waters to a deserted beach where they recline in the shallows kissing and hugging and...when he realizes one of Levent's eyes is open. That Levent is staring at him. Him, sitting hunched over on the very edge of the sunbed with elbows on his knees and one fist covering his mouth as if to stifle a moan: him staring at Levent. Who's staring at Luke.

"Günaydın!" Luke chirps, one of three Turkish words he remembers, dropping his hands to where his dick yearns to burst through his boardies' Velcro fly.

"Good morning." Sitting up, Levent stretches and yawns. It's even harder to make anything out with him blocking the sun entirely, just a glowy nimbus around the Levent-shaped shadow. "Your father decided not to wake you. It is pleasant to sleep under open sky and stars—yes? Would you like coffee?"

"I don't think anybody else is up." Luke means Altan Efendi's, the captain's, wife, who served him coffee yesterday morning. Luke means he doesn't want Levent to disappear into the galley, though it would be wonderful if he moved just enough so Luke could see him properly.

Stretching again, Levent stands. Luke half imagines he can make out something stiff making interesting folds in the stretchy fabric of Levent's trunks. "Roisin Hanım is happy for me to make my own coffee," Levent says, turning toward the stern. Luke is even more sure of Levent's morning wood when he casually adjusts it with his big left hand. Sunlight catches the tattoos on the inside of his forearm, making the blossoms glisten like fresh paint. "You prefer it without sugar, I remember," Levent says and starts away.

Luke watches him go—that ass! Red fabric straining to contain the lush muscularity of it. "Teşekkür ederim!" Luke gasps.

Looking back, Levent grins broadly, sun glinting on wet teeth. "No problem," he says like an American, and keeps going.

Luke imagines himself saying *Augh!* as he collapses face down on the sunbed, but really he doesn't utter a sound. He's touched a few nice asses. Well, two. Wanted to do more. Four months ago he thought Douglas was working up to suggesting they do more but what he was really working up to was breaking up. Breaking Luke's heart.

Not really. Bruising it a bit.

Luke's dad thought Luke's heart was broken. At least that's the only reason Luke can think of why Sam insisted his seventeen-year-old son come along on this trip, this Blue Voyage. Luke hadn't been at all sure about a two-week Turkish vacation with his dad and new stepmom but he wasn't offered a choice. It would have to be better than the alternative: staying with his mom and her prick of a husband. He wonders if Perla had a choice. She's far from a wicked stepmother and as best he can tell likes him almost as much as he likes her, but it *is* pretty much her honeymoon.

They're down below him right now, in the master cabin, his dad and Perla. Sleeping or...not sleeping. Which isn't anywhere Luke wants to go.

When he abruptly sits up, he thinks he hears water running—splashing. Standing, he looks aft past the mainmast, through the wide windows and open door of the deckhouse. Levent's standing at the taffrail, standing tall and stalwart on the cushioned bench with his back to Luke, right hand on hip, left hidden. After a moment the splashing stops and Luke vividly imagines him shaking himself off, tucking himself in, tying up the drawstring of his trunks. Before he can turn around, Luke looks away.

No way *he's* brave enough to piss over the side but now the thought's in his head, the need pressing at his bladder. When he gets to the deckhouse door, Levent's already inside, hovering over the galley stove. He flashes another big grin as Luke edges past and down the companionway.

In the tiny head next to his cabin, Luke does what he needs to do, brushes his teeth, washes his face. No shower, but he swipes deodorant under his arms. Before he can stop himself, he spritzes himself with the really expensive French cologne Douglas gave him for Christmas, when they were still boyfriends. It's too much. He knows it. *If* Levent's gay (he probably isn't), *if* he's the least bit attracted to Luke (how could he be?), *if* Luke can muster the nerve to make a move (like that's going to happen), how do they manage to get up to anything interesting on a sixty-foot boat under the eyes of Levent's bosses and Sam and Perla? Plus, while sex would be have to be fantastic with a guy as handsome as Levent, there's no chance of any kind of relationship. Luke's going home to California in less than two weeks.

He climbs back up the companionway. The coffee must be done because Levent isn't in the upper cabin. On the stern deck under the canvas awning, a tray sits on the bench below the taffrail, just where Levent stood to piss. But no Levent.

Then Luke hears footsteps overhead. He ducks through the door, looks up. Crouched on the deckhouse roof, Levent beams down at him. "Coffee is served, sir. I will be down momentarily." He's holding a pitcher, watering a clay pot of something as green as the foliage painted under the skin of his left arm.

"What's that?"

Levent inspects the shrubby plant as if he has no idea. "Keklikotu. Cooking herb. In English, I think...oregano? Good luck for sailors: earth and herb from Efendi's garden to ensure we return home safe. Also Hanım uses it in the excellent meals she prepares."

Pointing behind Levent toward the flying bridge, Luke asks, "What about those?"

Levent glances over his shoulder. On either side of the bridge stand two old olive-oil tins overflowing with fiercely red geraniums. "Just flowers, for beauty. Those I irrigated first."

"And that?"

That is a round, shallow, closely woven basket perched on the edge of the roof two steps from the keklikotu. The first evening aboard, returning from a trip to the head, Luke saw Roisin Hanım up there, carefully scooping dirt from a bucket into the basket. She was murmuring something Luke couldn't hear—he had more trouble anyway with her Irish brogue than her husband's or Levent's accents and maybe she was speaking Turkish. Or Gaelic. As he watched, she sprinkled water over the soil, then scattered seeds from four different packets. She seemed completely intent on what she was doing, entirely oblivious of anything but earth, water, seeds. Feeling obscurely nervous, Luke didn't say anything and moved away before she looked up, joining his dad and Perla on the foredeck. With Sam's amused permission, Perla poured Luke a glass of Turkish white wine.

"That"—Levent doesn't even look, his expression blank, his voice flat—"is woman's business. Hanım's business." He jerks his chin up and back, a quick gesture Luke's already learned means the same in Turkey as an American headshake. "I am not to know. Not to inquire. Not to touch."

"Oh." Weird.

But Levent shrugs off whatever disturbs him and smiles again, crinkling the fine skin around his eyes. "Coffee?" Setting the pitcher aside, he swings nimbly down the ladder rungs bolted to the bulkhead. Somehow he misses the last step and staggers onto the deck, crashing one shoulder into Luke's chest. Startled, Luke grabs hold to steady him, then doesn't want to let go. He'd thought Levent was taller but it must have been an illusion of his beauty: they're the same height.

"Pardon my clumsiness!"

"No—" Luke doesn't want to let go. The warmth of Levent's flesh, slightly greasy with sweat and yesterday's sunscreen, sears his skin. He thinks he can feel Levent's heart beating. He *knows* he can feel a woodie working up in his own shorts. He lets go. "No problem."

Grasping his hand warmly, Levent leads him to the bench, sits him down, sits himself down really close, hips and thighs touching. Dumbly, Luke wishes his boardies were as short as Levent's trunks so it would be naked thigh to naked thigh. Levent releases his hand, but it's only to reach over Luke's lap to the tray. "Coffee! I remembered: no sugar. I hope you like it."

Luke can't taste anything but the sweat-sunscreen-saltwater fragrance of Levent fighting with his own cologne, but he sips from the little cup and says, "Very nice."

"Excellent." Holding his own cup with his right hand, Levent lays the left on Luke's leg, just above the knee. The visible fragments of tattoo look as bright as the hibiscus blossoms printed on Luke's boardies. "Are you enjoying your Blue Voyage, Luke Bey?"

Before they left California, Perla had sat Luke down for a little talk. She knew the Turkish Aegean coast well—her mother is an archaeologist specializing in the bronze-age Lycian city states, so Perla had spent pretty much every childhood summer in Muğla province. It wasn't archaeology she wanted to talk about, though. It was Turkish men. "They're really friendly," she said, "really affectionate and touchy-feely among themselves. So you'll see lots of very handsome men holding hands and hugging, but you absolutely can't assume they're gay. It's a different culture. If you get friendly with some kid he'll want to touch you, be close to you, but it's never about wanting to be your boyfriend or anything like that. Okay? It's different social norms, different conceptions of personal space."

So Luke knows he shouldn't make any inferences out of Levent getting so close. God, how he wants to, though. Throat tight, he says, "I'm having a great time."

"That is good. This morning, I believe, we sail a few more kilometers down the coast to a protected cove with a pleasant beach. No hotels and package tourists like here—" Levent waves his coffee cup vaguely toward shore, where rows of green canvas parasols and folded sunbeds mar golden sand, waiting for tourists from the hotels above the beach to descend. "Tomorrow, Perla Hanım and Sam Bey plan an excursion to ancient ruins a little inland."

"Perla's mother is working at those ruins, I think."

They're having a conversation, Levent and Luke, which is somehow astonishing until it's just a conversation. Before Roisin Hanım comes up from crew quarters below the stern deck, Luke learns that Levent isn't from Didim, the *Esin's* home port, but his father is and Levent's known Altan all his life, crewed for him on the gulet every summer since he turned thirteen. The rest of the year, he lives with his family in İzmir. His English is so good because, except for Turkish literature and history, all instruction at his high school was in English. He graduated a month ago—he's just a year older than Luke. They laugh, amazed, when they figure out they share the same birthday.

Luke remembers only now and then that he's totally infatuated. When Levent's face falls into brief repose, his features as classically regular and handsome as an ancient marble bust of Adonis. Or when he leaps up to make more coffee and half turns to beckon for Luke to come with him, the torsion and symmetry of his nearly nude body as elegant as the Diskobolos, but alive and human. When the sun hits his eyes at the right angle and Luke sees the opaque black rings around his irises, gleaming, lucent caramel brown bleeding into golden-green mandalas around the pupils. Sees sun glistening on thick black stubble rising through the flushed gold skin of his cheeks, chin, above his finely molded lips. Beautiful.

Levent interrupts his latest reverie with a question and Luke explains he's lived with his dad the last four years because he doesn't get along with his mother's husband. He doesn't say that Roger (he won't call the man his stepfather) is a homophobic born-again asshole and he despises the woman his mother's turned into since she married Roger.

"Have you thought about college?" Levent asks out of nowhere.

"Not really. Not yet. Why?"

"Because....." Levent looks away. Luke's struck dumb by the impression his profile makes against pale blue sky, then dumber when Levent squeezes his hand and goes on, "Because this autumn I will be attending the University of California at Berkeley."

Half a minute of utter shock later, Luke blurts, "That's half a mile from my house. I mean—less than a kilometer."

"I know." Still gazing out to sea, Levent smiles very slowly. "Not that it was so very close, that is, but that you live in Berkeley. It would be lovely for me to have a friend nearby when I go to live in your country. Shall we be friends, Luke Bey?"

There's no hope of throttling down the insane hope pounding in Luke's chest. "Yes!"

Levent squeezes his hand even harder. "Of course, I would wish to be your friend for this short time that you are aboard *Esin*, but perhaps in California we may become very good friends."

"I think that would be...excellent, Levent Bey."

Chuckling at the Turkish honorific, Levent turns the full force of his grin on Luke. "And then, you see, it would be quite sad for me if after a year my good friend were to go away to Princeton or Yale."

Brain racing, Luke's been thinking the same thing. Not Princeton or Yale, his SATs and grades aren't that stellar, but the little he's ever contemplated college has always involved running far far away from the Bay Area. *Maybe* he can get into Berkeley. San Francisco State for one safety school and, and...and he's *almost* certain Levent is just about to kiss him.

"Good morning, boys."

Roisin Hanım's cheery greeting makes Luke flinch and he wants to think he hears dismay in Levent's "Günaydın, Hanım."

"Levent made coffee for you, Luke? Lovely. Did you sleep well?"

"V-very well, thank you."

And then Levent's jumping up to help Roisin with breakfast—"Turkish breakfast or Irish breakfast?" she asks of the air. And then Altan Efendi is pacing around checking out every square millimeter of his beloved gulet—he clucks with mild disapproval over the dew-damp blanket Luke left crumpled on his sunbed and hangs it over the foremast's boom to dry. And then, slightly bleary looking, Luke's dad appears from below, plops down on the bench next to his son—not as close as Levent—and asks earnestly if it was okay for him not to wake Luke last night and insist he go below. Luke assures him it was just fine. He'll probably want to sleep on deck every night it doesn't rain. Then Perla, carrying a book, radiating calm pleasantness. Then breakfast, which Luke assumes must be Turkish because he can't imagine olives being part of an Irish breakfast.

It's a jolly meal, full of plans for the day, though Luke never says much of anything and realizes after a bit that he goes perceptibly blank every time he looks at Levent. So with a certain amount of conscious effort he stops doing it. He was never so moony over Douglas.

But Douglas had been loudly out since seventh grade so there was never the same kind of doubt. He waited to pursue Luke until after Luke came out years later, so no doubt there either. And Douglas was, is, merely cute, not as beautiful as a demigod.

Luke catches Perla peering at him, wonders if she's guessed he's doing what she warned him not to. Wonders if she'd been on the *Esin* before and Levent is exactly who she was warning him about.

That's a horrible thought. He won't allow it toehold in his brain. He wants to be Levent's friend. More would be awesome but you don't turn down an offer of friendship just because the guy isn't interested in messing around. Luke and Douglas are still friends.

Sort of.

Into a moment of silence, he says, "Will there be time for a swim before we set sail?"

Altan appears about to hem and haw, but Roisin says something in Turkish, then, "We're in no hurry, surely. But the cove where we plan to stop for lunch is much more pleasant—" she gestures toward the now crowded beach—"so perhaps just a quick dip. I won't need help, Levent, why don't you join Luke? Refresh yourself before my husband puts you to work."

Levent offers her the intoxicating splendor of his smile. "Teşekkür ederim, Roisin Hanım."

Half a minute later, both boys tumble over the side, crash into the deep blue water. When Luke surfaces, ears ringing, he hears a jocular "Watch out for sharks!" from the railing far above and flips his dad a cheerful bird.

Then something grabs hold of his ankles and he's going under again. He knows it has to be Levent so he doesn't panic but his mouth was open and his lungs empty so he does panic when salt water floods his sinuses. Looking up when Luke starts to thrash, Levent goes wide eyed. He lets go immediately. One powerful frog kick later, his arms are around Luke's chest, two, and both heads break the surface again and Luke's coughing on his shoulder.

"I'm sorry!" Levent bleats, sounding really frightened. "I'm sorry! Are you all right?"

"I'll—" Luke coughs again. "I'll be fine in a minute."

"I'm so sorry. I won't let you go."

Luke knows he ought to put his hands on Levent's head and push *him* under, that's what a roughhousing straight boy would do, but he's queer and though his throat feels flayed it's just so lovely to be safe in Levent's embrace. "I'll be fine," he grumbles again, "you just surprised me," and turns his head to rest his cheek in the crook of Levent's shoulder.

Levent murmurs something. Luke catches his name but the rest is Turkish garble. "What?"

"Nothing, really."

Lifting his head to catch Levent's eyes, Luke demands, "No, what did you say?"

Levent blinks. "I said, it is my very great pleasure to hold you like this, my friend." And then Levent lets go.

He isn't convinced he actually fell asleep but what he remembers was awful. He was thirsty, so thirsty, in a place where there was no water, just dust. An endless ocean of sepia dust broken only by distant outcroppings that might be isolated mountains, might be stupendous buildings. The air was so thick and sere, the oppressive brown sky so low, he couldn't really see, but he felt that if he could reach one of them he'd find something to drink. Eternal ripples and waves of dust brushed over his ankles as he slogged, billowed up to his knees. He couldn't see his feet. It shouldn't be a surprise that he would eventually trip, but it was a dream so it was a surprise.

He stumbled and fell headlong on top of something that wasn't dust, but dust puffed up all around, choking. Voices like sandpaper whistled, *We mourn. We mourn him, cut down in youth and beauty.* The fall knocked tears from his gritty eyes, though he felt certain he was too parched even to spit. He tried to lift his head so the tears would run into his mouth but the springs were already stopped up again. Desperate, he was ready to search with his tongue for damp residue in the soil or wet spots on stone, but he hadn't fallen on soil or stone. He'd tripped over a corpse.

A mummy. His knees had pulverized its pelvis, one fist broken into its rib-cage. Glittering like mica, tiny flakes of fossilized skin and flesh clung to his own lean, desiccated arm. Impelled by dream logic, instead of leaping up with a shout of horror, running away, he bent closer to search out traces of his tears on the cadaverous face. Black as pitch, lacquered by time and dehydration to the glistening imperviousness of chitin or obsidian, the craggy surfaces and angles appeared unmarked, as if the tears evaporated before they struck. The air was that dry.

Slow-rising fear made him wish to flee but flight seemed impossible. With a tremor of dry nausea, he saw marks on the mummy's glistening black cheeks, stains where varnished skin appeared to be decaying, crumbling from black glass to brownish powder. It was only a moment—if there was time in this place—before the bruises were disturbed further, from within.

Threads or tendrils like writhing fingers poked through dissolving skin, white flushed a sickly pink at the blunt tips, wriggling, reaching.

He wanted to pull back but could not.

They had heads, the tendrils, like minute serpents, coiling, seeking. But then, one after another, the heads split open and unfurled tiny leaves, ghostly pale, yearning for a light more nourishing than they would find in this dim desolation.

Reassured somewhat that the tiny shoots were merely terrible, inexplicable, not malevolent, distracted by thirst and his consuming need to move on, he hardly noticed the continued flaking away of fossilized skin around the mummy's eyes. But as pallid seedlings grew and leafed out with unnatural vitality, a kind of radiance bubbled up within stony sockets, stirring dust and mica into minute whirlpools, and the broken, vine-cumbered mummy regarded him with brown eyes he seemed to know.

There's some stickiness because Sam saw part of what happened when Luke and Levent jumped into the Aegean. Sam's pretty amazingly laid-backly okay with his kid being a fag (polar opposite of Luke's mom) but he's not going to stand for Luke going all colonial predatory on somebody who's essentially their employee. Who can't say no. Eventually Luke manages to work his dad around to crediting the True Story of how Levent came to be embracing Luke in deep water off the stern of the *Esin*, but it's still sticky.

Of course Luke doesn't let on to any of the subtext. Like how much he absolutely does want to jump Levent's bones. After the fact, it occurs to him maybe Levent wanting a friend in Berkeley (*going* to Berkeley) might undermine the colonialism argument but he isn't going to bring it up again. Wary of being seen to admire Levent, all nautical and active and sexy as the *Esin* sails south, he buries his head in his iPod and a book Perla loaned him about the local ancient civilizations. He can't concentrate, though, because he keeps catching corner-of-the-eye glimpses of Levent's long legs and handsome big feet and wondering why, if it was such a pleasure to hold him, Levent had let go.

Can't concentrate until his eyes catch on a line describing exactly the horrible place in his dream: the endless ochre desert in half light, low sepia sky, distant peaks that might be palaces or ziggurats half seen through clouds of dust. No water anywhere, the unceasing whisper of unheard voices. He's never opened this book before—how did it get into his head?

He flips back a page, two, searching for context. There's a cross-hatched drawing of an ancient artefact, a broken stone slab engraved with the image of two women in elaborate costume standing either side of a bare-chested man (a crack runs through his face, ruining it) whose long lance or spear pierces the body of some huge animal. Luke can't make out what it is and the caption doesn't tell him: the women are named Ninnin and Llad, the man Dimuz.

The pages-long passage that follows is translated from a series of fragmentary records collated into *The Story of the Rivalry of Ninnin and Llad*. It's an academic translation, painful to read, impeded by square brackets around multiple possibilities for uncertain words, curly brackets around hypothetical reconstructions of missing phrases, footnotes full of scholarly quarrels. Luke figures out right away the sepia place is the land of the dead where Llad rules, but it's heavy going between the indirect ancient manner of telling a story and modern interrogations. After maybe a quarter hour's struggle, he gives up—he's on vacation!—and slaps the book shut.

But still, how did Llad's terrible kingdom get into his dream? Was it a dream? He truly doesn't remember falling asleep or waking, no transitions or interruptions in the Esin's skipping progress.

Luke looks up. No sign of Levent, possibly just as well. His dad lies flat out, oiled and basted, baking brown. Perla's propped on her elbows beside him, reading her own book.

Decisive for a change, Luke sits up. Putting the iPod to sleep and pulling out the earbuds, he says, "Perla?"

Her big sunglasses turn. "Yes, Luke?"

"You've read this, right?"

Perla nods, but Luke already knew it. It's a standard text. Her real life doesn't have anything to do with ancient Anatolian history—she's a financial adviser—but she minored in archaeology at her mom's university.

"I'm feeling really vacay-stupid. There's this myth, I guess, translated from original sources, that I can't make sense out of."

Interested, Perla sets her book aside and sits up. One of the things about his stepmom, in the four years Luke's known her, is that she has a higher opinion of his intelligence than he does. "Which one?"

"*The Rivalry of Ninnin and Llad.*"

She nods again. "Not Lycian—older. Probably Sumerian origin, though the Mesopotamian myths are interestingly different. Ninnin's a version of Innana, Llad Ereshkigal." Then she seems to see Luke's expression and laughs. "Sorry. Not helpful, huh?"

"I just want to know the story."

"Okay. You're right. That translation isn't meant for readers. So Ninnin and Llad, they're goddesses and sisters. Llad, the older one, watches over the dead in the underworld. It's not like our Hell, all burny and fiery and eternal torments—really, it's kind of worse."

Luke shudders, remembering. "Yeah, I got that."

"It's like endless boredom until you wear away from the tedium, and it's everybody who ever died, not just the bad seeds. No Heaven to balance it out."

"I don't believe in Heaven," Luke protests, *except maybe on earth.*

"You've been arguing with Roger, have you?"

"I don't *talk* to Roger." Uncomfortable, Luke stares at his hands. "I'm really glad to be here with you guys now instead of back home."

"Luke," Perla says. "A: Don't listen to Roger. He's an ignorant bigot terrified of a world bigger than he's willing to understand. B: You're here because your dad and I wanted you with us. No fear, I'll let you know if you get in the way. And C: Did you figure out *Ninnin and Llad*'s a gay-pride story?"

"Huh—*what?*" Whiplashed, Luke swallows. "And, uh, thanks."

"Luke," Perla says again, but doesn't go further.

After an uneasy moment, Luke prompts, "Llad's the goddess of the dead...."

"And her little sister Ninnin—" Perla sounds relieved—"well, Ninnin's responsibilities aren't so well defined. She's a fertility goddess. One of her traditional epithets is *mother and daughter and sister of passion.* Somehow she comes into possession of a baby boy named Dimuz, it's not clear how, nor why she decides it would be better for her sister to raise him in the underworld instead of her doing it in the high houses of the gods."

"A baby in that place?"

"It doesn't seem to warp him much, but you can't expect psychological coherence in ancient myths. Dimuz grows up to be the most beautiful young man ever, a noble paragon in every way those people valued, and when he's around your age Llad sends him back to Ninnin in the upper world. Inappropriately, at least according to our way of looking at it, she tries to seduce him. He spurns her."

"He's gay?"

"They don't come out and say it. Didn't have the words. He prefers to spend time with his men friends, warring and hunting and drinking and so forth, and there's never any talk about him enjoying temple prostitutes or other women like all the other heroes. So, yeah, most open-minded scholars read Dimuz—the Dimuz in this story, there are others where it's not so obvious—as the least ambiguous strictly homosexual figure in the ancient record."

"Score!" says Luke.

"Jesus, Luke, sometimes you're just too adorable to tolerate."

From his prone position a few feet away, Luke's dad says, "I know, right?"

"Shut up, both of you." Luke's squirming inside his skin.

Perla and Sam both laugh. Sam gets up to sit by his wife. "Enough embarrassing the kid," he decides. "Get on with the story."

Grinning, Perla leans against him. For just a second Luke's envious of them for having each other. Acceptance and positive reinforcement are all very well—no, spectacularly excellent (Roger and his mom glower in the back of his mind), but he wants somebody to lean against. Levent. He imagines this ancient gay culture hero, Dimuz, might be almost as handsome as Levent.

"Ninnin decides it's her sister's bad influence that turns Dimuz away from her," Perla is saying, "so, rashly, she goes down to the gates of the underworld. Even though she's an immensely powerful goddess, she has to abide by the rules: she can't enter death in all her living, divine glory. The demon guardians strip her of her splendid clothing and jewels and send her off into the endless desert as naked as any of the uncounted dead souls wandering there. It takes almost forever for her to walk to Llad's palace. By the time she arrives she's just like the other dead, remembering nothing of her life or who she was, only that she desperately wants *something*. Llad doesn't recognize her.

"Meanwhile, back in the real world Ninnin's absence is having terrible effects. Without her divine vitality, an unending chilly drought overcomes the land. Crops and animals die. Famine spreads. The remaining gods become alarmed. They decide only Dimuz can fetch Ninnin back from death and rescue the upper world, so they carry him off from whatever good time he was having to the gates of the underworld.

"The guardians recognize Dimuz as their old playmate and their mistress's ward, somebody who belongs, so they're pleased to let him through with all his honor and glory and humanity intact. When he tells them why he's come, they search out Ninnin's fine clothing and jewels in their treasure house and adorn him like a queen. Then they send him out into death.

"Because of who he is, it takes Dimuz much less time to reach his foster mother's palace. He finds the shade of Ninnin right away. When he dresses her up in her own robes, she begins to remember who she is. He takes her to Llad, who agrees to escort her back to the world of the living. And then Dimuz reacquaints himself with the companions of his youth and proceeds to have himself a fine time."

"In Hell?" asks Sam.

"It's not Hell," says Luke, annoyed by his dad's interruption.

"He's a hero, having a fine time is the point of his existence." Perla shoves Sam a little with her shoulder. "And like I said before, you can't expect coherence or verisimilitude or plausibility in the fragments of ancient myth."

"Sorry." Sam is contrite. "Go on."

"While Dimuz enjoyed himself, the two sisters made the long weary journey to the high houses of the gods. All around them, the world came back to life—gentle rains fell, seeds germinated, baby animals romped. Both goddesses were dissatisfied. Ninnin recalled the burdens of her responsibilities in the world and felt a strange nostalgia for the restful unknowingness of death. Llad was confused, repulsed, by the vast vitality and multiplicity of the upper world as life returned to it. Ninnin was angry that Dimuz still didn't desire her, preferred death to her, and Llad slowly understood that she, too, longed for Dimuz's arms.

"But they made the best of it because, being gods, they had no choice. Fascinating sidelight. We've got Dimuz, one of the first gay men in recorded literature, and also one of the earliest clear references to lesbianism: the text says quite clearly that Llad and Ninnin *comforted one another* during the nights of their journey and continued so even after they reached the gods' precincts, because *only she recognized her sister's terrible longing for the man neither could have.*"

What Perla finds fascinating Luke thinks is squicky and demeaning, but she doesn't take it further so he doesn't say anything.

"The thing is, with Llad not in the underworld, the balance of the universe is off again. Now the upper world is *too* alive. Without death, it grows fat, rotten with excess, diseased. The other gods become alarmed again. They petition the sisters of life and death to make things right. So they return to the terrible gates and call Dimuz. He laughs at their attempts to bargain with him—they're gods, they only know how to demand—but ultimately agrees that if Llad returns to her place he'll spend part of each year in life, part in death.

"So Dimuz returns to his loves among living men—distant from but visible to the longing Ninnin—and then, after the season passes, goes back through the terrible gates into the welcoming arms of the dead, but not of death, Llad, permitted only to gaze on him from a distance, yearning."

"Whoa," says Luke. "That's really sad, in the end."

His dad nods—then brightens, with a sly glance at Luke. "For everyone but Dimuz."

"He is Adonis," gravely says the last voice Luke expects, "Dimuz. The beautiful youth all women mourn when he goes into death. You tell the story well, Perla Hanım."

Looking over Luke's shoulder, surprise unhidden by her sunglasses, Perla says, "Thank you, Levent Efendi. Yes, Dimuz is a version of Sumerian Tammuz, who's the ancestor of Adonis. The Greeks tried to rationalize the stories, though, according to their view of the universe."

Finally, still jumpy, Luke turns his head. Beautiful almost-nude Levent, handsome as Dimuz, meets his gaze and smiles sweetly. "Roisin Hanım asked me to tell you she's prepared a mid-morning snack."

The *Esin*'s sharp prow cuts through the Aegean. Spray billows over Luke and his dad and stepmom when they return to the foredeck. Sails boom and ropes clatter. Altan Efendi bellows basso-profondo Turkish commands from the bridge and Levent leaps to obey, or Roisin Hanım if she happens to be in position and not encumbered by a tray of fruit juices for the Americans. It's all very like the previous days' sails except no longer so novel, so Luke can imagine himself becoming bored.

Except he's wondering just how much of Perla's story Levent overheard. The gay stuff? And what was that about Adonis? All Luke remembers about that myth is that Adonis was beautiful, went hunting, got killed by a wild boar, and the wild anemones blooming at the time took on the color of his blood in mourning.

Anemones. He hasn't had a good look at Levent's tattoos. They're flowers—anemones? He's pretty sure none of the blossoms are blood red. He'll have to try to get closer (which he wants to do anyway, of course) because he'll recognize anemones. Perla used to grow them in her garden before she sold that house to move in with his dad.

It seems only a moment later—Luke deep in dopey fantasies of cavorting with Levent in a meadow bright with flowers, so he has to lie flat on his belly—when, under power, sails furled, the *Esin* putters between two small rocky islands into a round cove surrounded by high cliffs. Luke jumps up and runs to the rail. From the flying bridge atop the deckhouse, Altan Efendi lets out a bellow of satisfaction: no other Blue Voyage gulet is there before them. He has Levent drop anchor where the water is deep and blue, but only ten yards toward shore the bottom of the cove bellies up nearly to the surface, turning the water lemon yellow for another fifty yards before it ripples against the tawny beach.

Luke's antsy all of a sudden. He wants to plunge into the tempting water, rinse the scum of dream sweat and sunscreen from his skin. Wants to stagger onto solid land that doesn't rock and roll underfoot, just for a change, to find running fresh water and smell green growing things, not endless salt and himself.

As if divining Luke's impatience, from above Altan Efendi booms, "We will go ashore in a few minutes, genç efendim. Let my wife and Levent just finish loading our luncheon into the dinghy."

Startled by the voice breaking into his tunes, Luke looks up from the green-blue water and pulls one earbud out. The captain waves genially and Luke removes the other bud. "Can I help?"

"I believe they have everything in hand."

Nevertheless, Luke grabs his book and sunscreen, the tray of juice glasses because it's there, and wanders aft. Perla and Sam have already vanished—down to their cabin to pull themselves together or whatever. As Luke rounds the deckhouse, Levent is just lowering a big red cooler over the taffrail. He happens to glance up.

Levent's grin hits Luke right in the eyes and he stumbles, blinded. The tray goes flying. Luke hears an unlucky glass encounter the rare metal fitment and musically shatter. The other two merely thud on wooden deck. Somehow he's on his knees and one stinging palm.

The pang in his hand isn't just impact. Before he can determine what it is or whether it should bother him more than embarrassment, someone has an arm under him, lifting him up, somebody's concerned voice is saying something Luke doesn't understand.

"I'm sorry, I...tripped?"

"It was my stupid fault, Luke," Roisin Hanım is muttering, her brogue thick and melodious. "Some sailor I call myself, leaving things strewn about for the unwary to trip over. Sit up now, let me see." She has him sitting back against the deckhouse bulkhead, she's holding his hand in both of hers.

"I'm bleeding," Luke observes. It doesn't seem to concern him much although there's rather a lot of it pooling in the palm Roisin holds up, dribbling between numbed fingers.

"Yes. An unfortunate encounter with broken glass." Leaning over his hand, she's being very calm. "Levent."

"Here." Looking frightened but resolute, Levent sets the enamelled-metal first-aid kit on the deck, unlatches it. "What do you need, Hanım?"

"Your eyes, my dear. I don't trust my own. We wish to be sure there are no fragments of glass or splinters in Luke's wounds. Tweezers, if you find anything."

She's not simply holding his hand, Luke realizes: she's clamped fingers and thumb tight around his wrist in a kind of flesh-and-bone tourniquet. He wonders, should he be worried?

Breathing thinly through his teeth, Levent squints over Luke's palm, swabbing up blood with a wad of cotton, probing gently with fingertips, then the pointed tips of a pair of bright steel tweezers. There's a momentary wince when he pulls something out of Luke's flesh but whatever it is is so small Luke can't see it. Levent goes back to work.

Now nausea begins to rumble in Luke's belly and a fog of some kind of great weariness creeps up his unnaturally extended arm. If his tears nurtured vines within the fossil flesh of the mummy in his dream, he wonders, what would blood provoke?

"Ow," says Levent.

Luke blinks back to alertness.

"What is it, dear?"

Levent doesn't reply. Wielding the tweezers with the wrong fingers, thumb and middle, he picks out another invisible fragment and drops it into Roisin's free, open hand. "I believe that's all," he mutters, peering hard, then sets the tweezers aside. His fingers are gummy, rusty with thick stains. "Luke Bey's hand needs to be washed. Then we can look again."

"Yours too," Luke blurts just as Levent sucks the bloody index finger into his mouth. Roisin lets out a little gasp and Luke, angry with himself, says, "You cut yourself!"

When Levent withdraws his finger it's not really clean, filmed with saliva and diluted blood, but cleaner than the others. Knuckles left red smudges on his chin. He regards the index finger's tip for a moment, his expression blank, and mutters, "A minuscule scratch."

"Let me see!"

Levent smiles—not the grin that turns Luke into a quivering pile of yearning, just a twitch of the lips that's somehow more affecting. "Of course, Luke Bey." A tiny bead of blood forms on the pad of the finger Levent's showing Luke before it dissolves into red feathers penetrating the slick of spit. "See? It's nothing."

Roisin hmmphs and releases Luke's wrist. "Go wash your hands, boys," she says, pushing Luke away—into Levent's arms.

As Levent helps him upright, Luke sees the thing he must have tripped over. Kicked nearly into the scuppers, the flat basket had scattered crumbs of earth across the deck, but not much. Less than two days after he watched the seeds sown, the basket's already crowded with seedlings, their roots knitting the soil in place. Then Roisin moves into his sightline, hiding the thing. "Tread carefully, boys. Watch for more glass. I'll clean it up in a moment."

It can't have taken any time at all. Perhaps glasses are always being broken aboard the *Esin*. Altan Efendi didn't come running from the bridge to see what was up, Perla and Sam didn't pop out the door Levent's leading Luke through, his steady arm strong around Luke's back, holding him upright as though he was unsteady.

He is unsteady. It's just a scratch, a couple of scratches. He's unsteady because Levent is holding him. He's unsteady because Levent licked his blood, both their blood, off his finger. Sucked the finger into his mouth like it was something else.

Unexpectedly, Levent half pushes Luke right past the galley. At the top of the companionway, Luke almost balks but then clatters down, half dragging Levent after, and pushes open the door of the little head next to his cabin. There isn't really room for two full-sized people inside so Luke has to practically climb onto the toilet lid before Levent can close the door behind them. Clambering down, he wonders, hopeful, why the door needs to be closed, and pulls a mad notion from the back of his mind. "Let me see your finger again."

Just reaching for the faucet, Levent hesitates. His lips tilt into the unearthly, close-mouthed smile and he lifts his right hand. Before Luke quite sees the tiny jewel-like blob of blood, before he's quite sure what he's going to do, the finger's sliding between his lips.

It doesn't really taste like blood. He doesn't think it does. Salty.

Levent's eyes narrow a bit and his smile widens just enough to reveal the wet pearls of lower teeth. In Luke's mouth, the finger twists, scratching at his tongue. Lower, outside his mouth, Levent's thumb pushes into the fleshy spot under Luke's chin. Slowly, Luke's face is drawn forward. This time they're really going to kiss.

"Let's wash up, Luke Bey," Levent says, voice low and amused, and Luke realizes he's about to plaster a bloody palm print on Levent's chest.

The finger pulls free with a liquid slurp.

Shoulder to shoulder, they wash their hands under trickles of tepid water. The soap stings Luke's wounds. Levent makes sure he does a thorough job. When Luke's hand is clean, the tiny cuts welling sluggish blood, Levent inspects it meticulously. He finds no more glass. Before he smears it with antibiotic ointment (Luke hadn't noticed him bringing the first-aid kit with him) and mummifies it in cotton gauze, he raises the palm to his lips and kisses it. "I feel your accident was my fault," he murmurs.

Luke can't process the suggestion, as ludicrous as it is accurate, and merely gapes while Levent tends to his hand. Levent's fault? Because he's distractingly beautiful and Luke's an infatuated klutz? A glimpse of pastel colors prompts him. "Tell me about your tattoos," he blurts, desperate.

"My flowers?" Levent turns up his left forearm as if to inspect the tattoos himself, faintly surprised by their blossoming under his skin. "They're pretty, aren't they?"

They grow up from the tangle of blue veins at his wrist, five sinuous stems intertwined with shorter stems of foliage like Italian parsley, each surmounted by a single open blossom: lavender, white, blue, pale blushy pink, blue again. "We call them *mountain tulip*, dağ lalesi, though they aren't tulips. I don't know the English name."

"Anemone," Luke says, certain now.

"Really? We have a flower called anemon. It's similar, I suppose, not as showy, and it blooms in the spring, not summer like these."

"One variety of anemone—the prettiest." Luke grazes one of the blue blossoms with the tip of a finger. Its purple-black center gleams, surrounded by a corona of blue-black stamens. Levent's skin is warm. "Or windflower. That's the antique English name, because the petals bruise so easily. You don't have a red one."

"No. Or not yet."

Something's happening. Levent's other hand's coming up, open and defenseless as a windflower, to brush fingertips against Luke's stubbly cheek. "There's a story about the red flowers," he says, eyes still lowered, "an old, sad, Greek story."

Luke wonders if the tiny cut on Levent's index finger is still open, painting his own cheek with filaments of red. "The blood of Adonis."

Unsurprised, Levent raises his eyes, his chin. They kiss.

They jump apart when heavy footsteps sound on the companionway outside the closed door and Luke's dad says, "Luke? We're all waiting."

"Sorr—" Luke can't get in a breath. "Sorry, Dad. Just a minute."

Sam's feet thunder back up the stairs. Levent's grinning at Luke, as if they were merely friends, before he turns to latch and heft the first-aid kit.

"Kiss me again," Luke demands.

"Your parents and my employers are waiting."

"Kiss me again."

"Very well. With great pleasure."

Sam and Perla and Levent swim ashore but Luke's ordered into the dinghy with Altan Efendi and Roisin Hanım. He feels clumsy, the hand bandaged into a useless paw so he couldn't row if they needed him to—they don't, Altan powers up the noisy outboard—and gazes yearningly after Levent's supple golden back and flutter-kicking feet. That luscious ass, his trunks the same scarlet as an anemone's petals. Two brief kisses. No tongue, even. Barely an embrace.

It's hardly a moment before Altan grounds the dinghy prow-first on the beach. Luke's no help fetching out the cooler and baskets, not even spreading the beach blanket. "How did this happen?" his dad wants to know, inspecting the white gauze wrapped around his son's hand.

Luke's relieved not to see any blood spots seeping through. He imagines Roisin has already told the story and Sam only wants confirmation. "I tripped and broke a glass and fell on it. It's not much, really. Lev—" It's hard to say the name without making it a revelation, as if his friend were just anybody. "Levent overdid the bandages. It'll be fine tomorrow, just scabs."

Salt water drips from Sam's hair onto the gauze, darkening it. "You're sure?"

"Positive."

"Okay." Sam squeezes, then releases the bandaged hand. "Let's have lunch."

After they eat, a bewildering array of savory finger foods (some, Roisin confesses, from cans), and drink (Turkish beer for the grown-ups, sour-cherry juice for the boys), Altan and Levent ferry baskets and cooler and dirty dishes back to the gulet. Talking—what about? Luke wonders, then stops wondering—Perla and Roisin wander along the beach, Perla in her swimsuit splashing through the shallows while Roisin Hanım on dry sand is still wearing a shirt and white pants. Is her modesty, if it is modesty, Turkish or Irish, Luke wonders, Muslim or Catholic?

Looking away, he stops wondering. The *Esin* floats serenely at anchor on the blue bay. Tethered to its flank, the dinghy wallows when substantial Altan Efendi clambers down into it, casts off, steers back toward the beach. No Levent. Washing dishes in the galley, presumably. Disappointed, Luke sighs.

"Are you having a good time, Lukey?" Sam asks.

"Huh?" For a second, more than a second, Luke doesn't hear the question, doesn't recognize it's a question. "Yeah! Absolutely." He remembers something about his dad. "I don't even remember...wotzisname." He does remember Douglas. Fondly, even. He's not an utter amateur because of Douglas. Risking a glance, he sees Sam doesn't appear convinced. "Thanks for not leaving me with Mom and Roger for two weeks, Dad, really."

A crease folds the skin between Sam's eyebrows. "They're rather...unevolved, aren't they?"

"They don't believe in evolution. Let's not talk about them. What about you? You and Perla. I'm not getting in the way too much, am I? I mean, it's your honeymoon."

Sam shakes his head, a don't-worry-about-it shake. "You and Levent seem to have made friends pretty quick."

Luke persuades himself not to gulp or blush, not to look away from his father's regard. "Like Perla says, they're friendly people, the Turks. And he's a great guy, Dad. Really bright. Smarter than me, I bet, I can barely speak English—" Luke's best grades and SAT scores, his only admirable grades, are in English—"let alone a second language. He's going to college this fall, you know."

"That's good." In Sam's world every young person should go to college.

"In the States, Dad. Berkeley. Half a mile from our house."

Sam's eyes widen.

"So, like, it's not just these few days on the boat. He'll need friends in California. I like Levent a lot, Dad, and I think he likes me."

Sam shakes his head, an I-was-afraid-of-that shake. "Lukey, look—" Another shake, and Sam squeezes his eyes shut for an instant. "*That way*, Luke? Do you think you like him that way?"

Luke blinks. He hates when Sam talks to him like he was a little kid. It makes him angry and rash. "Levent is extremely handsome, Dad, he has a really great body, of course I'm attracted to him." *He's attracted to me, too. He kissed me. Twice.*

Looking intent and fierce, protective, like a papa bear, Sam reaches for Luke's arm, the wrist of his good hand. "His tattoos, Luke. Five flowers, here—" He traces their position on the flesh of Luke's forearm. "Altan Efendi told me, he was proud of the boy. One flower for each of the foreign tourist girls he fooled around with over the last five summers aboard the *Esin*. I don't want your heart broken again, Lukey."

"Oh." He can't think. *It wasn't broken the first time you thought it was,* he thinks.

"I'm sorry, baby. Better to know, though, right?"

He kissed me. Perla didn't say anything about Turkish BFFs kissing each other, just holding hands and hugging. "Yeah, I guess." He musters up some bravado. "Well, you know, I do have a couple of straight guy friends. Who're good looking enough I'd be willing to fool around with them if they were interested. So it's like that. Levent's still going to need a friend in Berkeley. It's fine."

"Is it?"

Of course it's not, you stupid man. The thought makes him feel bad as soon as it forms. He loves his dad. Sam loves him, cares for him, as he is, imperfect and dumb and gay, not as he *should* be. "It's fine, Dad. I'm fine. You want to go for a swim?"

"Your hand?"

Luke's already tearing off the gauze Levent wound with too much, with false, care. "Salt water's good for little cuts."

Dozing on the warm beach afterward, all sunscreened up (the stuff stung in his cuts worse than the sea's salt), Luke seems to recall another ominous dream. Dripping blood-warm salt water, he had clambered out of the cove onto the rocky, scrubby flank of one of the small islands. Any moment he expected to reach its crest and gaze out over the wine-dark Aegean. (*Wine dark.* What did that mean exactly?) But he kept scrambling and the moment never came. After a while he ceased smelling the sea, only the salt crust on his skin dissolving as he sweated. Salt made the scents of the dry brush he blundered through, the green herbs he trod on, more vivid and strange.

Suddenly he seemed to hear voices and rushed ahead. Suddenly he was running up a narrow, rutted alley instead of a hillside, with tall, plastered, windowless walls on either side, packed earth and pebbles underfoot. The voices came from overhead, yelling, keening, women's voices: *We mourn. We mourn him, cut down in youth and beauty.* He tried to halt, to look up for the grieving women, but found he couldn't. As he ran up the steepening street, panting, baskets and terra-cotta dishes began to fall from the sky—from the tops of the walls. Dirt scattered from the vessels as they struck the street, dirt and the wilted plants that had been rooted in them.

Something hit him in the back of the neck and he fell to his knees, crying aloud. But now the street had vanished, or he had vanished from it: his knees crushed fragrant green grasses and all around him ghostly white anemones bloomed, bobbing on their long, springy stems. He plucked from the grass a shard of red terra cotta, its surface crusted with dried soil engraved with the hair-thin worm tracks of countless roots. Littered across the grass were clumps of dying or dead young plants, earth still clinging to their roots, limp and yellowed as if they were rotting or dried out, grey.

He heard laughter, masculine laughter. It was familiar, he thought. It was Levent, he was certain.

When he rose and saw the youth standing at a little distance in the meadow of white anemones, leaning on a tall wooden staff, he nearly ran, calling, but remembered what his father had told him. Levent, if it was Levent—his back was turned, his naked ass as spectacular as Luke had imagined—was not alone.

One woman wore black, not black clothing but darkness, the other brilliance. They were arguing in voices like harsh, incomprehensible thunder, not with the young man before them but each other, and the subject of their argument—Luke couldn't doubt it—kept laughing, scornful. At last, he seemed to shrug, said something low and bitter, and began to turn away.

Both women roared. Luke didn't see how it happened. Instead of two unearthly women, a single enormous beast coughed, suddenly impaled on the tip of the youth's staff—his spear. It scrabbled at the ground with its hooves, tearing up soil and grass and pebbles, grunting horribly as it forced the lance deeper into its chest. Small eyes gleamed red and red blood drooled around its tushes. Although its foot was anchored in the ground, the youth could barely hold his spear as the huge boar—or was it a sow?—made it bow and tremble.

The spear splintered. Unprepared, the sow nearly stumbled before her stumble became a rush. The youth laughed again before her sharp teeth opened his flank.

"No!" Luke yelled, waking himself up.

We mourn. We mourn him, cut down in youth and beauty.

All the white anemones flushed blood red.

It's hard to be cold toward Levent, especially because he keeps seeing his friend ripped open by the wild pig's tusks, but Luke has a certain amount of self respect and manages somehow. Despite Levent's obvious confusion and hurt. After the long sail into dusk and then night to the next anchorage, after the very late supper, before Perla and Sam finish their coffee and Turkish white wine, Luke excuses himself and goes belowdecks. Angry with himself for being taken in, with Levent for encouraging his stupid delusion, he undresses, brushes his teeth, climbs into the narrow bunk.

Can't sleep. The stifling cabin still smells pukey. He'll never sleep again.

A very long while later, he hears his dad and stepmother come down the companionway. He knows it's them—they pass the door of his cabin to enter the honeymoon suite, not much bigger than his cabin and oddly shaped, the bed triangled into the Esin's pointed prow. Then, louder, Altan Efendi's tramping feet, turning at the bottom of the stairs toward crew quarters in the stern. Luke thinks, can't be sure, he hears Roisin Hanım's lighter tread echoing her husband's. He waits, counting seconds in his head until he loses track, then waits longer. Everybody aboard *must* be asleep.

Barefoot and naked, Luke slips off the bunk and eases his door open. Trailing the fingers of both hands along the bulkheads to either side, he tiptoes through the dark, manages not to stub a toe on the lowest step, climbs the companionway to the deckhouse. Still no lights. First he goes to the forward windows and peers through. Moonlight and starlight just suffice to reveal the slumbering lump of Levent on the starboard sunbed.

Coming out the deckhouse door, Luke's distracted by the smell of something stronger than the Aegean's salt—something green. The keklikotu? He doesn't think he's ever smelled fresh oregano, only dried from the shakers on the tables in pizza joints. It's not that, not as sharp and unpleasant until cooking tames it, more like lawns and January meadows after rain.

Oddly curious, he finds the rungs bolted to the bulkhead and climbs. Levent isn't going anywhere. He doesn't know what to say to Levent anyway. When his head rises above roof level, he smells the oregano, recognizes it—the pot is right there—but it's muted, overwhelmed by the other scent. Not the geraniums by the flying bridge, definitely not geranium. New grass and something blander, and something like the tongue-shrinking tang of licorice.

It's the basket, Roisin's basket. On hands and knees, cautious, Luke approaches. What did Levent say? *Woman's business. Hanım's business. I am not to know. Not to inquire. Not to touch.*

Moonlight and starlight bleach the overcrowded new foliage to silver. Luke didn't know any seeds sprouted and grew so fast—two, not quite three days. Slender blades like grass, tiny whorls of lobed leaves like fancy French lettuces, sprays of feathery stuff on swaying stems. He leans closer.

"Don't touch!"

Startled out of his wits, heart hammering, Luke collapses, rolling onto one shoulder. Darker and denser than night, eclipsing stars and half the crescent moon, Levent looms over him.

"I told you, it's woman's magic, dangerous for men."

"Magic?" Luke blurts. Then, outraged, "You like girls!"

A loud intake of breath. "I don't dislike them."

"You *don't* like boys. Me! You sleep with girls! Altan Efendi told my dad and Dad told me."

"In some ways, Efendi is a very stupid man." Levent hunkers down to his haunches. "Luke Bey. Is that what it is? I have slept with women—well, not much sleeping—any man can, you could."

"No, I couldn't. I wouldn't."

"It wasn't my choice, Luke. What I desire women don't have."

"What?"

Reaching before Luke can shy away, Levent strokes his cheek. "Stubble. Beard stubble on your handsome face. Sexiest thing ever. Drives me wild." His fingers feather down over Luke's chin, neck. "A flat, strong chest with a little hair on it. Or a lot, if you should happen to grow a lot as you get older. Muscles. Something else."

Luke chokes the word out: "Dick."

"In a word. In my hand, in my mouth, in— You're not wearing any clothes, Luke Bey."

Almost embarrassed but more thrilled, and hornier than that, Luke sits up. "Are you? Levent Bey."

"More than I could wish."

"Take them off."

"Willingly. When we get down from the roof, away from...*that.*"

Luke's already scrambling to his feet—keeping a safe distance from the innocuous basket of seedlings and earth—when he remembers he's angry. With Levent. Who just called him sexy. Beautiful Levent. Who sexed up a different tourist girl every summer. "What about your anemones?" he demands. "Like trophies, one for each girl."

"Please, Luke." Levent's already on the ladder, his head level with Luke's knees. "Not now and not here."

Unmollified but still horny and acutely ready to be convinced, Luke follows. Inexplicably, it's when he's hanging halfway down the ladder that it properly penetrates that he's nude—naked as a jaybird in mating-season display. What if his dad—or, horribly worse, Perla—were struck by insomnia and felt a need to stroll up on deck?

Levent has already vanished around the deckhouse. Luke scurries after, finds him waiting with apparent calm seated on the port sunbed. The one Luke slept on last night. The folded blanket sits beside him. Levent hasn't removed his swimtrunks.

Wanting more than anything ever to sit right beside him but stubbornly determined to remain angry, Luke snatches the blanket. Flipping it half open, he wraps it around his waist and sits on the other sunbed. Without sun, with a yard between them, he can't make out Levent's expression as the other boy launches into speech.

"When Adonis—Dimuz goes down into death, all women mourn. They use their private magics to call him back, ensure he returns life to the world—"

"No," says Luke, impatient with mythology. "Just tell me this. It's boys you really like? Me?"

Rising to his feet, Levent pulls apart the drawstring of his scarlet swim trunks, pushes them down.

"I had a fascinating talk with Roisin Hanım yesterday," Luke's stepmother says.

"Oh?" says Luke, not really interested. He's still glowing, thinks he is, though he's tried to keep the brilliance damped. Exhausted, too. They didn't really do anything, him and Levent on the sunbed on the *Esin*'s foredeck, nothing Luke hadn't already done with Douglas—didn't do, actually, quite a few of the things Douglas had taught him—but they were awake all night anyway. Barely remembered, when dawn began to grey the sky, that Levent needed to pull his trunks back on and pretend to have slept, Luke scuttle frustrated belowdecks to put on something himself.

"The *Esin* and the summer Blue Voyages aren't what support them at all," Perla goes on. "Roisin calls the boat Altan's charming, expensive hobby. Roisin's shop in Didim brings in the significant part of their income."

"Oh?" Just a polite noise, a prompt. Luke hadn't wanted to debark from Altan Efendi's hobby, ride in an open Jeep up to visit the Lycian rock-cut tombs in the cliffs above the little fishing village—lose sight even for a moment of Levent. Levent sat right beside him through breakfast, nudging him now and again, throwing an arm around his shoulders, all the jokily affectionate bro-touching Turkish boys were permitted, frustrating as all hell. But also, under the table, now and then caressing or tickling him, rubbing his calf against Luke's, knocking their ankles together, trailing his toes across the insanely sensitive tops of Luke's feet. Even more frustrating. "What does she sell in her shop?"

"Levent hasn't told you? Roisin's a tattoo artist—she did his anemones."

"Really?" Startled, Luke looks up. They're sitting, stepson and stepmom, at the base of a grey cliff overlooking the village on its bay far below. Luke had pled tiredness and a false soreness in his scabby palm when Perla's mother with unnatural vigor for her age wanted him to climb with her to the high, sheer tombs. Sam had been eager but Perla said she'd seen it all before and stayed with Luke. "Roisin Hanım doesn't have any tattoos. Altan Efendi either."

"Altan's old fashioned. Traditional Islam disapproves of body modification about as much as traditional Judaism." Perla regards the inscription engraved in ancient Lycian letters around her own right wrist. She confessed once that it wasn't entirely grammatical, something her mother still gives her grief over, but refused to translate it. "Roisin's ink isn't where you can see it. She didn't do it herself, of course. Her teacher in Cork city, before she came to Turkey on holiday and fell in love."

Luke wonders if *he's* in love, on holiday in Turkey. He knows he was never in love with Douglas. In the harbor below, he can pick out the *Esin* moored among other Blue Voyage gulets—the fishing boats left with the tide—but not any of the people aboard. If they're aboard. Is Levent thinking of him, doing make-work boat maintenance with Efendi or carrying packages in the market for Hanım? "Why anemones?" he asks, feeling a stab of terror as he recalls the unexplained girls the blossoms represent. "Why did she ink anemones on Levent's arm?"

"For Adonis, of course," Perla says, as if it were an explanation.

"What?"

"Look at the rooftops in the village, Luke."

"What?" He can't see that far.

"They don't call him Adonis, probably, or Dimuz either, the women of the Aegean and Mediterranean coasts, when they plant his midsummer gardens. It's just custom, tradition, what's always been done."

"Gardens?" Luke's trying to see anything on the roofs far below. "Roisin's basket of seedlings on the deckhouse roof?"

"It's a fertility ritual, of course. They're all fertility rituals. Older than Turks and Islam in Turkey, older than Judaism probably. Roisin learned it from her mother-in-law, I imagine. The seasons of fertility, for sowing and harvest, are very different here than in Ireland. As the killing heat of midsummer approaches, the women remember Adonis under all his names and none, the god who dies every year, taking the world's virtue with him, and then is reborn. In his memory, they plant small gardens of seeds that germinate and sprout quickly, grain and herb, wheat, barley, lettuce, fennel. They die quickly, too, young like ever young Adonis. Too hot, not the season, perhaps the gardeners *forget* to water them for a day or two. Then, midsummer night, in a cataclysm of grief, they hurl the withered little gardens into the street or the sea and mourn the momentary death of beauty. It's very cathartic."

She's done it herself! Luke thinks, surprised. Usually he thinks of Perla as a pragmatic businesswoman, less romantic and given to fantastical gestures than Luke's own dad. Also: *She's not telling me everything.* It's women's business, women's magic, not for men to know. They're grieving, those women, the beautiful men who don't desire them, working magic to change their natures.

"Are you absolutely sure about this?" Sam asks.

It's two months later and an old argument. Since Luke returned home he's had sporadic messages from Levent, when the *Esin* on its Blue Voyages moored overnight in a town with an internet café or cellular network robust enough to support his smartphone. They weren't all the same, the messages, but they said the same thing Luke replied: *I miss you, I can't wait to see you again.* Last week, from his own computer in İzmir where he was making final preparations for departure, Levent wrote: *It was the blood, yours and mine, strengthening my natural inclinations. Plus Hanım's bad luck in not reserving Efendi's boat for a family with a daughter those two weeks. Plus my good luck it was YOU instead. Or maybe she took pity on me and arranged it all.*

"I'm sure," Luke says. He's hyper, antsy. Levent's already in the States— he landed in New York last night, called from the airport hotel. His voice sounded more foreign, somehow, as if being in an English-speaking country exaggerated his Turkish accent. "Absolutely positively."

They've driven down from the Berkeley hills, Luke and his dad (Perla's at work), across the Bay Bridge, through the city, south to SFO. Sam expected Luke to want to drive but Luke didn't trust his dad to keep safe all the way the flowers he bought this morning: six perfect out-of-season blood-red anemones with dense black hearts. He's holding them now, Luke is, jiggling on his toes with impatience as they wait in the arrivals area.

"He's sleeping in the guest room, you know."

"Of course he is." *It won't be* sleeping *in my room.* For two weeks, until Levent moves into his residence hall on campus. Two weeks to learn everything else about each other, to explore and experiment, to fall ever more in love. "Thank you, Dad. So much."

"Well." Sam pats his his son's shoulder gingerly. "He does seem like a good kid and I can only applaud the good influence that has you actively thinking about college yourself. But promise me, Lukey, promise me you'll warn him in no uncertain terms that I love my boy very very much and will not tolerate him ever hurting you."

"There he is!"

There he is! Luke can't run to him because Sam's holding his shoulder. He holds up the flowers in their crackly cellophane cone, grinning like anything, squirming like a little kid. From the crowd of other passengers, Levent beams. He hefts the overnight bag on his own shoulder, then lifts his left hand to wave. On the pale skin of his inner forearm, upside down, five pastel anemones are eclipsed by the sixth, scarlet as blood.

✦ ✤ ✦

The Arab's Prayer

To Israeli singer Yehonathan and DJ El-Zi,
for the inspiration of "Waiting for You (Tel-Aviv)"

Whrrr-click. The door near the top of the white plastic minaret opened and the little plastic mannequin teetered onto the balcony. Its painted beard was black, its turban green, its lips unmoved. *"God is great,"* sang the speaker behind the door, *"God is great!"*

"Time for you to get up," said Yaffe, jostling Mus'ad. "Prayer is better than sleep."

Mus'ad groaned indistinctly. Yawning, he tried to sit up, but his boyfriend's arm had him pinned down.

"I attest," sang the device on the shelf across the room: *"there is no God but God!"*

They struggled for a moment before Yaffe gave in, kissed the back of Mus'ad's neck, and removed his arm. Momentarily saddened by the loss of that weight, Mus'ad blinked gummy eyes and rolled away from Yaffe's sticky warmth to the edge of their bed.

"I attest: Muhammad is the messenger of God!"

composed 2010, Pawtucket, Rhode Island
first published in M-Brane SF #24, January 2011

"God honor him and give him peace," Mus'ad murmured, lowering his feet to the floor and sitting upright. The only light in the bedroom came from the glowing dome of the miniature mosque on its shelf. The window was so dark he could barely distinguish the tessellations of the mashrabiya through the glass. "How is it," he asked, turning back to Yaffe, a dark shadow on shadowy sheets, "you may be a secular Jew but I not a secular Muslim?"

"It's not *my* alarm clock."

"Come to prayer!"

"It was a gift from my mother!" She'd been amused by it, he assumed—she was a secular Muslim. Assembled in Gaza from Brazilian bioplastics, Turkish and Indonesian electronics, running Egyptian software and catching its time cues from an Israeli satellite, it commented on the world in ways its producers had failed to consider.

"Come to salvation!"

"I honor your mother as my own!"

Mus'ad shook his head. "I know you do. I know she doesn't care two figs. Habit, I guess. Will you kiss me before I brush my teeth?"

"Prayer is better than sleep!" sang the plastic muezzin as Yaffe sat up. They embraced again, nuzzled closed lips to closed lips, and Mus'ad stood. "Go back to sleep if you can, habibi."

"God is great! God is great!" The clock's voice was sampled from a famous Turkish muezzin so its accent was off. *"There is no God but God!"*

Yaffe dropped back to the pillow. "Perhaps." Mus'ad imagined a thoughtful frown.

In the bathroom, he blinked, dazzled by the lamp over the mirror. He brushed his teeth, shaved, showered. After the shower, before drying himself, he ran a trickle of cool water from the tub faucet and crouched to perform the prescribed ablutions.

Dried but damp again for the morning was already hot and humid, still nude, he returned to the bedroom. Yaffe snored. Pulling the white dishdasha off its hook, Mus'ad smiled. He would have liked to kiss his man but that would mean doing the ablutions over. The clock's glow had dimmed. He checked to make sure it wouldn't wake Yaffe with the second call—*he* would do that.

Nakedness covered, he went to fetch his rug, rolled and propped by the flat's front door. It was Pakistani, not an antique, not precious except by being all he had of his father's, a childhood gift. Going through the door, he touched his fingertips to the mezuzah on the frame and kissed them.

On the roof of their building, he spread the rug out below the tallest white-brick malqaf. When they moved in, he had worked out the position of the holy city: from this point the qibla axis projected between two smaller wind-catchers, their verticals framing a mihrab in the air. It had seemed to him not quite right to say his prayers in rooms shared with a kafir nor fair to expect the unbeliever to observe them. He was not especially welcome at the most convenient mosque.

Before he began, he stretched and looked out from his height. Five years before, when he first said the fajr prayers on this roof, dawn had been hard to make out, quarrelling with the city's lights. But now, except for aircraft-warning beacons on their spires, the towers of Tel Aviv stood mostly dark, street lamps only blinked on when they sensed a pedestrian, and stars glimmered over the Mediterranean even as the sun's limb rose above the inland horizon. From a minaret's loudspeakers in Yafo, Mus'ad heard a faint voice proclaim the iqama, the second call. He sank to his knees.

Yaffe still slept, still snored, sprawled across half the bed. Mus'ad admired him for a moment, the lushness of his flesh pixellated by thin sunlight through mashrabiya, then went to the kitchen to make coffee. Both of them liked it Ottoman style, a finicky business. When the brass ibrik was balanced on the element, heating toward the first boil, he rooted through the basket by the door for his earpiece. He found Yaffe's first—they were distinguished by Yaffe's having a blue button. Another rummage found the 'piece with a green button. Tapping it into his right ear, he returned to the ibrik, not yet bubbling. The boot-up chime sounded deep in his ear. He waited for the second chord to indicate a connection established.

"Good morning, Mus'ad," the jinni in the cloud said in Hebrew.

They danced the call-and-response of ID verification, jinni and Mus'ad, while he watched the coffee seethe—the foam reached the ibrik's lip and he lifted it off the heat before the jinni was satisfied.

"Messages?" Mus'ad asked. The coffee needed to stew a moment. He turned away from the stove.

"Eleven professional, one personal."

The windows in the flat's main room faced north. No mashrabiya broke up the view. He looked down into the street. Indicators flashing, a van stood at the curb outside the bakery across the way. They might stop for breakfast.

"Personal."

It was Yaffe's mother in West Jerusalem, an early riser. "My dear, my dear," she sang in her lovely, not quite idiomatic Arabic, "the Knesset votes today. I shall endeavor *not* to say a prayer."

Mus'ad smiled, wondering whether Yehudit had left the same message in English with her son's jinni, or Hebrew. He took two cups from the tray that displayed the painted coffee service he and Yaffe had brought back from their first holiday abroad, Spain—Sfarad. Al-Andalus.

He replaced the ibrik on the element for the second boil. His own mother, fond as she was of Yaffe, would never think to echo Yehudit's hope. Nadiyya was a staunchly modern woman who had divorced Mus'ad's mad father without sentiment. In '18, faced with the choice, she had not hesitated to resign Israeli citizenship—crossed the border only infrequently for coffee and shopping with the Jewish woman she called *sister* or to visit their sons on the coast, a foreigner in the nation of her birth. None of her former husband's actions had surprised, only saddened and angered her. She had no use for marriage.

The coffee smelled good, dark and rich with cardamom, and Mus'ad preferred not to think of his father. He poured it out and carried the two little cups and Yaffe's earpiece to the bedroom.

Yaffe was awake, surly, sitting cross legged on the mattress. The backlight of his slate gilded his face. Smelling the cardamom, he looked up. "I have to go to Cyprus."

"Oh." Mus'ad offered a cup. "Today?"

"Have to be on the dock in three hours. Should be back tomorrow night."

Mus'ad sat beside him. "That's not so bad."

"Unless something goes wrong."

Mus'ad didn't entirely understand Yaffe's job. He seldom had to travel but it was always sudden, while Mus'ad's business trips were meticulously plotted out months in advance. "Three hours—time for a fuck?"

"Come with me, habib." Slinging the slate aside, Yaffe took his boyfriend's free hand. "We'll get married."

Mus'ad met Yaffe's fierce grin with a smile. "Your mother called."

"I know—me too." Yaffe frowned, squeezed Mus'ad's fingers, sipped from his cup. "Drink your coffee, then we'll fuck. The act won't pass, you know. The rabbinate's been calling in favors all month."

"I have to work today. The Arab parties are far from certain, either, even the leftists. If it doesn't pass, I'll catch the night 'foil to Famagusta. I expect it takes a day or two for formalities—we'll spend the weekend."

"That, my love," said Yaffe sweetly, "sounds like a plan."

Mus'ad and his co-workers Yael and Yoel left the office for lunch. "You know," he was saying, "all my favorite Jews have *yod*-names—the two of you, Yaffe, his mom."

Fumbling for her ID, Yael laughed.

"You know," said Yoel, "I feel Vered would find that statement hurtful."

The building's retrofitted low-carbon-debt climate control wasn't overly efficient outside the server cores—the lobby especially, designed in the bad old days, was routinely warmer or chillier than ideal. Low-e glass had only succeeded in making the atmosphere murky. It meant, though, that the transition to outdoor summer heat wasn't quite so shocking. Mus'ad submitted to the retina scan, waved his ID past the sensor, held the ante-lobby door for his friends. "I adore your wife," he told Yoel, donning his glasses, "but I don't know her well enough to rank her as a favorite."

In turn, Yoel opened the outer door. Mus'ad strode through a moment of brilliant blindness before the glasses compensated.

Yael caught his swinging hand in an anxiously friendly way. "You don't come out with us enough, that's why you don't know Vered or Amir."

"Dinner tonight," said Yoel, hearty, from his other flank. "You and Yaffe. We'll add a *vav* and an *alef* to your favorites list."

"Thanks, but another time. Yaffe's on his way to Cyprus. I'm thinking of joining him."

"That's why you were working so hard!" Yael was a romantic.

They waited at the corner to cross. K-cars and electric runabouts and vans purred past. "What's in Cyprus?" asked Yoel. "Besides Yaffe."

The light changed. In Rabin Square across the street, there appeared to be a demonstration, noisy, parts of it joyful or expectant. "Marriage," Mus'ad muttered, removing his hand from Yael's and stepping into the crosswalk. Maybe they hadn't heard.

Yoel had. "It's that important?"

"It is to *them*."

He didn't mean the crowd in ordinary, everyday clothes listening to an orator on the City Hall steps, though their presence demonstrated its importance, their banners and signs and noisemakers. He meant the unholy alliance of the righteous—the clots and pustules of dog-collared Christian clerics, Arab and European, of robed Muslim imams and their bearded or veiled followers, of angry Torah scholars in crow plumage. He'd never seen so many Haredim at once outside of Jerusalem. He hadn't seen them so angry since the internationalization of the Old City and the holy places, the division of the new between two nations. A distant cousin of Mus'ad's, a little girl, had died in the Jerusalem riots in '17.

He looked away from the demonstrators, those on the side of the angels and those who said they spoke for God—looked up. Looked away from the scaffolding that had served as City Hall's façade for four years.

"Our very first holiday together," he told his friends, "abroad, that is, Yaffe and I went to Spain." They were cutting across the square, well away from demonstrators and counter-demonstrators. "In Granada, I asked him to marry me. Because, you know, we *could*. There. Civilly. Legally." Not unconsciously, he thumbed the ring on his right hand, rotating it around the finger. "I'd bought rings! When we came home, we could register with the Interior Ministry like any couple who married abroad."

Yael took his hand again. "He turned you down."

"He was feeling idealistic. Some politician, I don't remember who, had floated another attempt to instate civil marriage. Yaffe said it was an immoral abridgment of everybody's rights for marriage to be under the thumb of the religious courts. If he was a woman or I was, we still couldn't marry in our own country."

Yoel, who had wed within the status quo, laughed. "I doubt the rabbinical courts would permit dear Yaffe to marry a Jewish woman even if he weren't gay. I doubt he'd put up with the rigamarole. I had my rebellious moments—" He laughed again. "But honestly, Mus'ad, why is it important? Vered and I only did it to please our parents. You and Yaffe, Yael and Amir—as common-law spouses you have all the same rights and privileges as me and Vered."

Mus'ad knew Yoel well enough not to be offended—Yoel was a conventional, don't-rock-the-boat young man—only vaguely hurt that Yoel didn't know him.

Yael was less patient. "If I could marry Amir without first convincing a pack of doddering nineteenth-century rabbis I'm a proper Jew, I would."

"Exactly. It's the principle." Mus'ad took a breath. "Also, I hate the term *partners*. I want Yaffe to be my husband."

Their path did not take them near the rebuilt memorial to the martyr Rabin. It did pass through the shadow of the newer monument that honored the seventy-nine civil servants killed in the City Hall bombing twenty-one years later. Yael squeezed Mus'ad's hand, making him cringe, and murmured too low for Yoel to hear, "It's nothing to do with you."

He should never have told her. *I was in Spain,* he thought. *In al-Andalus with my beloved.* Taken into custody at Ben Gurion, right off the plane, taken from

Yaffe, interrogated, drugged, the least contents of his mind opened to their view, pawed over. It wouldn't have been appreciably easier for Yaffe to protest if they'd married in Spain. There were no charges, he was released—had known he would be released as well as he'd known they would arrest him. He had had no dealings with his mother's former husband since the divorce, nearly ten years.

He walked faster. He didn't think about it. Everything was better now.

"So you wore him down?" Yoel asked.

"Sorry?"

"Yaffe. Willing to settle for an EU marriage certificate now."

"Knesset wore him down. How many times has an act been floated? How many times have the rabbis and imams and bishops got it shot down? He asked me. Here, if today's vote is successful. Cyprus if not."

"Congratulations! Felicitations!"

"Indeed." Yael was grinning, the '16 memorial forgotten. "Here would be better, in all ways. I should like to be on hand."

"We should—oh." Stopping short, Yoel shook his head, then hurried after. "No, I forgot. I suppose not."

"Yoel, my friend, if you buy a bottle of Champagne, I promise to drink a glass with glad and grateful heart."

He supposed he was tipsy. Not drunk—he had been drunk once. Yoel had insisted on calling Yaffe, speeding across the blue Mediterranean, and standing him a split from the hydrofoil's bar. He, Mus'ad, drank a second glass without noticing—he broke the messenger of God's commandment perhaps twice a year—and then a client's call interrupted the dickering over division of the bill. He waved his friends off, back to the office, ordered coffee, and unrolled his slate: the client was calling from Kuala Lumpur at, for her, a thoroughly inconvenient hour.

The rally and counter-demonstration on Rabin Square had not broken up in the interval. The same speaker or a different one addressed the crowds. The separate religious parties still refused to mix, oil and oil seething atop troubled waters, united only in their anger. Passions might be more elevated, but not in a way that suggested a clear result from Givat Ram in West Jerusalem. He could ask the jinni but he was reacting poorly to the heat and bright sun. And Champagne. He took off his glasses to wipe sweat from his eyes.

"Are you ashamed?" The words were Arabic, the voice unfamiliar. "I know you, ibn Hassan. Your father would be ashamed."

Ashamed? The man who had been his father? That was one explanation. Partial, invalid explanation.

"I have no father." Mus'ad put his glasses back on. "I do not know you, uncle. Let me pass."

The man was not so much older than himself—not old enough to be truly his uncle. In the tired fashion of a decade before, he wore a black-and-white keffiyeh loose around his neck, three days' worth of black stubble on his face. "It was to prevent such abominations—"

"That man, Hassan, was the abomination," said Mus'ad, weary. "Let me pass, uncle. I have work to do and an appointment to keep this evening."

"Filth," the stranger said, flecks of spittle pinging the lenses of Mus'ad's glasses as he crowded closer. "Faggot filth unworthy son of a blessed martyr."

It was not anger, not yet, simply sorrow. "Indeed. I am quite certain the martyr reclines in paradise even now, surrounded by houris whose touch revolts him." Mus'ad stepped back and raised his left hand, spoke deliberately, formally, in Hebrew. "I do not know you, adoni. I do not wish to converse with you. It would be regrettable if I were forced to request assistance of these public servants." With his chin, Mus'ad indicated the armed young woman in IDF uniform on the point of taking an interest, her male partner intent on the restive Haredim.

As much a relic of an ugly past as any stubborn Haredi, the man stepped back. Another man than Mus'ad might find him handsome—the martyr Hassan, perhaps. He spat at Mus'ad's feet. "You will not escape the judgment of God."

"Oh, surely not," Mus'ad murmured under his breath as the man strode away. "Nor will you, my friend." He nodded politely to the IDF woman and walked on, ignoring a change in pitch in the noise of the crowd.

"My dear," said Yehudit through his earpiece, "foolish Haredim are rioting outside the Knesset and you may marry my son."

"Oh?" Mus'ad closed his eyes and flexed his fingers before pushing his slate away, across the desk. "I've been busy, not keeping track." The Kuala Lumpur client's problem was nearly solved. "I'm a little surprised. Have you told Yaffe?"

"He's not accepting calls. Not from me, anyway. I left a message. Are you well, Mus'ad? You sound...weary."

"Work." Mus'ad shook his head. "Going to join Yaffe in Cyprus tonight, have to finish things up." He breathed in, breathed out. "That is excellent news. Thank you for letting me know."

"Every Jewish mother wishes her son happily wed. This Jewish mother has waited years to call you her son."

As often as it was repeated, the claim never failed to make Mus'ad flinch with gratitude. "Yehudit—"

"You should call your mother. Or I will, if you're too busy."

"It will be some years more, I think, before Palestine or Gaza acknowledge such marriages. Yehudit, earlier I was reminded...."

"Yes?"

A lawyer, Yehudit had been his advocate when he went to court to renounce nasab, laqab, nisba, the whole panoply of patronymics and family identifiers that so bewildered non-Arabs, in favor of a simple Israeli-style surname. "When I changed my name—I don't think I've ever thanked you enough. It was a difficult time."

She hissed air through her teeth—he'd seen her do it, many times. "That man. Hardly a man, a sad, broken boy never permitted to grow up or be happy. He and his family lost any claim to share a name with you, Mus'ad, long before he killed himself."

And all the others, but she was too kind to mention them. "Thank you." Mus'ad's voice came thin.

"You paid my bill. Thanks are superfluous. Get back to work, my dear. Give your future husband my love tonight and tell him to call his mother."

Time was short. He needed to be at the dock by 1630. Even with the world at peace, security screening was never swift. Particularly not for an Arab. Another day the Knesset might abolish the requirement that IDs and passports proclaim one's religious affiliation—that one declare an affiliation. Another day.

He had packed for a holiday weekend. Doubtless he'd forgotten something but he and Yaffe had ready funds between them for incidentals, even at EU prices. He glanced around the flat's main room again. He had watered the plants, shut off devices that drained power even when inactive, given the thermostat permission to allow the flat to get warmer than they generally preferred. The rolled prayer rug by the door caught his eye.

"You were nobody's father, nobody's husband. You died unloved."

He shoved aside the low table before the sofa. Its feet screeched across the tiles. When he spread out the rug, he made sure the mihrab woven into its pattern did not line up on the axis to Mecca. It wasn't handsome, the rug, its colors garish, its workmanship not fine—it was small, the table would hide most of it. They should buy a bigger carpet for their home, he and Yaffe. In winter, the tiled floor became uncomfortably chill. He'd heard that artisans in Gaza were weaving interesting carpets—not as cheap as those from Pakistan, not as precious as even new Turkish or Afghan rugs, but interesting. Modern. He lifted the table onto the rug. The pieces of the Spanish coffee service trembled, ringing against each other. He looked around again, went to the bedroom.

On the nightstand by the bed he shared with Yaffe, the photo frame blinked from a snapshot of them in the Alhambra's Court of the Lions, where Mus'ad had asked Yaffe to marry him, to one of them at the Western Wall. The frame's carbon debt was minimal but he reached behind the nightstand to pull its plug from the socket. He twisted the ring on his finger. Now he was just wasting time he didn't really have.

Before unplugging the plastic mosque his mother had given him, he opened its control panel. The buttons were easy enough to figure out. He shut off the voice of the muezzin, saved the action into permanent memory, closed the panel. Deprived of its purpose, the thing was tacky, but a gift from his mother. He pulled the plug.

A Muslim was permitted to marry an unbelieving woman so long as their children were raised within the ummat al-mu'minin, the community of belief. The restrictions on a Jew, he believed, were more stringent. An Israeli, as of today, had the whole world to choose from.

On his way out, Mus'ad brushed his fingers across the mezuzah on the doorpost, brushed them across his lips. There was sentiment and there was sentiment. Tapping the 'piece in his ear, he asked the jinni to let Yaffe know he was on his way.

✦ ✦ ✦

Then We Went There

"You're a faggot, Prester. A fucking pansy-ass little gay faggot." The voice was loud but sounded surprisingly reasonable, unthreatening, at cheap odds to the words. "I don't like faggots."

"I'm not, Sean, really I'm not." Prester Johnston's response was thin, frightened, high pitched. Perhaps he wasn't gay (Davey hadn't thought about it, barely ever paid attention to Prester) but he was the smallest kid in the class, half Sean Roche's size.

Davey was coming from the showers when he heard them in the locker room. Coming from the showers naked except for the towel that barely overlapped enough around his hips to stay up. It was the year Davey shot up from tubby barely five-two to over six foot and scary skinny. He was taller than Sean but Sean could break him in half without trying. Sean was hot in a Cro-Magnon sort of way, one of the images Davey beat off to sometimes.

"You know what little queers like you are good for? Two things—beejays and butt fucking. Which one's it gonna be, faggot?"

Davey looked down the row of lockers. There wouldn't be time to find an adult but he couldn't tackle Sean with nothing more than his bare hands and a towel. Lacrosse stick, baseball bat, *something*.

ᘒ *composed 2009, Pawtucket, Rhode Island* ᘖ
ᘒ *original to this volume* ᘖ

Nothing. All the lockers were shut. His own was two rows over but there wasn't anything in it but clothes.

"No, please, Sean, I don't—I really don't want to."

What the fuck was the kid doing in the locker room this late anyway? What was Sean doing here?

"Nothing to do with what *you* want."

The floor felt cold under Davey's feet. He'd stepped out of his shower sandals as soon as he heard the voices. Sure to pick up athlete's foot now. Least of his worries. He put a hand on the cool enamelled metal of the last locker and peered around the corner.

Sean stood between two of the fixed benches down the aisle. His hands planted on metal locker faces at shoulder height, he leaned forward, head down. He must have been drilling late, Davey thought: green soccer shirt lay on the floor where he'd thrown it aside but he was still wearing cleated boots and striped knee socks. Matte black shorts were pulled halfway down meaty thighs but his ass was covered by the shiny black skin of compression shorts. It was a pretty ass, full, round, powerful. His back was like a tree trunk.

His head went further down between his arms. "You want to look at me, Prester."

"Please. No." Little Prester in street clothes crouched below Sean, voice muffled by knees and elbows. "I'll do anything, Sean. I'll give you money."

A thick ribbon of saliva drooled from Sean's mouth, falling onto Prester's shaved scalp. Davey almost thought he heard the plop. His hand's grip on the corner of the locker tightened till it hurt.

"You'll look at me." Threat in the tone more than the words.

Davey had to do something. There was no more time to think or worry. *Do* something.

He was running. His feet slapped the tile, loud, but Sean wouldn't have time to react. The towel was off his hips, in his hands, spread wide. He threw it over Sean's head, just coming up, blinding him, and got an elbow under Sean's chin. Gagged and choking, Sean made horrible muffled animal noises. Davey pulled him back and away from the lockers. Hobbled by his shorts, Sean lost any balance he might have had and stumbled backward, hard into Davey's chest. He must weigh a third again as much as Davey, who almost fell under the collision.

"Get out of here, Prester!" Davey yelled. "Run!"

Sheer bad luck, one of Sean's flailing hands latched onto Davey's wrist. The grip was tremendous. *He's going to break it,* Davey thought, heard himself think, but then the spikes of one of Sean's boots and half his weight landed on a bare instep and that shocking pain made Davey furious. "Someone," he grunted—"someone your own *size*." There was no way he was getting out of this without immobilizing Sean. *Get him*, he thought distinctly, *in the balls*.

How? As they staggered backwards, Sean's shoulders jumped against Davey's chest, his ass rocked into Davey's groin. He was howling into the damp towel. Plastic spikes screeching as they slid on glossy tile, his dangerous boots stamped for purchase. The bones of Davey's wrist ground together in his grasp.

Davey reached around Sean's bulk with the hand that wasn't being tortured, going for the crotch, but his open palm slapped on the unbreakable eggshell of a hard cup stuffed down the pocket of Sean's compression shorts. "Shitfuck!" He slammed his fist into the soft pit of flesh above the cup but it was a bad angle, he couldn't get any force behind the blow.

He was going to lose the wrist. No help for it. He planted his feet wide and pulled harder against the other boy's throat, continuing to hammer on his belly. Sean's cleats slipped as he tried to push back and Davey slammed all his weight forward. Just a few little steps. Sean's knees smacked one after the other into the bench bolted to the floor.

He howled, toppling forward. Davey couldn't get free. Sean's skull hit the locker with a hollow, horrific boom.

He brought Davey down with him. In an instant they lay tangled together half on, half off the bench, like lovers, Davey involuntarily clutching the bigger boy, his naked prick jammed into Sean's firm, Lycra-clad ass. But Sean had gone limp. Davey wrenched his hand free and rolled off, fell, his ass landing hard on the floor and the bench jarring him sharply just below the shoulder blades. Just a minute. He was panting, honking. He didn't have a minute, he had to *get out* before Sean came to.

Nursing the blazing fire in his wrist, he pulled himself upright—almost fell again when he put the wrong kind of weight on the foot Sean had mashed. Recovering, he looked down at Sean crumpled over the bench, his top half twisted at a bad angle into the well between bench and lockers. Davey couldn't tell if the other boy was breathing. "Jesusfuck, no," he moaned.

Then he heard the muffled sobbing. Two benches down, Prester Johnston still huddled in a fetal crouch against the blue lockers, head between his knees, shoulders rocking.

"Jesusfuck goddamn! Prester! Dammit, I told you to run."

"No!" the boy wailed. "Please, I don't want to, leave me alone!"

Davey found himself standing over the kid in a stance as threatening as Sean's. "Do you have a phone on you, Prester? Call 9-1-1. I hurt him bad, I think. I think—" He swallowed, had to say it in his head before he could say it aloud. "I think Sean might be dead."

Prester lifted his head. "What?" His face was bloated and blotchy from crying.

Enraged, Davey yelled, "I saved your skinny worthless ass and I think I might have killed him doing it! Now give me your phone."

Cowering, Prester tried to make himself smaller, to burrow into the locker behind him. "I don't have one."

Davey did. It was in his locker with his clothes. "Stay here," he ordered Prester. He was going to need backup whether or not Sean was dead.

Not dead. When he turned for a last look he saw the body shuddering on the bench, heard wretched retching sounds from underneath. Shit, he'd choke on his own vomit and that would kill him. The sturdy legs kicked, convulsed, then slid off the bench after the torso. A locker door boomed again, struck by a flailing heel.

Sean lay mostly on his back between lockers and bench. The towel had come off his face. It was foul with puke and there was nasty slime smeared around his mouth. He stared wide eyed at the ceiling, panting harshly and shaking.

"Sean," Davey said, "I'm going to call 9-1-1. I'll get you an ambulance."

"I'll kill you." Sean seemed to have trouble focusing on Davey above him, moving his head from side to side and blinking. "I don't know who you are but I'll find you and I'll kill you and then I'll fuck your fucking corpse and then I'll fucking kill you again."

Flinching, Davey stepped back. A brawny arm grappled the bench seat. Sean sat up, holding on with both hands. His eyes were bloodshot and scarily blank, staring at nothing. The stain of mucus around his mouth looked like blood. Maybe some of it was blood. "I'll kill you," he said again.

When he put weight on his elbows, trying to lever himself upright, Davey panicked completely. There was no time for the phone, 9-1-1, clothes. He didn't realize he'd grabbed Prester Johnston and dragged the useless kid with him until he reached the end of the aisle of lockers. Prester was blubbering again but didn't fight back.

Davey risked a glance behind him. On his feet, Sean was trying to get out from behind the bench. He didn't seem to see well, didn't appear to understand it was the shorts around his thighs that hobbled him. He roared in frustration, no words, just fury, and swiped at the air with fists as big as boxing gloves.

"Oh, god."

It used to be easy. Deep in panic, Davey concentrated. When the bullies came after him, when he was still short and tubby, he could get away every time until they gave up. They didn't come after him anymore, though, not this year, now that he was taller than them. He hadn't needed to escape for a long while. Besides, it had got more interesting here: he'd discovered boys. And if he was going to moon after inaccessible boys he wanted some of them mooning after him, too, so he'd started working out. That was why he was at the gym so late. Though even with whole-milk protein smoothies and creatine supplements and two hours a day on the machines he'd put on barely ten pounds in six months....

Don't think about that, think about *this*.

Still holding onto Prester's shoulder, he took three steps, feeling for the corner. Found it.

His ears popped. A wallop of salty ocean air pounded into his nostrils. They staggered in deep, powdery sand. Prester yelped. Davey let him go. They were safe.

It was night but the moon was full and high, painting a white road across the strait. Sobbing as he suddenly understood how much he hurt, Davey stumbled across the beach. The sand was still hot when his feet broke through the crusty surface, the air was warm. Reaching the water, he found it pleasant and waded in, small waves splashing at his ankles.

"What happened?" yelled Prester Johnston before Davey was knee deep. "Where are we?"

"Somewhere else," Davey called without looking back. "Safe. Sean can't find us. We'll wait an hour or two, then I'll take you back."

Splashing behind him. Davey turned around just in time for the small, fully clothed figure to slam into him and bowl them both over into water barely deep enough to submerge them. Rearing back upright, Davey coughed the salt water out of his sinuses. When Prester, snuffling and horking, sat up beside him, Davey said as reasonably as he could, "What the fuck was that for?"

"Where am I?" Prester demanded, his voice shrill. "How did I get here? *What did you do?*"

Davey took a deep breath and moved his weight off the sore wrist. The water lapping against his rib cage was nice. "I don't know the name of this island. Never asked. There's a fishing village-slash-trading post about a mile down the coast but I don't think it *has* a name. Next island over, there's a big town—they call it a city—but I don't speak that language and I can't pronounce the name. If you look out to sea you can probably see the lights."

Prester didn't stand up to look. He coughed again. "We were in the school gym forty miles from the closest shore and now we're on some nameless tropical island in the middle of the night. And the moon's too freaking big. What just happened?"

"I saved you from being raped by that gorilla and then saved us both from being dismembered. Does it matter?"

"Yes. I am freaking out here." Prester sounded relatively calm. "I'm more terrified than I was with Sean pawing at me."

The warm water was helping. Davey flexed his wrist under the surface. It still hurt but he could manage the full range of motion with only a few twinges and all his fingers worked. He didn't think anything was broken. He didn't want to talk. He'd never told anybody about his escape route.

He'd never brought anybody else along.

He glanced at Prester. The whites of the other boy's eyes gleamed very bright in moonlight. His skin looked blacker at night than under sunlight or fluorescents. A flash of tooth as he opened his mouth.

"Used to be," Davey said, "I was short, shorter than you. And fat and clumsy. I was like a bully magnet. Nobody would be my friend and all the bigger boys ganged up on me. Musta been more than just short and fat, I don't know. Maybe they all knew I was gay before I did. I couldn't run very fast and I was too fat and stupid to hide very well so they always got me. They never hurt me bad enough I could report them or anything but it was all the time. Every day. Dad wasn't any help, said I should just man up and *fight back*." He lifted one hand and watched the water drain between his fingers. A piece of the moon remained, caught in the net of wrinkles on his palm. "One day when I was just completely desperate and hysterical, I chanced on how to come here. It was the middle of winter and I was all bulked up against the cold, you know, even more than just the fat and general patheticness, and the streets were all icy where they weren't slushy, I kept falling down, and these four guys were after me. They didn't try so hard. I guess it was *fun* chasing the fat kid, making me so scared if I'd had a minute to stand still I would have pissed myself. I was maybe a block ahead of them. I didn't know anywhere to hide—I was so frightened I'd got lost in a part of town I didn't really know. I turned a

corner, thinking, I don't know, maybe I can find some open door or a crowd
of people. Instead I found here."

"Where is here." Prester's voice was firm and flat. It didn't even sound like
a question.

"I don't know. Somewhere else, like I said."

Prester stood up out of the water. It came above his knees, lapping in little
waves against sodden denim. "It sure isn't New Jersey." The wet cotton of his
t-shirt clung to bony shoulders, skinny chest, a little pot belly. Turning away
from the shore, he looked out along the path of moonlight on the strait. "I see
lights—that's the city you were talking about?"

"It's not a city like Philly or New York, just a big town. All the boats are
sailboats. I don't think they've invented the internal-combustion engine yet
here."

"So it's like Narnia?"

"What?"

"Another world. A different world. Is there, like, magic?"

"What? Look, it's my safe place. When things get bad and scary, I'd come
here for an hour or two and just relax and get over it. It's warm and there's
an ocean to swim in and no bullies always on my ass. Then I'd go home and
maybe things would be better for a while."

Turning again, Prester looked down at Davey, sitting on the sandy bottom
in blood-warm waves that sloshed against his chest. "What we have here,"
Prester said, "is a failure of imagination. You don't explore? You don't think
about maybe staying here?"

"Why'd I want to do that?"

"Because New Jersey's hell on earth."

Not waiting for a reply, Prester headed back to dry land. When he reached
the shore, he wrestled his shirt off and wrung it out. He didn't look any less
weedy without it. He mopped at his chest and arms with the shirt and wrung
it out again, then seemed to pause for a moment to think.

Mild curiosity exhausted—he sure wasn't *attracted* to a skinny kid who appeared barely to have hit puberty yet—Davey lay back in the rocking embrace
of the sea. His heels dragged in the sand but torso and head floated, bobbing.
The dark sky was filled with stars, more than you ever saw at home unless you
went deep into the country. He supposed the constellations were different but
he'd never been good at picking out patterns, they were just glinting jewels
scattered at random. The moon was definitely bigger. He'd never thought
about that before. *Another world.*

Sure he'd explored. He'd found the fishing village his third or fourth time. The people were kind enough. They gave him something weird to drink and something weirder to eat, and there was one old guy who seemed to speak English—Davey could understand him most of the time, anyway. They were dark skinned, like Prester, but they didn't really look like Prester though most of them were almost as skinny, and most of them didn't really wear clothes so that was embarrassing. And he was white and fat and covered in clothes, no matter how hot it got, because he didn't want to get a sunburn (the old guy had given him a big hat woven out of some kind of grass), so he really stood out. Little kids pointed at him, amazed. Of course he wasn't fat anymore but he was still white. The old man mentioned another white person occasionally to be seen in the vicinity but Davey found the story hard to follow.

The villagers built their houses on stilts on the edge of a deep lagoon where a river reached the sea. Just thatched roofs on poles. The only walls were woven like his hat. No plumbing—when he saw a kid squat to shit in the shallows of the river and then wash his butt with the same water it really upset him. No plumbing, no cars, no electricity—no TV or phone or internet. Why would he want to stay? He'd got in big trouble at home anyway that time for going missing seven hours and upsetting his dad.

Anyway, he wasn't sure he could find his way back to New Jersey from anywhere but this stretch of beach.

All of a sudden the sea didn't feel as safe. It was choppier, he thought. A wave washed over his face and he sat up sputtering. There were clouds in the sky now, thin wispy clouds racing by really high, and thick dark slower clouds lower down, advancing from beyond the strait and the far island. When he stood up he felt the wind on his skin, chilling him. Storm coming. Maybe a hurricane—what did he know about weather patterns here? He'd better grab Prester and take him home.

Only Prester was gone. "Ratbastard," Davey said when he was sure. Moonlight clearly picked out where Prester had trudged away through the sand, away from the village Davey had told him about—away from the little Davey knew of this world, into unmapped territory. Serve him right if Davey did leave him behind.

He couldn't do that. He was responsible for the little shit. Had made himself responsible. And there was a storm coming. Looking out to sea, Davey saw the waves getting higher, faster, and saw lightning detonating in the dense pile of cloud that had overwhelmed the island beyond the strait. "Shitfuckpiss," he said, and looked closer at the marks Prester had left behind.

They were already harder to read as more and more banners of cloud whipped over the moon.

Two foot-sized pits in the sand, as if somebody had fallen from a great height and landed without stumbling. As he leaned over them, the moon broke free for an instant and he saw the imprints, deep in the holes, of soccer-boot cleats.

"Sean?" Davey looked around wildly, his heart ringing like a broken bell. The track he'd thought Prester's was Sean's, pounding over and obliterating the boy's smaller prints. Davey began to run. "*Prester!*" he bellowed.

Soon he was panting, fighting a stitch. Prester and then Sean (if it was Sean) had found the deep dry sand at the top of the beach too hard to run through and sprinted down closer to the water. Even with shifting, uncertain light, the path was easier to follow now—Davey could make out the lighter treads of Prester's sneakers interspersed with Sean's bootprints. Sean's stride was longer. Prester could not escape.

A few times the path was effaced by high waves but he always found it again. The waves were a lot higher, noisier, hitting the beach instead of sliding up it. He heard distant grumbles of thunder now and then and a wind was picking up, slapping at him. He looked up to see how close the storm was to swallowing the moon.

The frothy remnants of a wave washed over his feet and a black shadow creased his own shadow on the sand before him, briefly hid and then revealed again the single pair of sneaker prints running ahead. Panting, Davey looked up again. Something odd was crossing the broad face of the moon. It was big, or close, or both. No kind of cloud—it appeared solid, its edges sharp and hard against the moon's brilliance, but it was all silhouette with no contour and he couldn't work it out.

Lightning flashed over the strait and thunder rolled, much closer. Davey realized what it had to mean that only Prester was ahead of him now. A massive gust of wind nearly toppled him and then a wave tried to take his legs out from under him.

"Told you I'd find you."

Sean's big arm fastened around his neck, thick elbow forcing his chin up so fast he bit his tongue. His back slammed up against Sean's hard, wet chest. An immense hand came around to grab and twist at his junk. He could feel the cold impersonal shell of Sean's hard cup grind against his ass. Before his breath was choked off, Davey screamed.

Pale blue sky through a wide, many-paned window. Overhead, a high, vaulted ceiling that was pale silvery grey between thin wooden ribs, and some kind of hanging lamp that seemed to sway on very slow intervals. Sheets like hot water clinging to his bones. Davey felt so sore all over he couldn't determine which pain was worst. When he tried to swallow the saliva pooling under his tongue it burned his throat. He never slept on his back but felt too listless and uncomfortable to shift onto his side.

"You'll feel better soon." A face obtruding on his field of vision. It looked like Prester Johnston, dark skinned, darker eyed, fine featured, but not. Something off. A girl's face, not a boy's. "So they tell me."

The next time he woke, Davey sat up, still intolerably achey, and swung his legs over the side of a narrow bed shaped like a boat. The sheets, cooler now, still weirdly slippery, drifted off his naked skin. The sky beyond the window was still pale, cloudless. The window was odd—the wall it was set in was odd, bellying up and out from the floor in a curve so that ceiling, if it were flat, would have been wider than floor.

The effort to stand threatened to be too much but he made it and stumbled the short distance to the window. He saw nothing but sky, cloudless blue sky ahead and above and to both sides. Then he looked down.

He was too feeble to shout, to be terrified. Below lay a continent of angry cloud, black and grey and turbulent brown, roiling, bubbling, boiling. Deep within canyons of dark fog, lightnings cracked from gaseous promontory to vaporous cliff. Unthinking, he grasped at metal mullions and leaned forward. The pane framed by the mullions was not glass. It felt like water, cool water yielding to the pressure of his forehead, molding itself to his face and bubbling against his ears as he pushed into it, leaning out, leaning down.

Nothing but storm beneath him, as far as he could see.

It became difficult to breathe. The watery substance of the window pressed against his eyeballs, distorting his vision, crept into nostrils and open mouth. He half wondered whether it would be possible to push all the way through and fall, fall forever into the storm far below, but the endeavor was more than he could make. He allowed the elastic meniscus to urge him out and gasped in air that tasted stale when his mouth came free. The skin of his face tingled and his fingers, when he freed them from the mullions, burned.

He turned to survey the chamber in which he found himself. Another boat-shaped bed stood opposite the bed he'd wakened in. Someone lay in it. He took a step.

It was Sean Roche, lying on his back, peaceful, deep asleep and breathing slowly, quietly. Davey tried to summon outrage, the will to press a pillow over the handsome, brutally carved face, but outrage proved inaccessible. All he felt was sad and bewildered and alone. The impulse rose to climb into the little boat with Sean, to hold and perhaps be held, to float away from this place, but he let the urge rise and rise until it dissipated.

There was a door. It resembled a door. Passing between the feet of the two beds, Davey approached it. He saw no knob, no means of opening it.

The substance of the door dissolved, going translucent, transparent, vanishing. Prester Johnston stood before him.

Not Prester. A young woman who wore Prester's t-shirt and jeans and sneakers and uncannily resembled Prester. "You're awake," she said in Prester's voice and extended her hand. "Come."

She led him along strange passageways and corridors lacquered with dragonfly and butterfly wings that twisted and convulsed so that Davey could never see more than a few yards ahead, up staircases that spiralled within circular or square or multiply angled shafts. Sometimes, climbing, he felt convinced they were going down. He began to feel sick again.

At length they passed through a long vaulted hall and emerged into pale, cool sunlight and a broad lawn of emerald turf, enclosed on all sides by high walls that resembled milky satin. A circular pool lay at the center of the lawn and beyond it stood an open pavilion roofed with gaudy silks. The young woman drew him to it, encouraged him to recline on a couch upholstered in soft velvet. "Prester?" Davey said.

"Not my name. Never my name." The young woman sank into a pile of cushions and regarded him serenely. "When my...parents adopted me from, as they thought, Ethiopia, they attached that name to me as an academic quip. A joke. Not a terribly funny one, even to those who understood the historical context. My name is—" She uttered a sound he could not interpret, a bright, clear note that bothered his ears.

"I was adopted, too."

"Of course you were. As was our friend Sean."

"After my mother died, my father hated me." Davey had seldom admitted that aloud.

"A pity, I imagine."

"Where am I?"

"This is the Court of the Air, of which I am, as I have recently rediscovered, absolute ruler."

"I'm sorry?"

"I was disoriented, I suppose, when you brought me back, did not recall my life as it is and must be. It seems I was bored, as has happened far too many times. I made myself a new and different and complicated life in your New Jersey." Her pronunciation of the state's name was off, as if she had forgotten how to say it aloud, only remembered the look of it, printed on paper. "You were my key, you and Sean together, my *ticket home*, as it were."

Davey swallowed. "I don't understand. I would like to go back now, please."

"You can't." She revealed no regret. "I had no more use for that world once out of it and so it no longer exists."

It was shellshock that made him numb, Davey imagined when he could bring himself to think about it, PTSD. Though whether the trauma was losing one entire world or gaining another he couldn't say. The Court of the Air possessed ingenious plumbing, it turned out, though its people had never thought to pass the secrets of its engineering along to the lesser nations below. He discovered other compensations as well for the marvels of lost New Jersey, whether he understood their workings or not, which those unfortunates in this world who were not subjects of the Court would never know.

When he regained physical health and strength, he was enrolled in the Academy. His fellow students, small, slender dark-skinned young men and women, were amused, some of them attracted, by his pale complexion, pale eyes, how he towered over them—his remote, chilly affect that reminded them of themselves, although his had no humor in it. When they studied the histories of imagined worlds, his perspective was appreciated, deferred to, but they never studied the history of his own world, nor of this one.

It had no history, he was told (he didn't believe it): the world had always been as it was. The Court of the Air, that vast incomprehensible structure, had ever circled the globe, riding its mount of storm that wreaked destruction on the lands of lesser, earthbound people below. The woman—she was not young—whom he continued to call *Prester* in his mind long after he learned to pronounce her name, had never not ruled the Court except as it grew tedious and she made herself a temporary life elsewhere, in worlds she created for her own entertainment.

He saw her seldom, only at a distance, in formal circumstances. She wasn't reliably a woman, nor young looking. Davey never again spoke to her.

He acquired friends of a sort—he had never had friends—although they often dropped him for minor slights or simply out of inattention, and he learned to do the same. There were lovers as well, not infrequent, who found his dogged preference for men quaint and, if they were not men to begin with, adapted for him. That habit distracted him so he did not dwell on it, no more than he did his inability to do the same. After the first time, it became known that mindfucking him was inadvisable and he was left alone in his own head. Often, when it occurred to him his lover too much resembled the Prester he had once briefly known, the fucking abruptly stopped.

He continued to grow taller although, since the Court of the Air did not measure by feet and inches, he could not determine how much. The food he was served and the Academy's athletic disciplines toughened him. He grew strong, muscular, as he had long ago in another life despaired of ever becoming. Once, encountering him at random during a ceremony neither yet understood, Sean Roche told him, surprised, "You look good. I wouldn't have expected it."

They were drawn together, Davey and Sean, by their shared history in a world nobody else remembered, but they were also mismatched for Sean was more drawn to women (although he dearly treasured being fucked) and the affair did not last. Nevertheless, years later, they encountered one another again in a tavern of one of the poor, primitive cities on the ground, and plotted revolution.

Firooz and His Brother

They were all merchants, the men of his family, caravan masters, following the long road from Samarkand to the great city of Baghdad at the center of the world. A youth on his first journey, Firooz often did not know quite what was required of him. Because he wrote a handsome, legible hand and could do sums in his head, before they left Samarkand he had helped his uncle prepare the inventory: silks, porcelains, spices from the distant east; cottons, dyes, spices from the hot lands south of the mountains; carpets, woollens, leather and hides, books from local workshops. On the road, such skills commanded little respect. He could shoot, could manage both short and long blades, but the paid guards knew him for a liability if bandits were to strike: he was his uncle's heir, they had been instructed to protect him. He made coffee when they camped, tended and groomed the horses of his uncle and the other merchants, cared for their hounds. Mostly he felt superfluous.

Along one of the many desolate stretches when the plodding caravan was days away from the town it had last passed through and the next, his uncle told him to take his bow and one of the hounds, ride away from the bustle and clamor of the caravan to hunt. Fresh game would be a treat.

Before they had gone very far, the hound sighted a small herd of deer grazing on the scrub. When Firooz loosed the hound, she coursed across the plain,

⟨ composed 2005, Rehoboth, Massachusetts ⟩
⟨ first published in The Magazine of Fantasy & Science Fiction, May 2008 ⟩

silent. Holding his bow ready and drawing an arrow from the quiver, Firooz spurred his horse after. On an abrupt shift of the breeze, the deer caught the hunters' scent. Lifting their heads as one, they turned and fled, leaping and bounding across the plain.

The hound had her eye on a particular animal she must have sensed to be weaker or more confused than the others. She pursued it relentlessly, leading Firooz farther and farther from the caravan, into a broken country where strange spires of jagged rock thrust up through the loose soil, twisted little trees clinging to their flanks. All the other deer had vanished. The young buck they followed cantered nimbly among the spires and towers and bastions. Steep shadows fell from tall spires and scarps, filling narrow passages with dusk. Springs and streams flowed here, watering the soil and nourishing seeming gardens of wildflowers in bloom, more lovely than anything Firooz had seen since leaving Samarkand. There were trees as well, protected from the winds of the plain, tall and straight and broad, and lush stretches of green turf. If he had not been intent on the deer's white rump and the hound's feathered tail, Firooz should have been astounded.

The deer's strength was failing. It staggered, leapt forward again, ducked around a steep formation. The hound sped after it. Wrenching his mare around the corner, Firooz entered the deep, cool shade of a woods cramped narrowly between two arms of rock and slowed to a walk. He saw neither deer nor hound among the trees. There was nowhere to go but forward, however. The mare's hooves fell muffled on leaf mould. Firooz did not recognize the trees.

After a time, he heard barking ahead and spurred the horse into an easy trot. The barks broke up, became distinct: two different voices. Over the hound's melodious baying, which echoed from the high walls of the canyon, sounded the sharp, warning yaps of a second dog.

Firooz was ready, when he passed between tall trees into a small clearing, to rein in the mare and leap to the ground between the two animals. He grabbed for the collar of the sand-colored bitch but she, startled and snarling, eluded him, bounded over the sweet grass and leapt upon the other, smaller dog. Courageous or stubborn, it shook her off the first time and stood its ground, growling ferociously. It was scarcely more than a puppy. Wrapping the excess fabric of his jallabiya about his forearm, Firooz stepped forward to separate them but stumbled and fell. By the time he regained his feet, the bitch hound had torn open the puppy's throat and stood over her fallen foe, jaws red and dripping. Still growling, the puppy lay on its side, panting from the new scarlet mouth in its throat as well as the one it had been born with, bleeding heavily from both.

Saddened by the bad end to such outsize courage, Firooz cuffed the hound aside and severed the younger dog's spine with a single stroke of his Damascus blade. For a long moment, he regarded the small corpse, while the hound lay at her ease, licking her chops, and the mare cropped at the grass between her feet. Clearly, the dead dog was not wild, native to the desolation—had been cared for, tended, for its woolly black coat gleamed where not matted and dulled by blood and it appeared well nourished. Heavy shoulders and sturdy limbs suggested it had not been a courser; though not fully grown, it would not have become large enough to threaten big predators, bears, wolves, leopards: it was surely not a hunter's dog.

Puzzled and regretful, Firooz did not at first properly hear or understand the muffled wailing that rose almost between his feet. The hound had returned, to nose interestedly at the corpse. He shoved her away again and gently lifted the dead dog aside.

It had died protecting its charge. In a perfectly sized depression in the grass lay the crying babe, naked but for spatters of the dog's scarlet blood. Firooz's first, terrible impulse was to kill it, too, and ride away.

The hound was back again, licking the blood from the baby's perfect skin. Her soft, damp tongue seemed to calm it—him—and after a time the babe ceased wailing. Looking away, Firooz cleaned and sheathed his sword. He didn't know what to do.

He knew what to do. Removing his rolled prayer rug from the mare's back, he wrapped the dead dog in it and fastened it again behind the saddle. The horse bridled and shied at the scent of blood. He took a clean scarf from the saddle bag. Kneeling by the baby, he nudged the hound aside for the last time. He moistened a corner of the scarf to wipe away the remaining traces of blood. The quiet baby stared up at him with a knowing, toothless smile. Picking up the baby, Firooz wound the scarf about his pliant body—somehow he knew how to hold him so he didn't complain. Firooz couldn't figure out how to mount the mare while holding the baby, so he took the reins, called the hound to heel, and set out walking back to the caravan. Along the way, he decided to name the baby Haider, after his grandfather.

Stranger things than discovering an abandoned child in the wilderness had occurred in the hundreds of years since caravans began travelling between Samarkand and Baghdad. The doctor who accompanied the caravan proclaimed Haider fit. A nursing goat was found to provide milk. The dead dog was buried with dignity, its grave marked by a cairn of stones beside the road. Firooz's uncle said he should raise Haider as his son, to which Firooz replied, "I am unmarried and too young to be a father. He shall be my brother."

Haider grew and prospered. Firooz, too, prospered. In time, he married his uncle's daughter as had been arranged in their childhood. In time, he took his uncle's place at the head of the caravan. His wife did not travel with him, but his brother Haider did. In all this time, Haider had become a handsome, pious, merry young man; he, too, was appropriately and happily wed, and when the brothers departed for distant Baghdad their wives remained together in the comfortable Samarkand house, caring for Haider's children, two small boys and a lovely girl. For the elder brother's marriage, though happy, remained childless: his wife quickened readily enough but always lost the baby before its time. Their family—indeed, the unhappy not-mother herself—urged Firooz to take a second wife, but always he refused. He loved his wife well, he said, and as for heirs he had his young brother and his brother's sons.

The caravan was heading again for Baghdad. Reaching the spot marked by the dog's grave's cairn, Firooz called a halt, although it was scarcely noon. There was a spring here and often game nearby. He called his brother to him. "You have often heard of how, by the will of God, I found you," he said. "We have passed the grave of your first protector many times, but I have never shown you the place where I found you, not so far away. While our companions hunt, let us go there."

They took with them two fine hounds, descendants of the first bitch. Now and again they sighted game but, though the hounds complained, did not loose them. Firooz felt he knew his heading exactly although it was now twenty-one years since he followed the long-lost buck deer. They entered the broken country, then the region of strange spires and canyons and lush vegetation. Haider exclaimed at the beauty of the place, but Firooz felt an odd urgency pulling at him and led his brother on without pausing. When they came to the narrowly enclosed woods, the hounds strained at their leashes and, as they progressed farther among the tree shadows, bayed.

They were answered by furious barking, of a timbre Firooz, twenty-one years later, recognized. Keeping a strong hand on his hound's leash, he spurred his horse forward.

Awaiting them in the clearing, stalwart, as if the years had not passed, was a half-grown dog fleeced like a black lamb, which Firooz could not distinguish from the dog he had killed and buried. The two men dismounted hastily. Without needing to be asked, Firooz took the leash of the second straining hound. The black dog continued to bark as Haider gingerly approached, but these were clearly cries of joy and welcome. Falling to his knees, Haider embraced the animal. When he looked up at his brother, Firooz saw tears on his cheeks. "I seem to know this dog," he said.

"It cannot be the same one," said Firooz, but he was confused by the marvel.

Properly introduced, the hounds made friends with the black dog, which Haider began calling Iman as if he had always known her name. Iman gratefully accepted several pieces of dried meat, and showed the men a spring and small pond as artfully placed under the overhanging cliff as if an architect had designed it. Beyond the high scarps around this place, the sun was lowering. Firooz and his brother washed at the spring, laid out their prayer rugs toward Holy Mecca, and made the declaration of their faith. Firooz's rug still bore faint stains of blood.

Haider built a small fire and prepared coffee. The hobbled horses grazed contentedly on grass sweeter than any they had encountered since departing Samarkand, while the three dogs lay about—Iman always near her master— panting, happy. The brothers reclined with their coffee, talking of matters of no importance, but not speaking of marvels.

After, heated with the spirit of the coffee, they removed their garments and embraced. They were men, they were fond of each other, they were long away from their wives. No words needed to be spoken as each gave pleasure to the other, as none had ever been spoken.

Yet afterward, when they woke from slumber and lay side by side, content, Haider said, "My brother, do you truly not regret having no children?"

Firooz considered. It was not a question he had not had to answer before. "It saddens me," he said, "that my wife cannot bear our children safely, for she so wishes to be a mother. And yet, one day she may, for I myself was my father's late, unexpected child, after his wife had been barren for many years. As for my own wishes—it was God's will to grant me a brother after both my parents had died. My uncle told me to call you *son*, but it was a brother God gave me and I have never not been glad of you. Now, moreover, there are your sons and daughter at home, whom I could not value more if they were my own."

"This is what you say, and it is a fine answer. Is it what you feel?" Haider rose to his feet, as naked as the day Firooz found him. As Firooz admired him, Haider said, "I believe I can give you a child of your own blood—and mine," and as Firooz watched, amazed, the handsome young man was transformed into a beautiful young woman. "Ask no questions," she said, kneeling at his side and placing her hand on his lips, "for I cannot answer them." She kissed his mouth.

They made love again, and it was not so very different than before, except that Haider gave only, did not take. Indeed, when he remembered it later, Firooz felt he preferred the manliness of Haider as he had been or the different womanliness of his own wife.

When both were spent, the woman who had been his brother kissed him again, and rose, and gathered up the garments of a man. As she drew them on, her form appeared to melt within the fabric, assuming again the guise of Firooz's brother Haider. Beard grew on cheeks now more wide and flat, around lips more thin and hard. The long sable glory of the woman's hair drifted away, leaving only black stubble on Haider's well shaped skull. "We should return to the camp," he said, offering a hand to help Firooz up.

Grasping it, Firooz held the small, smooth hand of the woman. He started and, as he blinked, saw for an instant the woman encumbered in outsize man's clothing, but the vision fled when his brother's gripping hand and strong right arm hauled him to his feet. Numbed by astonishment, frightened, he stumbled about, donning his own clothes while Haider rolled up their rugs and repacked the coffee service. The younger man mounted his horse easily, called to the dog, Iman, who came readily, keeping a sane distance from the horse's hooves.

Haider appeared to remain Haider, a man, for the rest of the journey to Baghdad. Still, Firooz continued troubled. Perhaps it had been simply a dream, his brother's transformation—they did not speak of it, nor came there again an occasion that he might touch his brother, see him whole and nude and prove that vision false. Yet sometimes, regarding Haider over an evening's fire, Firooz thought the younger man looked ill, drawn and pale; sometimes, as they rode, the straight-backed youth appeared for an instant to slump in his saddle and to resemble more a weary woman than an energetic, cheerful man. The black dog—which followed Haider everywhere, received choice morsels from his bowl, sometimes rode perched before him on the saddle, held safe by his strong arm—would bark, Haider would smile and shake his head, and Firooz blink.

In the great city of Baghdad, Firooz conducted his business out of the caravansary maintained by the merchants of Samarkand, selling, buying, bartering, trading. It was already a profitable venture. For some days business occupied him to the exclusion of any other concern. Then a late-arriving caravan brought him a sad letter from his wife in Samarkand: she had not told him before his departure that she believed herself with child and it was just as well for, by God's will, she had lost this baby too, soon after he left. Yet she was well, recovered from the injury to her body if not the wound to her soul; her sister (by which she meant Haider's wife) was a constant comfort, Haider's children constant joys. She awaited her husband's return with fond resolve.

Haider entered Firooz's chamber as he finished reading the letter and set it aside, his eyes wet. "You are once again not to be an uncle," Firooz said.

"I know. My wife, also, wrote to me." Haider poured cool water for his brother, offered a scented kerchief to wipe his eyes. "I grieve with you."

Firooz drank. "Nevertheless," he said, "I meant what I said, the day you found Iman." (Hearing her name, the dog yapped, before curling up for a nap.) "I should like a child, for my poor wife's sake, but I have no need of one." He held out a hand for his brother to grip.

Though Haider's well known, well loved face did not change, it was a woman's hand Firooz grasped, small boned and soft, and a woman's full, quickening belly to which his palm was pressed. "You are to be a father, brother," Haider said in his deep, full voice, "and I a mother." He held Firooz's hand to his belly a moment longer, exerting a man's strength to prevent his recoiling. "Although I should prefer your wife raise the child, as I have other responsibilities."

"How is this possible?"

"Do you question the will of merciful and compassionate God?"

"Are you a jinni? An ifrit?"

"I am a creature of earth even as yourself, not a being of fire. I am a man: your brother. And a woman—not your sister or your wife, but the mother of your unborn child. Firooz, my dear, there is no more I can tell you. I mean you only good."

Firooz recoiled when Haider approached again.

"I came," Haider said with a gentle smile, "to take you away from your new sorrow and your weary business. Tomorrow we go to the Friday Mosque to say our prayers among the ummah. This evening I intend to dedicate to your comfort and ease. Come, brother. This other matter need not concern you for some months yet. Come."

Still troubled, Firooz gave in. Leaving the disappointed Iman behind, Haider led Firooz out into the streets of the city, first to a hammam as splendid as the finest mosque. Here they bathed—Firooz felt immeasurable relief when he saw that Haider, wearing no more than a cloth around his hips, appeared no less masculine than he ought, his belly flat and firm, his chest and shoulders broad. Attendants massaged them in turn; others shaved the hair from their scalps and bodies, as was meet, oiled and perfumed their beards; still others brought coffee when at length they reclined on soft couches and did not speak.

From the hammam, they went on to the house of a gentleman of their acquaintance, an elderly merchant who left the travelling to his sons and nephews, where they were fed dishes from distant lands and offered conversation of the kind to be encountered only in great cities.

Finally, pleasantly weary and replete, they returned to Firooz's rooms at the caravansary. Iman greeted them with great joy, not lessened by the little bowl of tidbits Haider had smuggled under his robes from their dinner. Firooz seated himself again before his accounts and inventories.

"No," said Haider, firm. Drawing his brother to his feet, he undressed Firooz and laid him down on the couch, removed his own clothing, blew out the lamp.

Making love, Firooz was uncertain from moment to moment whether the person in his arms was a strong, slender, forceful man or a soft, yielding, fecund woman. For one night, it seemed, it didn't matter.

A month later, they departed Baghdad at the head of a caravan laden with the goods of all western Islam as well as infidel Europe and savage Africa. Some months into the journey, they came again to the cairn of stones by the road and here again they halted. As camp was set up, the black dog Iman became agitated. She circled the grave of her predecessor several times, then, barking and whining, made Haider accompany her in investigating it again. She led him to the edge of the encampment and gazed long across the plain where, beyond the horizon, lay the place she had been found. At last, Haider went to his brother, the dog whining and yapping at his heels, and said, "I must go. Will you come with me?"

The place, when they came to it, had not changed, but Haider had. Dismounting from his horse, he was no longer a sturdy young merchant but a frail, weary woman whose inappropriate, ill fitting garments did nothing to disguise the belly round and full as a melon, the brimming breasts like ripe pears. Frightened as much for as of her, Firooz ran to take her arm. "It is early, I would have thought," she said. "I should have known God would lead me here, again, to bear my child."

"There is no midwife," Firooz protested, "no shelter."

"We shall manage."

Her labor was short, though she bit her lips to bleeding from the pain and clenched her fists so tight as to leave bruises on Firooz's hand and cause the dog that lay on her other side, shoulders under her hand, to yelp. When his son came, Firooz was ready to catch him, marvelling, weeping, to lift him, all bloody and damp, to his cheek. He severed the cord with the blade that had killed Iman's predecessor. The mother pushed out the afterbirth onto the rug stained by much older blood and lay back, resting her aching legs. "Is he beautiful?" she asked.

"He is beautiful," the father said, tender, cleaning the baby with fresh water from the spring.

"Give him my breast," she said, "for I think I shall not keep it long."

While the baby suckled, the man washed the woman, prepared a clean place for her to lie and coffee to soothe and revive her. When the baby slept, tiny hand curled around a lock of Iman's fur, the woman rose slowly to her feet. "Bring me my clothing, please, Firooz," she said.

As she dressed, the transformation occurred, so subtly Firooz could not determine the instant he saw no longer the mother of his son but his brother Haider. The young man knelt by his nephew but did not touch. "What will you call your son?"

"Khayrat."

Haider smiled. The old word meant *good deed*. "A fine name." He stood again. "We should return to camp. It will be dark soon."

"Will you carry him?"

"No, brother. I meant him for you."

There was no other man in the caravan who remembered Firooz's finding Haider twenty-two years before, none to call his finding Khayrat other than good fortune for fatherless babe and childless father alike. When, months later in Samarkand, Firooz's wife took Khayrat from her husband's arms, she was nearly reconciled to her own barrenness.

Haider never again, to his brother's knowledge, became a woman; never, in word or action, admitted to being more than Khayrat's fond uncle. The dog Iman was spoiled and petted by children and adults alike, though she never forgot where her love and loyalty lay, never slept where she could not hear Haider's breath. She bore litters to passing dogs, and every puppy resembled her, and when after a long life at last she died, there was another fleecy black bitch to be his companion.

The years passed, between Samarkand and Baghdad, bringing the family instants of joy and good fortune, sorrow and bad luck, as God had written in their fates. Haider's wife died of a fever, her children still young. The family mourned but went on, as it must. Haider did not marry again. When they were old enough, his sons—and later Khayrat—journeyed with the caravan to and from Baghdad. Grown to manhood, they led it, and their fathers remained at home.

They sat in their garden by a singing fountain, Firooz and his brother. Haider stroked the flank of his dog and said, "Long ago, Firooz, I told you I was no jinni or ifrit, but a creature of earth like yourself. But unlike, as well. Beneficent and compassionate God made many worlds, interleaved like the pages of a great book. Some lie as close to another as any two surahs of the Holy Qu'ran, others as distant as the beginning from the end. In some, things that are impossible here are commonplace; in others, everything we take for granted is entirely unknown. There are worlds that contain no miracles at all, worlds where a new miracle is born every morning. The earth from which God molded my ancestors, brother, lies in another world. It is time, I think, for my dog and me to go home."

"Haider?" Firooz gripped his brother's hand to prevent him from rising.

"I believe there is only one Paradise, Firooz. We shall meet again in not too long. Let me go, brother." Tender, he kissed the back of Firooz's hand and raised it to touch his own forehead. "I cannot love you less, here or elsewhere."

"I should die before you!" Firooz closed his eyes, desolate.

"It is not to death I am going. Give my blessing and my love to my sons." Gentle, he removed his fingers from Firooz's hand, kissed his brow. When his brother opened his eyes again, dog and man were gone as if they had never set foot on the earth of Firooz's world. The elder brother wept, and then, as he must, went on living until he died.

✦ ✦ ✦

Turning

Serkan did not understand the music. He hadn't expected pop or electronica—he hadn't known what to expect. The single flute, its tone thin and whiny, edgy, marked no rhythm he could count and lapsed only at odd short intervals, as if by accident, into melody. He did not understand the audience around him, ranked behind a low fretwork fence on the eight sides of the wooden floor. Hushed, expensively dressed men and women simply waited, many—as he looked from face to tranquil face—with their eyes closed, still as porcelain figurines. He did not understand why he had accepted the invitation to attend this outmoded rite, this performance by Konya's renowned whirling dervishes. The invitation had been extended by a man he ought to hate. Did hate. His mother's brother's son had ruined him when both were just boys.

The man who had rescued Serkan, offered him a home, taught him a trade, Cem—bitter Cem had urged him not to go. When Serkan chose not to hear his advice, Cem commanded, then pled, then turned haughtily away to wrap himself in the frayed remnants of his dignity. He refused to reply when Serkan wished him a pleasant evening and went to the door.

At one side of the open floor, the Mevlevi dervishes were not so still as the audience. They fidgeted: fussed with the hang of their black mantles, adjusted

composed 2009-2010, Pawtucket, Rhode Island
first published in Chelsea Station #1, November 2011

the seat of their tall flowerpot hats, scratched at itches on their noses or in other places. Not even the old grandfather, their master, was still. He dipped and swooped from dervish to dervish like a moulty black pigeon after crumbs. Serkan saw very well that the master spent a particular amount of time with his cousin. All these years later, both of them grown, Zeki looked nervous and small, the lenses of his spectacles catching light and dark from overhead, now reflective, now black and opaque.

The old man wandered out to the center of the floor and one by one the ten younger men doffed their mantles and ambled after him, out of step, all matte white except for their tall brown hats. Several of them somehow reminded Serkan of Cem, fragile with age and poor health, although he did not believe they were also petulant, querulous, like the sad fellow waiting in the ruin of his family's mansion for Serkan to come home. Zeki was transparently the youngest of the dervishes.

Concerned—but why should he be concerned? his cousin was nothing to him, less than nothing, his enemy—Serkan noticed that Zeki had removed his glasses with his mantle. Zeki saw as acutely as a mole without spectacles. He looked little and strange on the floor, stumbling after his elders. Closely tailored, his white jacket somehow made him appear bulky and it hit oddly high above his waist, shortened his torso so that the legs imagined under the draping white skirt of his gown became freakishly long.

The maddening flute played on. One dervish received his master's blessing and stepped away, started his turn. Unimaginably, the audience became more quiet, more still. Serkan distinctly heard the thuds of the dervish's left foot striking the floor, the audible friction of his right: the pivot. Right hand went up, left out and down. Spinning slowly like a child's top, the rightward tilt of his head exaggerated by his tall hat, he wobbled away from the master. His skirt flared as he spun faster, belling out at the hem to expose close-fitting white trousers above black shoes. The one swivelled jerkily on its ball, squeaking, while the other slapped the floor.

Another dervish followed, and another, a lengthening chain around the circumference of the floor. Each revolved swiftly about himself: all formed an irregular moving orbit around the nodding old man at the center. One after the next, they passed by Serkan's seat.

He was not sure what he was seeing. The sema was advertised as performance, a word that suggested to Serkan drama and narrative. The music of the flute continued maddening, making no points, following no progression. It was a very ragged affair, Serkan thought. Some evenings when nostalgic Cem insisted Serkan not go out to ply the trade the elder had taught him, their only income, they watched ballet and folkloric dance performances on the television. Cem had once, long ago, meant to become a dancer, until his father forbade it. The dancers on the television worked together, moved together, made something beautiful of their whole—or faded back, anonymous, and permitted the soloist to exploit the vacuum of the glowing screen.

Here, now, each dervish whirled alone, rapt in himself. As a group, they made no patterns on the floor. They held their arms and hands in different postures, turned at different speeds, made their great circles with no acknowledgment of the others so they ought to collide.

Serkan's cousin Zeki spun before him now. Blind at the best of times, Zeki had closed his eyes. His features were bland, composed, thin red lips parted in his patchy black beard as he breathed—grunted, distinctly, each time his left foot hit wooden floor. Zeki had demolished Serkan's life, slowly, inevitably, a gathering destruction that broke like a tremor in the earth and cast him into darkness, out of the world of godly men. Serkan loathed his cousin, trembled with rage, with horror and despair. The odd-looking little man whirled before him, embodying serenity in furious motion, and salt burned the margins of Serkan's eyes.

He looked up. The dervishes, turning, were a formation of radiant spinning stars, a field of white flowers.

❧

> *I dreamt that the Beloved entered my body,*
> *pulled out a dagger,*
> *and went looking for my heart—*
> *He couldn't find it.*
> *So he struck anywhere.*
> —MEVLANA JALAL AD-DIN RUMI

The man didn't want to use a condom. He was German though his name (the name he'd given Serkan) was Turkish. His parents and grandparents had raised him in Turkish but he didn't speak it easily.

"I can't do that," Serkan said. It wasn't the first time a john had demanded to fuck him raw. "I'll put it on you. You'll enjoy that."

Batting his hands away again, the man grunted. He was older than Serkan but still young, big and handsome, with a big, handsome dick that Serkan had sucked on until its owner whimpered, also not part of the bargain. "I'm clean," he said.

"You don't know that I am. I'm a whore. You don't know where I've been, who's been in my ass." Except the very first, unforgiven, no man had fucked Serkan unprotected, but the German didn't need to know that. His dick was slick and ready, pretty. Serkan actually wanted it for a change or he wouldn't have volunteered his mouth. Cem said that risk was minimal even if he came down your throat but you didn't want to give it away. You had to agree to it beforehand, add it into the cost.

This time the man grabbed his wrist with one big hand and squeezed until it hurt, until the unwrapped condom fell from Serkan's fingers, lost in the sheets between the man's thighs. "I said no."

"Please," said Serkan, breath coming fast.

"No. I paid to fuck your ass, not a rubber." He hadn't paid yet.

"We agreed."

"I agreed to pay you."

Beginning to be frightened, Serkan tried to pull his hand free.

"Stop fighting." Smiling, the man lifted his free hand to brush Serkan's hair out of his eyes. "I'll hurt you."

"No." The smile frightened him. "Please."

"Pretty little boy." Serkan was not so little but without much effort the German dislodged him, twisting his arm up around his back as he pushed Serkan into position, his cry muffled by expensive hotel pillows. "Pretty little whore." Easy and confident but not releasing Serkan's wrist, he clambered up, kneeling between Serkan's thighs, forcing them farther apart. Serkan felt the dribbly tip of the john's cock trace cursive graffiti on the plump muscle of his ass as the man leaned over him. "Pretty little ass."

The hard grip on Serkan's wrist let go but the man's other hand pushed between his shoulders, holding him face down in the pillows so he couldn't beg. A finger found his slickened asshole, probed. "Oh, you're ready for me," the man muttered. "I like that."

He wasn't brutal. Was firm, insistent, inevitable. Knew what he was doing, knew how to give pleasure as well as take. When he slobbered on Serkan's neck, when he pressed his comforting weight into Serkan's back, when he reached under with one hand to twiddle at Serkan's nipple—when he reached with the other and found Serkan hard, he made a fist and pushed Serkan's prick into it with the thrust of his own hips. "Sweet," he murmured, "so sweet."

Once it happened, or perhaps it did not, centuries ago when Seljuk sultans reigned over the land of Rum, that Mevlana set aside his verses and went out into the town. As he walked through Konya's marketplace, merchants and shoppers called respectful greetings. Approaching the alley where precious things of gold and silver were made and sold, Mevlana heard the tapping of the smiths' mallets as they hammered patterns into soft metal. La illaha illa'llah, he thought the mallets sang, *There is no God but God.*

Mevlana paused, rapt.

La illaha, the hammers tapped, illa'llah.

"La illaha," sang Mevlana, crossing his arms across his breast, "illa'llah." He lowered his head, then raised it again and watched in wonder as his right hand lifted up, opening to the sky for God's blessing. "La illaha illa'llah." His left arm extended, he fixed his eyes on the hand, palm open to the warmth of the earth under his feet.

Mallets continued to tap out the rhythm of the testament. The men around Mevlana stood back. Balancing his weight on the ball of his right foot, Mevlana began to turn. Awed, shoppers and merchants moved farther back to give him room. He spun about in a circle, the skirts of his kaftan lifting to form another circle, white and billowing, tilting with his movements. In the crowd happened to be a musician carrying his reed flute, which he raised to his lips. Blowing, he caught the notes of Mevlana's devotion and the rhythm of the hammers.

Mevlana continued to turn. The men around him had never witnessed such happiness on a man's face, such rapture, such peace.

Serkan's father and mother came to his uncle's household in Konya from their poor upcountry village in search of a better life. Eventually they found it, better if not good. His father worked for a man who built hotels and apartment blocks, his mother worked for that man's wife, cleaning and cooking, but they continued to live with Serkan's uncle Kadri. Kadri was a widower, he had nobody else to care for his household or help raise his young son. Zeki was four when Serkan was born—seventeen when Serkan was thirteen.

They slept in the same room, of course, Zeki and his younger cousin. Serkan never told when his cousin, frustrated beyond measure by a beautiful girl at school whom he daren't approach, raped him. He never told his parents or Zeki's father that for three years, once a week, sometimes twice or three times, Zeki continued to fuck him. Zeki bought a tin of olive oil before the second time and then it didn't hurt so much. Then, if Zeki, inattentive, neglected to be cruel and call him ugly names, curse him for not being the girl he wished to dream of that week, it felt good. If Zeki caught him touching himself, he merely laughed, pitying. Except one time when Serkan's come splattered on him. That time, he punched Serkan in the belly until he wept and couldn't breathe. "Not for you," he said, covering Serkan's gasping mouth with his right hand, and slapped him hard between the legs. The blow hurt like the evil one's touch but Serkan didn't dare bite down on the tender flesh that filled his mouth.

Still he didn't tell, although he was more careful, waited to find his own release until Zeki left his bed and fell asleep.

When Serkan was sixteen and believed himself nearly a man, his cousin almost twenty, one night after Zeki fucked him and then rolled off, ready to cleanse himself and sleep, Serkan grabbed his cousin's hand. When Zeki was excused from the national-service draft on account of his miserable eyesight, Serkan had been emboldened, for *he* suffered no physical defect.

"Don't touch me, faggot," Zeki snarled and tried to shake him off.

"I'm not a girl," Serkan said. He brushed Zeki's trapped fingers over the hair on his chest. "I'm no longer a boy. You should find me ugly, undesirable. Why do you continue to fuck me?"

Zeki did not reply, struggling to free his hand. He was a small man, though, smaller than his young cousin had grown.

"I think you like it—more than you'd like a girl. I think you like me, like giving me pleasure. It is pleasurable, you know, for me. I think—" Serkan drew Zeki's fingers between his own legs, made them tickle his prick until it began to stand up again—"I think you would like my dick. It's bigger than yours. I think we should find out how much pleasure it might give you."

Finally breaking loose, Zeki staggered away. Naked, he could not flee their room. "I will never...do that again," he said, his voice small, quavery. "I swear."

"Put on your glasses, Zeki." Serkan rose to his feet. "Look how big it is, how much it wants you."

"It's wrong." Zeki backed up to the closed door, could go no farther. "It would be very wrong for a boy to do that to a grown man. A terrible sin."

"To do what? Say what you mean, Zeki. It would be wrong for me to fuck you." Serkan took a step toward his cousin. "Wronger than you fucking me for three years, I wonder? It's a terrible sin to fuck any person but your wife, so the Messenger of God said, peace be upon him."

Fearful, fascinated, Zeki appeared unable to remove his gaze from Serkan's prick, though it must not be much better than a blur without his spectacles. Trembling, he shook his head, still staring. "Şeytan is in you, cousin," he stammered, slurring the *sh*-sound. "Whispering in your heart. Call on God and the angels to help you resist." Tears stood out in the corners of his eyes.

"Was Şeytan in you? Three years ago? Just now?"

The tears began to stream. "It's *different* when a man does—"

"Fucks, Zeki. When a man fucks a boy. Rapes a boy. I'm bigger than you now, Zeki, I need to shave more often. Beside me, *you* appear the boy."

"I was weak! I'm sorry. The evil one tempted me and I was not strong enough to resist."

Disgusted, Serkan turned away. "You're still weak. I won't bother you." He lay back on his bed and, in full view of his cousin if his cousin could see—but he would know what Serkan did—teased and caressed himself to climax. He smeared the emission about on his chest and belly, raised hand to mouth and licked the fingers. Then he wrapped the bedding about himself and settled toward sleep. He was aware of Zeki stealthily donning pyjamas and glasses, creeping out of the room, but slept before his cousin returned, if he did.

In the morning, Zeki spoke to his father. In the afternoon, Kadri spoke to his brother-in-law. In the evening, Serkan's father shouted at him, called him filth, pervert, monster, devil. "Kadri took your mother and me in when he need not. He helped to raise you. His son has been your brother. How you have abused their hospitality—how you have shamed us! You are not my son. You are nobody's son. Get out before I rid the world of your stain."

"Baba—"

"I am nobody's father. Get out."

"My—"

"Nothing in this house is yours. One last time I tell you: Get out."

There were clothes, books, a few CDs, outgrown toys in the room Serkan had shared with his cousin. Sad and afraid, Serkan knew his father would, if pressed again, kill him. Attempt to kill him. He could not bring himself to cause his father to commit that sin. He turned away and left his home.

Mevlana's family and friends and followers were jealous of Shams, the master's beloved, who first showed Mevlana that knowledge of God was not to be found in books but only through recklessly allowing oneself to drown in God's love. Shams had led Mevlana into madness, they felt, as the evil one leads men into error and sin. They whispered against Shams. They conspired. They implored Shams to depart the city and free their master from his spell.

Giving no warning of his departure, leaving no word of his destination, Shams travelled to Damascus. Distraught, Mevlana asked news of his beloved from every traveller, sent messages to every city of every nation of the House of Peace. At last a reply came from the city of jasmine that spoke of the new saint who had taken up residence there.

When Mevlana stood once again in his teacher's presence, he threw himself at Shams's feet. "I cannot be parted from you," he cried. "You are my sun and I merely your moon."

Yet the distrust and jealousy of Mevlana's disciples did not dwindle in the light of their master's surpassing love for his master. It kindled into hatred.

One night, Mevlana and his beloved sat together, speaking of love, of God, of drunkenness, of the world as it is in the light of the intoxication of love, and the world as people believe they see it. Shams was asked to come to the door: there was a messenger, he was told. He did not return.

Some say Shams went travelling again, in search of deeper wisdom, in fear for his life. Some say he went to the ancient heart of Persia. Some say he journeyed to the far uncertain fringe of the House of Peace, to India. Some say the followers of Mevlana carried him away into the winter night and murdered him, buried him shamefully in barren earth with no prayers.

Some say one among Mevlana's disciples who tore Shams from the house of his beloved was Mevlana's son Ala al-Din: some say Shams turned to Ala al-Din in the wilderness, the light of love shining in his eyes, and said, "La illaha illa ana." *There is no God but I.* That mystery, that heresy, that declaration of unending love spoken, Shams vanished from the earth as a jinni, an uncanny entity born of smokeless fire rather than the fertile earth that birthed men and women, might vanish, never to be seen again. Some say.

The earthly body of Shams-e Tabrizi, Mevlana's beloved and master, was laid to rest in Khoy, ancient capital of the Azeri kingdom. His tomb stands there still.

The earthly body of Shams-e Tabrizi was laid to rest in Multan, city of saints and beggars, in the Punjab. His tomb stands there still.

The earthly body of Shams-e Tabrizi mouldered away to dust within the mausoleum dedicated to his memory in Konya, not far from the place where, many years later, Mevlana himself would be interred. You may visit his resting place if you choose.

When we are dead, seek not our tomb in the earth, but find it in the hearts of men.

Afterward, the German dozed, his sweaty weight heavy on Serkan's back, his prick still buried in Serkan's flesh. In time—it seemed to Serkan a very long time—the thing softened, shrank, withdrew. "Please," Serkan murmured, as tender as a lover, "I wish to clean myself. I'll fetch a cloth to clean you."

Grumbling like a lover, content as a lover, the man shifted his weight, permitting Serkan to struggle free. "Come back soon," the man muttered. "In a little, we'll do it again, when I'm recovered."

Crossing the room, Serkan paused to rummage through the pockets of the clothes he had thrown on a chair when the man asked him to undress. He found what he wanted and went on. He sat on the toilet and voided himself of the man's sperm, as much as he could force out—crouched over the bidet to rinse his ass with the hottest water inflamed tissue could bear. He washed hands and face, dick and balls with soap and hot water. Gazing at his naked person in the hotel's vast mirrors he felt he was the same man, the same whore, who had agreed to the German's proposal. He picked up his pocket knife from the counter where he'd laid it.

It counterfeited a Swiss soldier's utility knife though he knew it had been made in İstanbul. One by one, he went through the tools. Few of the blades were sharp enough to cut any substance firmer than cheese, none long enough to pierce but only to slice. Pondering, he regarded the awl. It was perhaps ten centimeters long. When he pressed its point to the tip of his forefinger, it took an instant longer for pain to register than for metal to enter flesh. He watched red blood well up around invasive steel. It would serve no purpose to have his blood tested soon: seroconversion took a month or more.

Setting the pocket knife aside, he sucked his finger for a moment until the bleeding slowed. He soaked a hand towel in scalding water and wrung it out. Carrying steaming towel in left hand, knife with the awl locked outward in the other, he stepped back through the door.

The man had fallen fully into sleep. Sprawled on his back, vulnerable, he snored sweetly, untroubled. His extended left hand wore silvery crusts of Serkan's semen. Unlike a properly reared Muslim, he did not shave between his legs. Nested in tangled, unclean pubic hair, wrinkled and shrunken, his prick resembled a worm wriggling out of the earth, fouled with gummy drying lubricant, his own semen, Serkan's excrement.

Kneeling on the bed at his side, Serkan first wiped the left hand clean. The man only muttered without waking. Gentle, Serkan swabbed and scrubbed the genitals. The penis began to wake but the man did not until Serkan laid the warm, dirtied cloth across his mouth and nose. He found the throbbing pulse in the man's throat and, precise as a goldsmith, drove the awl in, up through the jaw.

Dying, the john woke. Fury and terror shone from wide eyes, muffled gurgles attempted escape from his covered mouth. His limbs thrashed, bruising where they struck. There was a great deal of blood, pumping and vital, when Serkan removed the awl from his throat and stabbed it into one eye. He felt the thin bone at the back of the socket puncture as jelly and fluid and more blood burst from the eyeball, and then he pierced the other. Over the iron reek of blood he smelled sudden shit. "I said *no*," Serkan murmured.

He waited until convinced the German was dead, then returned to the bathroom. He stood under hot water in the shower for a long time before he began to scrub. At length, he stepped from the shower and dried himself. He attempted to rinse the pocket knife clean, though he knew blood must have coagulated in the crevices where blades and tools folded. He could not bear to use it again for any purpose, in any case. Wrapping it up in another hand towel, he resolved to toss it through the grate of a storm sewer, the first he passed.

The room smelled bad when he returned, so he went to one of the windows and fumbled through the drapes to open it. Turning back, he noticed on the writing desk a squat crimson pillar candle, beside it a box of matches. The perfume in the wax was stifling, fruity and artificial, but he lit the wick anyway. For moments he contemplated burning the place down. But the hotel's other guests had done nothing to offend him and it was a new building (perhaps his father had helped build it), doubtless riddled with sensors and alarms and sprinklers. He refused to look at the pile of meat on the bed.

It required only a few minutes for Serkan to dress, only a few more to find the wallet in the dead man's discarded trousers. Passport, ID, credit cards from German banks were of no use or interest to him but there was a surprising, stupid amount of cash, both lira and euro. Without thinking it through, Serkan rejected the notion of taking only the sum they had agreed.

He found the man's suitcase in the closet. None of the clothing was of excellent quality and, though it was all neatly folded, the garments were wrinkled and smelled of his sweat. He had been on his way home after his holiday, Serkan supposed—a supposition confirmed when he encountered a velvet bag filled with vulgar gold jewelry, bangles, necklaces, earrings, which Serkan might see any day in the shop windows on the street of the goldsmiths. Girls and women in Germany would not appreciate receiving gifts from a dead man, so Serkan set the bag aside to take with him, knowing he could not expect to receive a fair price for any of it.

The last thing he found, swaddled in a tourist shop's plastic bag and many gaudy silk scarves, was a small glazed porcelain figurine, a spinning dervish of the Mevlevi order. The sentimentality of the object startled him. The expression painted on the figure's face, intent on its downturned left hand, was insipid. He turned it in his hands but the belled porcelain skirt of the dervish's gown did not ripple or rise higher, the expression did not change, he heard no ecstatic music. He kept the scarves, bundling them back into the plastic bag along with the jewelry, but placed the vapid dervish on the desk beside the burning candle before walking out the door.

Mevlana sat reading by the fountain in the courtyard of his father's madrasa. He was not yet beloved throughout the House of Peace—his dead father, from whom he inherited the school, was far more renowned—not yet called *Mevlana* except by his own students. In the marketplace, at the Friday Mosque where he often led the congregational prayers, in the sultan's court, he was known merely as Jalal ad-Din Muhammad, son of Baha ud-Din Walad, Sultan of Scholars.

Everybody knew the story of their encounter on the road from Khorasan, father and son, with the poet Attar of Nishapur. Seeing the father walking ahead of his son, the poet had proclaimed, "Here comes a sea followed by an ocean!" But that was over twenty years before and, though Jalal was respected in his city as scholar and teacher, there seemed little likelihood of his fame ever eclipsing his father's.

He was studying a work of Attar, *The Parliament of the Birds*. Beside him on the fountain's rim sat several other precious volumes. He heard the sound of footsteps, the tapping of a staff, and looked up.

The glare of the sun was such that for an instant he believed he saw the sun walking into the courtyard of the madrasa, but it was merely a man. A man of advanced years, clothed in dingy, ragged wool patched here and there with faded silks. Coming to a halt, leaning on his staff, stranger regarded scholar. "What are you doing?" the stranger asked.

Annoyed by the intrusion on his peaceful study of a wandering beggar who doubtless couldn't read at all, Jalal replied, "Something you cannot understand."

His lips cherry red within a bushy grey beard, the stranger smiled. "Is that so?" he asked. "May I see?"

Ashamed of his discourtesy, Jalal rose to offer the stranger the book. Even an illiterate might appreciate its craftsmanship, the loveliness of fine calligraphy, the beauty of the volume's painted illuminations. But as he held it out, open to a splendid gilded panel depicting the hoopoe addressing all the birds in the world, the pages burst into flame.

Crying out, Jalal dropped the book. In an instant, fierce flames subsided and nothing lay on stone pavement but a pile of ash, grey flakes whirling in the breeze. Horrified, Jalal raised his eyes to the stranger's.

Still smiling, calm, the beggar lifted his staff and used its foot to push the scholar's other books from their precarious perch into the pool of the fountain.

"What are you doing?" cried Jalal, plunging his hands into the pool to rescue his books. "What have you done?"

Yet each noble volume, as he withdrew it dripping from the water, became instantly bone dry, without blot of ink or smear of paint, and when he set them lovingly aside and turned on his knees to the pile of ash, he found Attar's *Parliament of the Birds* whole, entire, undamaged. He opened the ornamented binding: his eyes fell on a line of verse he had never properly comprehended and it was transparent, pellucid. "What have you done?" he asked again.

"Something you cannot understand."

Jalal lifted his eyes to the stranger's face and it seemed, somehow, that he had always known this man. "Who are you?"

"I? I am only Shams, from Tabriz."

In the language of poets, the beautiful tongue, *Shams* meant *Sun*. Recognizing the face of his beloved, Jalal understood that his first impression of the man had been correct. He rose to his feet and embraced his laughing master.

Departing forever his uncle's apartment, Serkan did not know where to go. He had nothing, no home, no family, only a few lira in his pockets, the clothes he wore.

All his life he had lived in Mevlana's city, known of the poet's fame, in school studied translations of Mevlana's verses into words and letters he could read, if not always understand. Yet he had never found time to visit the museum that had been made of the poet's mausoleum and the lodge of his disciples. Serkan knew the landmark, the Green Tomb, but he had never entered the gates.

He could not think why he should visit now. He could not think of anywhere else to go.

It was a long walk, trudging busy city streets. When finally he saw the conical turquoise dome of the tomb, he was weary and long summer dusk had deepened to night. Of course the museum was closed.

Despairing, Serkan purchased a bottle of water from a sidewalk vendor. Miserable, he sat on a bench within the park that surrounded Mevlana's monument. As he drank he wept, silent.

After a time, a person sat on the bench near him. Serkan did not look up until the stranger said, "Friend, I believe I know you."

Serkan felt quite sure they were not acquainted. The man was slender, not young, attired in finer garments than any of his family's friends. The lamps in the park scarcely illuminated the unfamiliar face but it seemed to him that contours and coloring were enhanced by paint and powder. There was something false about the hair.

"I'm Cem," the painted stranger said. "Why are you not dining in comfort with your family?"

Serkan looked away again. "I am dead to my family." Ashamed of himself, overwhelmed, he uttered a single quiet sob.

Cem took Serkan to his home. He fed the youth well. He bathed Serkan with his own hands and, with his own razor, carefully shaved the boy's stubbly beard and all the hair from his body so that he almost appeared a boy indeed. But when Cem took Serkan to bed, although man taught boy, it was the boy who fucked the man.

Mevlana and Shams had closeted themselves in an inner room, windowless and with only one door. It was early on a winter morning. Mevlana's wife peered through the crack at the door's jamb, curious. Shams and her husband sat quite silently on opposite sides of the room, each man's eyes intent on the other.

Without warning, the solid back wall of the little chamber seemed to split open, emitting a blaze of brilliant light that somehow did not blind the witness. Out of the light paced six radiant persons, clothed in light, whose faces were so dazzling their features could not be distinguished. The figures bowed and greeted Mevlana and his master in an unfamiliar language like bells and birdsong. They placed in the center of the floor a vessel that appeared to be fashioned of radiance, not glass, which contained flowers of surpassing beauty. Then the six disposed themselves about the room and sat and all were silent again for a time.

The hour of morning prayer arrived. One of the shining persons bowed to Shams, but he demurred. The person then gestured to Mevlana. All turned toward the city at the center of God's world and Mevlana led the company through their prayers (outside the door, his wife repeated the holy words under her breath), then spoke a lesson of such simplicity, humility, and beauty no listener's eyes could remain dry.

Mevlana's wife was wiping the tears from her eyes when the six splendid persons rose, bowed again, and departed through the shining door. The wall became solid again.

Before his wife could recover from her astonishment, Mevlana had opened the little room's only door. He bundled the supernal flowers into her arms and said, "Take good care of these, hatun." Retreating, he closed the door behind him again.

The fragrance of the flowers intoxicated her. In a daze, she found a place to put them. Throughout the day she stole moments from her duties around the house to wonder at their beauty and inhale their perfume.

The next day, Mevlana's wife took a branch of the miraculous blossoms to the perfumers' market, hoping to discover their source for she had never encountered flowers to compare. All the artists of scent were astounded by them—none recognized the blossoms, none could guess whence they came—all wished (none was impolite enough to utter the wish) a great supply of them to distil into perfume.

By chance, a spice merchant of distant India happened to enter the market, bearing rare woods and essences and resins for the perfumers. Seeing the flowers in Mevlana's wife's hand, he exclaimed in wonder. "Here it is the middle of winter in chilly Konya," he cried, "yet these rare flowers bloom only in one small glade in the most southerly part of my country, where it is always balmy, for a single week in spring!"

Amazed, the woman returned to her home, where her husband again urged her to care well for the flowers. They were a precious gift, he said, from the gardeners of the earthly paradise.

All her life, for years after her husband's death, Mevlana's wife watched over the flowers. Their petals never bruised nor withered, their fragrance never faded. Anybody who smelled them, however ill or sorrowful, felt at once revived. If, to succor a person who could not travel, she gave a branch away it did not require replacing. When Mevlana's wife at last laid off her earthly form, the flowers were not seen again by ordinary women and men. It was said they had accompanied her soul into God's presence.

Emerging into winter night from the hotel lobby, Serkan recognized the floodlit green faïence cone of Mevlana's tomb above the trees across the street. He had still never entered the museum but it would be closed now. Pacing the sidewalk, eyes down, he watched for a drain in the gutter. When he saw one, he shook open the towel in his hand and watched his pocket knife clatter through the grate. He looked up, around. No passerby appeared to be paying attention. It perturbed him to feel so unperturbed.

He crossed the street to the park, dropping the towel on the tarmac halfway across. Walking, wandering, he came to the bench where Cem had found him two and a half years before and sat, though it was too chilly to sit long. He had no doubt he would share his new little fortune with Cem but for a moment he wished to contemplate possibilities. For a moment he wished to imagine buying a bus ticket to Ankara or İstanbul or one of the Mediterranean resort towns—to imagine being a young man, almost nineteen, with a life ahead of him. To imagine not being a whore, not making only a whore's choices.

He would return to Cem's house. He would wrap one of the pretty silk scarves around Cem's bald head, adorn his ears and neck and wrists with gold, count out half the cash. Cem had inherited house and fortune but the fortune was nearly spent.

First, though, Serkan would use a small part of the new fortune to buy himself dinner. A dinner such as he had never eaten, such as Cem had enjoyed long ago when he was his wealthy family's pampered only son. Serkan knew precisely where to go. It was not far. The place served dishes devised to tempt the jaded palates of sultans in imperial İstanbul, subtle, elaborate, painstaking.

The factotum who greeted him at the door was clearly not impressed. Serkan was young, solitary, and, though clean, not well dressed. A brusque waiter led him to an out-of-the-way table and gave him the menu. The dishes' names resembled poetry which would require a concordance to understand— *the imam fainted, thighs of a maiden*—but there were also descriptions. By the time the waiter returned with fresh, cool water and a plate of simple meze, Serkan had made his choices.

The waiter had seated him so that, while he was largely unnoticeable to other diners, they were laid out for him like the figures in an old painting. He sipped his water, chewed fried anchovies and cold beans and fresh cheese, and regarded his fellow citizens. Not all citizens, of course, some were foreign tourists, and likely none fellows. If they knew who he was, what he was, they would scorn if not stone him.

In one place, two tables had been pushed together. Here sat a party of eleven men, all dressed similarly in dark jackets and white shirts. They were not gregarious or voluble. A pall of calm seemed to cover them as they ate, drank, conversed quietly. The waiter who served them—not Serkan's waiter—appeared respectful in the manner of a polite child attending his stern, old-fashioned, but loving grandfather. He deferred especially to the man who sat at the head, a hale, kindly looking elderly man with a large white beard. A small brocaded cap perched on his cropped white hair.

When Serkan's waiter brought the first dish and placed it before him, Serkan asked, "Who are those gentlemen?"

"Mevlevi." The young man's tone was awed. "They performed the sema earlier this evening at Mevlana's lodge."

The mystic dervish brotherhood, followers of Mevlana. Legally, they were performers merely, licensed to spin at prescribed times for the entertainment of tourists. The Republic had appropriated their lodge and dissolved the order, banned it, when that old man was only a child or not yet born. Yet every resident of Mevlana's city knew it was merely their public face that changed at government decree: they met still, as a private group, accepted acolytes, worshipped, found God in surrender to the unrelenting movement of the world. The old man would be a direct descendant of Mevlana himself.

It was nothing to do with Serkan, a sinner not in God's eye. He had not even witnessed the sema. He turned his attention to the plate before him.

A person began to pass his table, heading toward the lavatories, but halted. Serkan raised his eyes from the voluptous meal. A small, abnormally small, agitated young man gazed at him, one of the Mevlevi by his clothing though he was not presently serene. It was not possible to recognize him, impossible not to. "Serkan?" Behind the thick glass of his spectacles, Zeki's eyes were wide. "I feared you were dead." The wispy, patchy beard did not flatter Serkan's cousin's face.

"I am dead to you and your family, Zeki Efendi." Unsettling enough to be rediscovered, but for it to be a dervish, a holy man—how could the boy who crippled his life become holy? Serkan lowered his eyes to his plate, schooled his pounding heart. "I did not intend to offend you with my presence—I will leave as soon as I finish my meal. Forget you saw me."

"Serkan!" Anguish sounded in Zeki's voice. "You hate me. You have many reasons to hate me." Suddenly Zeki went to his knees. "Serkan Efendi, I wish—since that day I have wished to beg your forgiveness."

Serkan swallowed the ash and dung in his mouth. "You have it. Please, get up and go back to your friends."

Slowly Serkan's cousin rose to his feet. "But how will I find you again? We must talk. How have you lived? Serkan—I am sorry to offend you: you are in my heart. I feared you were dead."

"You must not find me again." In his heart? Serkan dwelled in nobody's heart except an old queen's who feared dying alone. "Please, go back to your friends. Forget this encounter happened. *Believe* that I am dead."

"Serkan—" Zeki inhaled sharply, held his breath for a moment. "Very well. May merciful and compassionate God hold you close. I wish you well." He went away. Some minutes later, returning from the lavatory, he passed without speaking.

The food was spoiled. Its subtle flavors were vile on Serkan's tongue. With every swallow he must force himself not to gag. It took a considerable time to get through it—the Mevlevi had long departed before he was done—but he couldn't bring himself to let it go to waste. When the waiter finally produced his bill, on the dish with the reckoning lay a turquoise-green pasteboard card. "The young dervish sent it," the waiter said, his voice thin with envy, when Serkan picked up the ticket to the performance of the sema the following evening.

⁓⁊⸲⸱⁊⁓

I was buried and rotting
in the grave of myself.
When you came to visit me,
I raised my head and
climbed out of my tomb.
—Mevlana Jalal ad-Din Rumi

Surprised the tomb's door stood wide, Serkan passed through. He should have left the shrine immediately the sema concluded, flushed, sweated dervishes stumbling one by one past their master to some inner chamber of the museum. The audience, departing the hall, was subdued. Serkan should have left immediately—walked home to fretful Cem's or visited the likely establishments to pick up a john. Zeki was nothing to him. He despised Zeki as one was meant to abhor Şeytan. Zeki was dead to him.

The anteroom was decorated with ancient manuscripts. A silver door invited him to the next chamber where an overwhelming richness of gold and cobalt tile soared to the high dome. Golden brocade covered the coffins of the poet, his family, followers. Perched atop Mevlana's sarcophagus, directly below the dome, a stone dervish hat was wrapped about its base by a stone turban.

It was all very holy, very solemn, very beautiful: there was nothing for Serkan here. He turned to leave. There was money to be made—men to fuck him or for him to fuck. He was a whore, now a murderer.

Zeki stood at the silver door, hands behind his back. Out of dervish gown, no flowerpot hat to make him tall, he was not impressive. A little, narrow-shouldered man in white shirt and dark jacket, the shirt buttoned to his throat—his hair lank and beard unfortunate. He resembled some of Serkan's clients. He could never be a whore himself. The lenses of his glasses reflected gold—there was no seeing through them. "Serkan," he said.

Approaching, Serkan smelled his cousin's pungent sweat. "Why?" There was another scent, a fragrance. Serkan couldn't catch it.

"I wronged you. Over and over. Cruelly. I lied to my father and to your father and caused them to wrong you worse than I."

"I didn't mind the fucking, after the first time." Serkan supposed he shouldn't speak of fucking within the tomb of a saint. "Zeki, I forgave you last night, don't you remember? I must go. It would be better not to see each other again."

"What do you know of Mevlana?" his cousin asked. "Mevlana and Shams."

Serkan looked over Zeki's head at figured golden tiles, rich blue tiles inscribed with unreadable gold calligraphy. "Nothing. Less than nothing. What I was taught in school."

"This is for you." Bringing his right hand from behind his back, Zeki extended it to Serkan. A flower lay on his open palm. Just a flower, a single blossom shorn from its stem.

Serkan could not name the colors painted on its filmy petals. He had never seen such a blossom, in none of the expensive florists Cem wished he might patronize again. It was beautiful in a way flowers *weren't* but men, infrequently, might be. He leaned toward his cousin's hand. The blossom's perfume encompassed them. Serkan's breath failed—or he was all breath, nothing but breath.

"When Mevlana first met Shams, the day love was discovered to him, he led his beloved to a private room. They did not emerge for sixty days. Serkan, please? Come with me."

Reaching for the flower, Serkan grasped Zeki's hand. Crushed petals bonded one flesh to the other.

❧❧

I tied a noose around the neck of my soul
and brought it to Him:
"Here is the one who turned his back on love—
Do not let him escape this time."
—MEVLANA JALAL AD-DIN RUMI

Haider and His Dog

The convoy of clockwork-cog barges had been beating north up the coast for what almanacs and the crew's timepieces marked as fifteen days. The ever-slowing sun hung halfway down the western sky but it would not set for another six almanac-weeks. At the bow of the lead barge, Haider and Iman, his faithful companion, stared north. Haider pulled out and consulted his time-piece: the navigator had promised landfall within the quarter almanac-day.

He knew the deserts between Samarkand and Baghdad in that other world, but in this world he had never seen a place as desolate as the coast to his right. On this voyage, he had seen—had ridden through—great storms piling in from the west that refilled the convoy's cisterns in a matter of minutes. He had watched in confusion as the winds and clouds and rain halted a parasang short of shore and roiled there like a pack of wild beasts frustrated by a fence. "No rain falls on that coast," the convoy weatherworker had told him. "It has been so as long as anybody knows—since before the sun began to slow, at least."

"Why? How?"

"As you see—" The weatherworker, Sagal, a hardened, preoccupied woman, gestured toward the line where the latest storm was breaking up. "There is a barrier. Myself, as a weatherworker, I am always aware of it but cannot under-stand it, nor contemplate even attempting to breach it. It is as it is. There is no

composed 2007, Pawtucket, Rhode Island
original to this volume

rain, no fresh water at all, between ocean and the mountains to the east—no-body can live on the Empty Coast."

"But Iyivë...." Iyivë was the city to which the convoy brought its cargo of grain and timber.

"Iyivë is the fortunate exception. You will see."

Iman had fallen asleep on the warm deck at Haider's feet. Haider turned from contemplating the westering sun, which bloated as slowly as it slipped down the sky. What would the world be like, he wondered, when, as it seemed it must, it ceased turning at all? He would not live to see that world, a thought that disappointed him only a little. He had seen a good part of his brother's world, and more of this world of his birth since his return. Although he had not tired of marvels, he had tired.

Resting his hands on the rail, he sighed and looked north and east again. A new marvel met his eyes. A range of low, sandy hills or dunes rolled from the desert into the sea; beyond their crest, a shining white tower spired into the blue sky. Its height he could not begin to gauge: taller than any man-built structure he had ever seen. Taller and more slender and elegant than any build-ing he could have imagined.

From his basket on the mast behind and above Haider, the watch called, "Iyivë!"

Startled from sleep, Iman barked and struggled to her feet, glaring about wildly. Haider laid his hand on her white head and she calmed. She was old. She had not been young when she led Haider back to this world and now it was fifteen almanac-years later and her fur had been entirely white for the past four. This voyage, he suspected, would be her last if it was not also his. Encouraging her to follow, he went to find the bargemaster.

"Iyivë?" he said when he found her. "What is that tower?"

"You have not heard of or read about the temple of Iyivë?"

Haider shook his head. "I prefer to be surprised than to have my expecta-tions disappointed."

He offered the master his wineskin. They sat at the chart table and, af-ter a healthy pull at the thick black wine, the master traced out the Empty Coast on the map before them. North of the glyph that represented Iyivë, a high range of mountains ran from the east, a spur of the great north-south range. Reaching some parasangs into the ocean like an arm, the east-west range cast out a handful of pebbles: a chain of islands. "From here south is as you have seen—desert. Storms in from the west halt at a barrier nobody can explain—"

"Sagal told me."

"From the east, these peaks perform the same service. That, of course, is entirely explicable. And so the coast has been barren forever."

"Yet there is this city, Iyivë. A great city, I believe."

Leaning back in her seat, the master gave a few turns to the crank of the magical little device that kept the barge's clockwork wound. "Back in the days when the sun's passage over the world required no more than a day and gods were common in every land, two thousand years or more? A fishing boat out of the islands was driven south by a storm. It did not founder, it wasn't wrecked, but when it finally passed the barrier into calm waters it was two hundred parasangs south of its home port. It had only gone out for the day, you understand, so carried little water. The storm had not broken and even if it were to do so the winds were against them—they had no clockwork then, you know, only sail." Reminded, the master turned her crank again.

"In despair, preferring to die on solid ground if die they must, the crew beached their boat. There was, it seems, just there, a god named Iyivë who had been waiting for people to come to her since the world began. She succored the sailors. They required drink, so she reached into the earth very, very deep and brought up a spring of good water, the sweetest water they had ever drunk. They had fish to eat, of course, and kelps and weeds of the sea, and she gave them ever-burning coals over which to cook. She took the seeds from their last few lemons and oranges, caused them to grow overnight into a bearing orchard. It's still there, as you will see."

"The great tower?" prompted Haider. He did not like this talk of gods, for he knew there had ever existed but one. That there were—or had been—uncanny beings of great power in this world he did not doubt. He supposed they were jinn, whose existence in his former world he had never doubted either.

"When the storm offshore finally broke, many days later, the fishers wished to return to their homes. This displeased the god. A few weeks of companionship had reconciled her to the previous eon without, but not to a future of solitude resumed. One of the fishers, too, a youth who had become her lover, wished to remain. Why could they not found a town, she said. The fishing was good, there were never storms within the barrier, with irrigation the soil was far more fertile than on their rocky islands. Finally, she said, this god, Iyivë, is far more sympathetic than the crude, quarrelsome gods at home.

"The other fishers discussed this suggestion but no decision was made before they lay down for the night. The young woman went to the god, and after they had coupled in the fragrant orchard she told Iyivë she feared her companions would reject her plan and return home. But she would stay! she exclaimed, for she was a romantic. Iyivë pondered for a time, then told her to sleep."

Haider felt impatient. That the master liked to tell stories and appreciated her own voice he knew. He would have asked one of the common bargees but their suspicion of a foreigner from the lustrous east (as they thought) made them short tongued. He suspected, too, they were nervous of his dog. He reached down beside his chair to fondle her ears.

Coming into the world, he had been surprised to find that people recognized his companion and guide. It seemed Iman was not to be seen as merely a friendly, clever dog of no particular ancestry. No, she was of a very particular breed, rare but widely known and, if not feared, respected: nearly an object of awe. Dreamherd, they called her, and made the warding gesture appropriate to their cultures. When Haider pressed for explanation, he was invariably rebuffed with many signs of nervousness. He had been travelling about from city to town to village for more than an almanac-year before an unworldly scholar of the great library of the hidden city exclaimed, "I believed them to be extinct!"

Dreamherds, the scholar told him, were an ancient, uncanny breed. Each pup, upon being weaned, chose one particular person to be its charge, a bond that could be broken only by death. Such uncompromising loyalty, of course, was scarcely unknown in the dog tribe. What distinguished the dreamherd was the talent its name alluded to: it influenced its master's dreams, marshalled and guided them, provided, through ambiguous vision, hidden knowledge. "But the woman of the snows—" in his travels Haider had heard much of this demonic figure—"seems determined to exterminate the breed. It is said her son was chosen by a dreamherd pup. When the child was stolen, she blamed the puppy for not keeping him safe and would have slain it had it not slipped out of her grasp into another world."

For no more than a minute Haider had wondered whether *he* might be that lost child, carried off to a different world as a babe, but dismissed the speculation as fruitless. He saw no profit in putting the question to this amenable scholar. If he, Haider, were indeed the son of the woman of the snows and inspiration for the evils she visited on the world, he preferred not to know.

The scholar had led him and Iman to a hidden vault within the library. "You are fortunate," he said, "never to have been discovered by agents of that woman, for they would destroy your dog at once and take no care to preserve your own life. I believe this will be of service." Opening a tiny casket of intricate design, he removed a charm in the shape of a man carved from deep blue stone. "This will confuse her uncanny agents, so that they will see an ordinary dog of no moment. Fasten it to her collar, please." Bemused, Haider had knelt to comply. "Merely human agents, however," the scholar continued, "cannot so be fooled. I can only advise you to be wary, watchful."

Now Haider felt along Iman's neck for her collar and held the blue charm in his fingers for an instant. Reassured, he turned back to the bargemaster, who regarded him strangely. "The temple of Iyivë?" Haider said.

"Yes, of course." The master shook her head, gave several furious turns to the crank of her device. "When the castaways awoke in the morning, they discovered a marvel. While they slept, a tremendous white marble tower had been raised over the spring the god had dug for them. Down channels carved in each of its eight faces poured an unceasing flow of sweet water. Would such a wonder not be the envy of any city in the world, said the god. Bring your families here from your poor islands to establish a great town and I promise the source will never fail.

"Astounded as they were, some among the fishers continued hesitant. Though their homes and livelihoods were mean, the gods of their islands petty and demanding, they feared such great change. The god said, Have you not noticed how you feel after drinking this water? Are you not invigorated and content? Is it not more refreshing than wine, than the waters you have known before? The water of this spring is proof against all contagion, all poison. Live here under my protection, drink my water, and you will never fall ill. You will live to ages that will astonish people of other lands and remain vigorous and healthy until death finally takes you. All this I offer."

"Merchants in many towns have tried to sell me water of Iyivë," observed Haider.

The barge master laughed. "Doubtless it was not the real thing. More than one great prince has been bankrupted by the price of a case. In any event, the virtue of Iyivë's water is reduced by bottling and transit. Nevertheless, it is the source of the city's wealth—and mine!" She laughed again. "May Iyivë not founder entirely before I die."

"*Founder?*" Haider began to ask, but a young bargee had approached: the master's attention was required. He knew the answer, in any case, if he only thought. As the sun slowed, it dragged great tides around the globe. Any coastal city was at risk: every coastal city that had no convenient high ground had constructed tidewalls against the swell.

Left to their own devices, Haider and Iman visited the galley to filch a pair of blood oranges and a string of smoked lamb. The man inspected his timepiece, decided it was time (if not past time) to make his devotions to the God Who had, it seemed, not found it needful to gift this world with a blessed messenger or His revealed word. Returning to his cabin below deck—for he had long since learned it best not to advertise his faith—he washed in mere rain water and laid out the rug his brother Firooz had given him in another world. In this world, there was no Holy Mecca to face so any direction was as good—or bad—as another. He said his prayers. He asked God's blessings for distant Firooz and their children. He felt refreshed.

Naturally, Iman had gone to sleep. Haider regarded her white form with affection, smiling when she snored. Since her fur had begun to fade, she offered fewer dreams and those more resistant to interpretation, but her companionship could not be questioned—or, to Haider's mind, equalled. He stroked her neck and back, scarcely disturbing her, and then laid himself in his swaying hammock. Although it was customary to use one's timepiece and almanac to maintain the ancient twenty-four-hour cycle, Haider found it difficult to sleep long during the months of daylight, instead taking naps as he found them.

He did not recall dreaming, but woke to a powerful sense of dread. Iman stood by his hammock, her expression more alert and wary than he had seen for years. She failed to wag the snowy plume of her tail until he rolled out of the hammock and caressed her head. Above them, the thumps of running bare feet reverberated through the deck. "What is it, Iman?" Haider asked. She merely whined.

He took his swords and belt from the travelling chest and buckled them on, long, slender shamshir to the left, shorter kilij to the right. There were spring-loaded weapons that shot poisoned glass darts, but he had never learned to use one. Long ago in another world, he had been a fair archer but his eye was no longer sufficiently keen. If weapons were needed, the swords would have to serve.

They climbed to the deck. He saw that the barge had rounded the sandy headland, but the screws that propelled it were silent, still. The weatherworker Sagal stood nearby. Haider followed her gaze. The first thing he saw, of course, was the stupendous white tower. Now he could make out that it was faceted, not square or round. The water channels engraved down the three visible faces glistered like molten silver. He had never been good at gauging measures but he felt it must be at least seventy-four arsani tall—an improbable height, doubtless impossible without magical aid for a structure so slender. No other building in the city stood even a third as high.

He lowered his eyes from the tower's cloud-scraping (if this shore ever saw cloud) summit. Attenuated cranes like great insects stood idle over the tidewall. The sun's slow setting had lowered the floating dock below each crane, but there were only a few small boats moored, and one larger vessel." Is something amiss?" he asked.

Sagal did not turn, intent on the shore. "We await the pilot. We have been waiting—" she checked her timepiece—"an hour and a quarter since the harbormaster should have sighted us. The banner of welcome has not been raised. It is...perplexing."

"That ship," Haider said. "It appears to be burnt out."

"Also troubling," replied Sagal shortly.

"There are no people on the tidewall or the docks."

Impatient or perturbed, Sagal shook her head. "I know no more, see no more than you."

"But you have visited Iyivë before."

"It is not a great or busy port, Master Haider, but yes, I can report that on previous occasions it has been busier and we have not had to wait. Further than that, I cannot tell you. I am the weatherworker merely." With a curt nod, she walked away.

At the chart table on the sterncastle, the bargemaster was speaking with navigator and mate. As Haider and Iman approached, the mate said, "Very good," and turned away, starting when he saw the foreigner and his dog. He made his nation's sign of protection against the uncanny, a matter of kissing his thumbnail and brushing it across his eyelids, as he passed. Bargemaster and navigator looked up at Haider from their seats, the former's expression tolerant yet tense, the latter disciplined to trembling blankness.

"As you see, Master Haider," said the bargemaster, "we have reached Iyivë. Is the great temple not a marvel?"

"I have not seen its like in any country," Haider agreed. "Yet something—perhaps several somethings?—is amiss."

Maintaining her precarious equanimity, the master shrugged. "Our draft is too deep to take any of the barges in without pilots. The sandbars, you understand, are changeable. I am sending in a boat. I'm sure there is no real problem."

"Your dog," the navigator blurted. "It is a dreamherd, everybody knows, whatever its color."

The master slapped her palm on the table, making compasses and pens jump and clatter. "The dog has given us no trouble. The voyage has been uneventful—even pleasant to this point, yes? No secret assassin or uncanny being has attempted anything. I am weary of this."

Haider nodded to the master in gratitude. To the navigator, he said, "She is of that breed, yes."

Wringing his hands, the navigator said, "I meant only to ask, have your dreams told you anything of Iyivë?"

Haider knelt to put an arm around Iman, who leaned against him, panting happily. He thought of the dread that had wakened with him. The weight of the swords at his hips would not allow him to disregard it. "She is old," he said, looking up at the two faces that regarded him over the table. "Her guidance remains trustworthy, but there is less of it than when she was young and agile and it is, indeed, more difficult to understand. I can tell you nothing specific of conditions in the city—in that way, I know far less than you, who have visited before. But I have received a warning of danger—" He rattled the shamshir's hilt against the chains that fastened it to his belt. "Whether to myself alone, to ship or convoy or crew, I cannot say."

The master pressed her lips together, nodded. "The landing party will go armed," she said, rising from her seat.

"I should like to accompany them."

"Is that wise?" The master's expression said clearly that she saw before her a man no longer young, creaky at the joints and of no known competence.

Abhorring the drama of it, Haider drew his kilij with a flourish and deftly presented it. Spry and eager despite her age, confident of her duty, Iman sprang to her feet and snarled, showing teeth as curved as the kilij. It was a form of sabre this world did not know, and the bargemaster knew him to be right handed. "It may not be wise, but I will not handicap your party and may be of some assistance."

She gave in gracefully. After he scabbarded his blade, she led him down to the foredeck and over to the side, where the landing party had gathered under the mate's eye. The small, unpowered boat had already been lowered; it made a hollow *thunk* against the barge's flank now and then. "Master Haider has warned us of some danger in Iyivë," she told the mate, "else I should send you in armless and unsuspecting. For this we owe him thanks, although—" she glanced aside at Haider—"I am not entirely convinced the favor he has asked is wise. He *and his dog* will go along with you. He has assured me he can protect himself if there should in fact be...difficulty. I therefore say, in your hearing and his, in the event of attack or other trouble, you are not obliged to endanger yourselves in attempting to protect him or the dog. Is this understood?"

With a glare for Iman, the mate agreed. All the small party was armed, each carrying one of the spring-loaded sidearms holstered at the hip, most also a short, two-edged sword against close fighting. The bargees went over the side first, clambering one after another down the rope ladder, then Haider. When the mate made no move, the bargemaster scooped up Iman and lowered her carefully to her master. As they settled down in the waist of the rocking boat, Haider heard the master say a few sharp words to the mate, who looked chastened when he in turn made his way down.

It didn't take long to row into the harbor. There was still no sign of activity on any of the docks or on the tidewall that rose higher as they approached, cutting off view of any of the city's buildings except the beetling temple. The silent ship tied up to one of the docks was a type unfamiliar to Haider; it was no longer than the barge but much higher, with a tall sterncastle ornamented with many windows, their glazing shattered. Extensive charring marred the upper third of the hulk. All four of its masts were jagged stumps. As they pulled in closer, Haider saw that its bowsprit also was broken, but the figure fastened to the prow below was undamaged: a gigantic woman, artfully carved, her blonde wooden hair rippling in a frozen breeze, her painted lips parted in a smile of delight.

"Flag of the Iyivë fleet," said a bargee who had noticed the direction of his gaze. "The woman's a representation of their god."

"Their god? Do they worship her still?"

The bargee laughed, disbelieving. "Of course not. What living person has ever met a god?"

The rowers feathered and raised their oars and the mate leapt onto the dock. Still, no heads were raised above the parapet of the tidewall, no hails or challenges raised. When the boat was tied up, Haider lifted Iman over the side and clambered after. The dock bobbed as the remaining crew followed. Without a word, the mate drew his sidearm and gestured with it toward the foot of the stair that climbed the tidewall. Haider and his dog went last.

From the walkway at the top, they looked out over the quiet city. Besides the stiff breeze from behind them and waves hushing against the foot of the wall, the only sound Haider heard—it took a moment to determine what it was—came from the water rushing down the channels of the high tower. It hurt his neck to gaze up to its peak. He saw now that aqueducts had been raised to catch and distribute some of the liquid bounty, marching on their tall arches out from the temple at the city's center to the farthest suburbs. Iyivë was not the largest city he had seen, in this world or the other, but its extent impressed him. To see such a fine city silent and deserted disturbed him: as if all its population had fallen dead in an instant (there rose no charnel smell, circled or quarrelled no carrion birds) or, as one, stepped across a threshold to another world.

The party made its way down a comfortable stair to the shadowed street. All the bargees carried their weapons at the ready, peered about narrowly, nervously. Iman paced calmly at Haider's side, scorning the puppyish indiscipline of rushing about and sniffing at exotic new smells. Nevertheless, her master noted the nostrils in her black nose working as she glanced from side to side.

They passed a warehouse with its business door ajar. At a nod from the mate, one of the bargees slipped in, soon returned, shaking her head. "Where is everybody?" exclaimed the mate, frustrated.

"The fleet is out," ventured the bargee who had spoken earlier to Haider, "except for the flagship."

"The fleet couldn't transport a quarter of the town's population if they packed them in like salt fish." The mate spat on the clean pavement by his feet.

They continued, turning onto a wide boulevard that led inland. Sandalled and bare feet slapped loudly on stone paving until the mate, annoyed or nervous, stepped onto the strip of turf that divided the street and the others followed. They had passed now out of the shadow of the tidewall but tall trees with broad crowns shaded them as they walked and obscured their way ahead. Handsome buildings with grand porticos flanked both sides of the boulevard, but they were as still and silent as the warehouse.

The amiable bargee fell back to walk at Haider's side. "You have travelled widely, I believe," he said. "Have you seen or heard of such a thing?"

"A city depopulated?" Haider shook his head. "Not such as this, without evidence of destruction or massacre. The town is in good order, is it not?" He glanced past the bargee's profile at another noble building. "An invader willing to slay every inhabitant would scarcely be satisfied with burning one boat— would scarcely clean up after himself. Nor would he, having conquered such a prize, walk off and leave it empty." He shrugged. "Indeed, whence could arrive such an invasion? Not out of the desert, surely."

"There are...entities that have no need for fresh water," the bargee muttered darkly.

"Why then take a town whose only reason for being is its famous spring?" Feeling very nearly cheerful, Haider patted the man's shoulder. "In all my travels I have never met such a being, my friend."

Iman growled.

At first sight, Haider believed the creature to be a human woman. She stepped out from the black entrance of one of the grand palaces and halfway down its sunwashed stairs, seeming to glare through leafy shadow toward the landing party. She wore no clothing, but it had been some years since Haider allowed himself to be shocked by simple human nakedness. But the eyes in her sharp, severe face were entirely black, gleaming and oily like beads of tar. Then Iman barked, angry and scared as a living person could not make her, and the watching woman reacted not at all: she was either deaf or unnatural, unable to see Iman, protected by the scholar's charm, for what she was.

"Vlithant," whispered the man at Haider's elbow.

Deaf and uncanny, both—blind, as well, in daylight. The creature lifted its chin and, with a shudder of primitive horror, Haider saw its nostrils flare and flutter as, like a dog, like Iman, it quested for the scent of prey. He knew of these things: in the cruel and beautiful court of Asudhodh had indeed seen one, first created and then destroyed, for the queasy entertainment of the magnates. "Hold, Iman," he said as the dog whined and shivered, then, to the man, "Your gun is useless against such."

"I know." The bargee's voice quavered.

The rest of the party, including its leader, had halted when Iman barked, drawn together in a clump, nine pointless weapons aimed at the still, sniffing vlithant. It was aware of them, clearly. "We must go back," Haider said.

"We should kill it," said the mate with stupid bravado. "It cannot see nor hear us."

"It can smell us. We stink of humanity, my friend."

As if it had heard him, the vlithant cocked its head again and opened its mouth, revealing jagged teeth gleaming as red as oiled cinnabar. Its incongruously human tongue, pink and moist, lolled out: an organ in the palate distinguished odors more sharply than could its nose. It raised its hands, clawed fingers outspread, as if it might sense their presence through the currents of the air.

"If—when—it attacks, we shall attempt to release it from its flesh, of course." Haider had drawn both his blades, shamshir in the right hand, kilij in the left. A vlithant could only be killed by taking off its head or digging out its heart or lungs. In the arena of Asudhodh, after all its limbs had been hacked off, the magnates' plaything had yet contrived to bite out the throat of the penult gladiator when she bent to deliver, as she hoped, the coup de grâce.

"We must retreat. Count on it: it is not the only vlithant in Iyivë. We may have roused but the one as yet but others will be stirring."

The vlithant made a noise, a thin squeal, still rocking its head about and snuffling for flesh. Its own skin had begun to blister and smoke where sun hit it most fiercely. With clear frustration, it darted back up the steps and into the shade of the portico.

Haider nudged still growling Iman with his leg, the nearest bargee with his shoulder. "Now we will retreat."

"Can we outrun it?"

"It would be fatally foolish to try." He pushed the woman again, began himself to back slowly toward the sun-bright paving of the street. "We will go carefully, keeping watch in all directions. So long as we can remain in sunlight, they will hesitate to attack even after fixing our positions."

From the street, with the trees between them, they could no longer observe the one vlithant they were sure of. It—or perhaps another on the far side of the boulevard—squealed again.

All the fight seemed to have gone out of the mate. Eyes glassy and face pale, he stumbled along with his crew, still holding his sidearm—he had not troubled to carry another weapon—but not attempting to hold it ready. His lips worked silently as he prayed or cursed or fruitlessly begged. A third squeal made him start and wave the pistol about wildly. Concerned, Haider was on the point of sheathing one of his blades to take the man's gun from him when he moaned aloud and raised the barrel.

Ahead, two new vlithant had appeared, one on the right at the door of another building, one on the left, keeping under the shade of a tall tree. They swivelled their heads and snuffled nostrils and tongues after the unctuous scents of human fear. Haider and his companions would have to pass between them to reach the treacherous shadow of the tidewall.

Senseless, the mate shot. The trigger mechanism of his weapon made a sharp noise and the glass dart seemed to utter a thin, windy whine as it pierced the air. By some miracle, it struck home in the left vlithant's upper chest. The creature staggered and twisted half around but did not fall. Squealing, it lifted a clumsy hand to its breast and pawed at the dart fixed above its left nipple. Its own thick, slow, black blood distracted it: it dabbled at the welling wound without dislodging the dart, then lifted bloodied fingers to its lips and licked, suckled.

The mate had raised his pistol again, aiming for the vlithant on the right, which had ventured a few steps closer to the street, its face working as it scented its fellow's gore. "Fool!" snarled Haider, and knocked the man's hand down with the dull back of the kilij, uncaring whether he broke the wrist. "You can't kill a vlithant with poison."

"It's you!" the man cried, shaking his hand without releasing his weapon. "You and your monstrous beast!" Moving with a grace and conviction unsuspected, he raised the pistol again, supporting his injured wrist with the other hand. The slender barrel did not waver from its aim on Haider's chest. The poison on the darts was sufficient to kill a man. "Because of you we will be *food!*"

Before Haider could react, before the mate could shoot, Iman had leapt. Her paws struck him in the belly, bowling him over, and her teeth slashed his forearm. Howling, he shot. The dart whined and thudded home in Iman's flank. Haider's kilij opened the mate's chest. Dropping both swords, he reached through hot, spurting blood to gather his stricken dog into his arms.

Blood had spattered his face. Cradling Iman to his chest, he licked his lips. "The blood will draw them," he said without looking up at the others. "Save yourselves if you can."

"Master—"

"Go! I want nothing to do with you or your deaths!"

He hardly heard them leave. Iman panted harshly. Scarlet blood, her own and the mate's, painted her white fur. Three earlier Imans had died in Haider's arms, in the other world, comfortably, in the fulness of age. This was the last. The poison would not allow her to go easily. Weeping, Haider bent over her and took the dart in his teeth. It shattered as he drew it out, slivering his gums and lips with the toxin's bitter flavor. Splintery barbs would have broken off in Iman's flesh in any case, bearing their evil freight. His mouth flooded with spittle and he swallowed, feeling the burn and the scrape down his throat, then spat.

Soon the blind vlithant would find him and his dog, soon they would bitterly feast. The late sun was hot.

✦ ⟨✦⟩ ✦

Jannicke's Cat

To Betty Harrington

OLIVES-TOWN, AWAY: YEAR OF THE COLONY 181 ZIZDY 53

"Grandie, what's this?"

"Not yours," she said without having to think, without turning from the long view of the bay and the volcanic cone outside the bay, from memories she hadn't left behind. "Fredo, go away. Grandie's tired and irritable. Knock next time."

"I did knock!" Goffredo protested.

"Did I say *come in?*"

"I didn't hear you...."

"I didn't hear you knock." Jannicke knocked her own knuckles on the wooden rail, heaved a sigh meant to inspire guilt—although, if she remembered her own children, Goffredo was too young to comprehend guilt—and turned around. "What is it, Fredo?"

Goffredo stood just inside the open door from her bedroom, attention half divided between his great-grandmother on the porch and whatever had disturbed him. He resembled Zé more than he did Jannicke's grandson Kamen, her family's pallor overcome by Zé's more dramatic coloring. Kamen, of

composed 2008, Pawtucket/ Little Compton, Rhode Island
first published in M-Brane SF #10, November 2009

course, looked like his father, being Matvey's clone as his brother was Radoš's. But the technology of reproduction had evolved beyond cloning: Goffredo was an individual, the son of both his fathers. "This, here on your worktable," Goffredo said, unsure. "It's got *eyes*."

"Pruta?"

"What?"

Leaning back against the rail, Jannicke felt old. "Bring her here, Fredo."

"*Her*—?" His grandie was the only *her* Goffredo knew, discounting the great-aunts he'd met once. He shook his head. "It smells bad. I don't want to touch it. It's got eyes."

Jannicke sighed again, involuntarily this time. "When I was a girl, Pruta was my favorite toy. I found her unpacking."

Goffredo squinted, then clearly recalled that *girl* meant Grandie-when-little, two improbable concepts. "But what is it, Grandie?" He edged out of the door.

"She's a cat, Fredo. A toy cat."

Another word encountered only in history lessons. "There aren't any cats," said Goffredo. "Like cows and dogs and sheeps. They all died."

Like women, soon enough. "Yes, Goffredo, that's true. As I said, Pruta is a toy. She doesn't even look so much like a real cat." Stiff, Jannicke pushed off from the rail. "Why don't you come all the way outside? I would like to sit down now."

She didn't want to go in. Jannicke's room (the whole house) smelled new and it saddened her. Eventually she would get used to it, or it would stop smelling new, or she'd die. Her own belongings made it almost bearable but she still preferred to stay outdoors. When he moved her over from the island, Kamen had wanted to give her all new furniture. "I made your father and his brother in that bed," she said, knowing it would make him uncomfortable, "and both your aunts." Not as uncomfortable as it made Zé: her grandson-in-law had not in his lifetime, until he married Kamen, been related to a living woman. "When Auntie Llora's daddy broke his head in the storm and Emergency Response couldn't get across from Olives, I made Dinu comfortable in that bed. I intend to die in it as well, Meny." The childhood nickname made Kamen uncomfortable too. Guilt was a remarkably effective tool, once the child grew old enough to comprehend it. There was no more argument. The bed came—everything she insisted on. "*They*'ll just burn it—" *They* being the new owners, that perfectly pleasant couple, who had spent five years with her, learning and doing what she had to admit she could no longer expect herself to do on her own. Though they disliked her house and planned to raise their own—perhaps already had—she almost trusted them (almost) not to allow her lemons to die if there were a frost this winter.

Her lemons? Not hers anymore. *They* had leased her name for marketing, a concession she hadn't really wished to grant, but income was better than sheqels in a Haven bank. Anyone who cared knew, next harvest, Jannicke's lemons wouldn't be *Jannicke's*. Olives were all very well, but lemons had been Jannicke's life.

She settled on the bench Jacenty had made for her one winter when their twins were smaller than Goffredo, looking out over the olive groves below the house, toward the island. "Don't you have any toys like Pruta?" she asked her great-grandson.

He hadn't decided whether he was allowed to sit or, if so, where. "No. I don't think so. A toy *cat*?" Goffredo twisted his hands together, looking worried. He was polite, at any rate, most of the time. Zé's influence, certainly. Whether or not he liked or approved of her (she didn't believe he did), Zé was dependable, accommodating (really, Kamen had married a man just like the father who'd raised him—the father who wasn't Jannicke's son). Astonishingly accommodating in supporting his husband's insistence she move off the island, to share their new house and make their lives miserable until she got around to dying. Gave up the west bedroom because Grandie wanted the view....

Jannicke blinked back to the present: Goffredo was acutely uncomfortable. "Do sit down, Fredo." She patted the cushion beside her. "Grandie's neck will get achey if I have to keep looking up at you. Unless you need to pee?"

"N-no."

"Go do it. Maybe you'll find me something nice to drink when you're done, if you think you can carry it."

"Yes, Grandie." Goffredo scuttered off.

She wondered for all of two hundredths how closely his concept of *nice to drink* would gibe with hers. It was an unproductive avenue. With a groan she felt in her bones but heard as though another old woman uttered it (they were all old, all the women alive in the world...her own daughters were old), Jannicke stood up again. After a moment's light headedness, she turned to the open door.

Pruta lay on the worktable just inside. Jannicke inspected her old toy: battered, dirty, loose stitches at the shoulder—*she* still saw the cat in the pointed head and pointed ears, four floppy limbs and floppy tail, especially in the silk-stitched lemon-yellow eyes, but the resemblance wasn't close if all you'd seen was images, still or moving. No modern man considered nostalgia for the impossible past a virtue. Going back out, she sat with the toy in her lap and stroked its back.

The cat's stuffing was lumpy. Stains mottled the faded grey velvet, its pile worn off in irregular patches and blotches. Besides the loose stitching on the shoulder, Jannicke found a short split, a centimeter or two, in the seam where a strip of paler velvet was pieced into Pruta's throat and belly, a tuft of yellowed fiber working through. The smell, too, damp and mould—it had got onto Jannicke's fingers. For some reason, evidence of the toy's age distressed her more than the lentigines and lumpy veins on the backs of her own hands. She closed her eyes for just a moment.

Dada had made the toy: she knew that, but she thought she ought to remember him doing it. There were so many memories, big and small, important and not, there for the taking. She remembered Dada's big, clever hands, though in other memories (later, she supposed) they weren't so big. Dada hadn't been a big man. She didn't remember him working out the pattern or cutting the fabric or stitching the pieces together. She could imagine a needle in his fingers, the tip of his tongue protruding between thinned lips as he concentrated, squinted, but that wasn't memory.

"I brought you some lemonade, Grandie," Goffredo said.

"Fredo." Jannicke opened her eyes, not really startled. She took the tall, cold glass from his small hand. "Thank you." When she raised the glass, for an instant the mould smell on her fingers threatened to sicken her, but then the clean fragrance of lemons and sugar drove it away. Chill bubbles tickled her palate: the syrup was diluted with sparkling water. Zé or Kamen must have been around to help Goffredo. "Thank you," she said again after swallowing. "That's very pleasant."

"May I sit down?"

"Please." She took another sip of lemonade, snatching at another memory.

Careful of his own glass, Goffredo clambered onto the bench, close enough to Jannicke that both would be aware of the other without looking, not so close she could complain: he knew she didn't like being crowded. He slurped and swallowed his lemonade, loudly. Sometimes she wished the physicians weren't so assiduous in keeping her hearing acute—the muffledness had been restful until it alarmed her and she brought it up. That had been...when? Fifteen years ago? Long after the first, now semi-annual, retunings of her eyes. For clear vision she continued grateful.

"What were we talking about, Fredo?"

"You asked if I had a toy cat," he said. "I said no."

Where had she been going with that? Oh. "Maybe not a cat." Not quite unconsciously, the thumb of her free hand stroked velvet. "Maybe a puppy?" There had been a man in the Windwards who made puppies, long ago. Jacenty had ordered four of them when the twins were born, four different colors of plush pelt, shipped at ridiculous expense. They resembled real puppies more than Pruta did her model. At nine, Llora was really too old but accepted her stepfather's gift with grace—she had been graceful once. She might even have remembered living dogs. "Some kind of animal?"

"I've got a bird! It sings and flies and comes when I call it! It's pretty."

"Is it soft?"

"Not really. Parts of it, maybe. I think it's a robot."

"It sounds like a very nice bird." Really, in a way, it did. "Does it have a name?"

"No—should it? It's the only bird I've got."

Another unproductive avenue. Jannicke had never named her own toy dirigibles or earthmovers or boats, toys that *did* something, that didn't invite personality. "What about when you go to bed, Fredo?" she asked, turning to regard her great-grandson. "Don't you have something soft to cuddle at night? When you're sad or worried or afraid?"

"When I'm scared my daddies let me sleep in their bed with them," Goffredo said simply, puzzled. Then he brightened. "My pillow's soft and cuddly!"

Jannicke sighed, knowing she was doing it, unable not to. "Of course it is. Let's be quiet now, for a little." She looked away again.

She was too old. If there were a god who knew her name (it seemed unlikely and unfair), that deity was unkind to make her live through so many years. She should have died long ago—with Jacenty. Was it nearly twenty years? It was. Over sixty since Dinu, but Llora's father had died unconscionably young. She should not have lived to watch her daughters turn bitter, to see one son disappear, the other die.

JANNICKE'S ORCHARD, CITRON-ISLAND, AWAY'S ATTENDANTS: YC 152 FIVER 63

Kill himself. She was too old to be sentimental. Deror had killed himself with full deliberation, without malice. Unhappy as he was, if he'd thought it through, if he'd been able to foresee how badly the act would damage his twin, her sweet boy would have hesitated. *It's broken*, he wrote. *The world is broken and it's broken me. It won't be fixed in my lifetime.* Had Deror understood that sentence or merely written it? *I love you all.* Knowing only his mother of those he loved was on the island and she in the orchards without her journal, he released the missive into the aether, then threw his own journal into the hydrothermal vent and followed after.

Jannicke didn't carry her journal into the groves, but the phone went every-where with her, bonded to the jaw, under her skin. "Mother! Find Rory now!" Deror's twin yelled from the nursery in Haven where he and Radoš were meeting their own twin sons for the first time.

It was too late. It had always been too late. Since before they could walk her children had all been warned against the hot spring that warmed their home and the glasshouses in the winter, ran the turbines that provided power to the whole island. Heated by the pocket of magma under the volcano, the water spurted up boiling. The leader of the Emergency Response team that came over from Olives shrugged sadly. His instruments could pinpoint the instant Deror went in and his phone failed (Deror must have failed before the phone) but without special equipment that would have to be imported from Glass Falls, a day's lag or worse, he couldn't begin to attempt retrieving the body.

Matvey had not forgiven his mother for forbidding the attempt. His deso-late rage scared the babies, even when he wasn't shouting—scared his young husband, already nervous simply by virtue of becoming a father. It was little wonder the marriage hadn't lasted. Jacenty, bless the old man, had tried to help Radoš with the babies: he wasn't blamed, he'd been on the big island. Llora and Ebru pitched in as well, but the elder didn't like babies and the younger worried about her own sons, at home with their father half the world away. (That marriage hadn't lasted either.)

Exhausted by rage, by grief, by his mother's stubbornness (heartlessness, he called it), at last Matvey was persuaded to go to bed. Exhausted herself, too angry and tense and sad to contemplate sleep, Jannicke made herself a strong drink and took it out of the house.

It was spring. The lemons were in blossom, their fragrance thick and sharp, layered over and nearly obscuring the scent of damp humus and the thin in-eradicable reek from the fumaroles up the hill. Mourning her two lost sons—she knew she had lost Matvey as well—Jannicke strode between the widely spaced trees. If it were daylight, she would be watching for damage, deadfalls, disease, without realizing she was doing it, but it wasn't daylight. She came out through the trees, came to the outlook on the cliff above the channel. She sat on the bench Dinu had placed there when he still believed he had a hope of persuading her to leave the volcano and her family's orchards. Jannicke's grandmother had planted the first trees seventy years before Jannicke's birth—the first human person to settle on Citron: she had named the island.

From Dinu's bench, on a clear morning, you could see the buildings of Olives-town across the channel on the big island, at night their lamps. Dinu didn't want to go to Olives but it was a town. At least it hadn't been the volcano that killed her first husband. He'd so feared it would.

Jannicke sipped her drink, sparkling lemonade over-fortified with rum from Godemiche-island in the Australs, and waited. No moons competed with the veils of stars across the thick indigo of the sky. Like a small cluster of fallen stars, the lamps of Olives burned over the water, below the black peaks and massifs of the Spine that cut a negative relief against the starry sky. Nobody had ever told her and she had never asked which quadrant to search for the tiny yellow jewel that marked humanity's home solar system. She supposed sons must kill themselves there as well.

"I don't understand," her son-in-law said. Radoš settled beside her, heavy.

"Boiled meat," said Jannicke. "You aren't old enough to remember meat on the bone, meat from an animal. I couldn't ask ER to risk themselves for a memory I'd rather not have."

"No." Radoš coughed. It wasn't so many years since squeamishness destroyed the market for eating-fowl: perhaps as a boy Radoš had gnawed the flesh from a turkey's or chicken's drumstick.... "No, I meant—he seemed so happy! When we got married, when we told him he was going to be an uncle—"

"My dear." Jannicke didn't want to touch her son-in-law, though she felt she ought. He was a solid, pleasant young man, not, she thought, terribly thoughtful or imaginative—although there must have been some leap of the imagination involved to make him believe marrying Matvey a good idea. She patted his knee, twice, then withdrew her hand. "My dear, he *was* happy—for you. Deror felt sure he would always be alone. It was a great comfort to him, a delight, that his brother wouldn't be. And he became fond of you very soon."

"Then why?" Radoš coughed again. "I was fond of him!"

Jannicke looked out over the waters. "The rate of suicide among young men rose one thousand per cent in the five years after—" she paused: no easy term for the phenomenon had established itself—"after we learned no more women would be born. It's declined in the twenty-five years since but it's still unprecedentedly high. Especially among men your age—Matvey's age, Deror's age, the first generation."

She knew she sounded cold but wasn't prepared for Radoš to bolt up from his seat and step away from her. "You looked it up!" he exclaimed, as if accusing her of helping Deror.

"I looked it up," she agreed, resigned. "The rate among young women, the *last* generation, is much higher."

"Ebru and Llora are last generation." He was glaring at her, she imagined. "They haven't killed themselves."

"Yet, at any rate." For a moment she contemplated happy Dinu's happy daughter—she would have liked to blame Llora's unhappiness on Dinu's death....

"Deror," said Radoš.

"There was a girl—a young woman, older than you, of course. Ebru's age. Deror met her in Emils-port when he was on global service, building ships. She liked him well enough, I suppose. I never heard her side. *His* side: she was everything, everybody, the light and breath of the world." Jannicke sipped her drink, savoring the rum, savoring a memory of feeling that way herself, long ago. "Radoš," she said. "There isn't a woman in the world who isn't thirty years or more older than your boys. Who will they fall in love with, when they grow up?"

Radoš took another step away. He wasn't close enough to the cliff that she needed to worry. "I would hope—" He inhaled deeply, a kind of moan. "I hope they'll take after their dads and fall in love with other boys. *I* knew I was all about boys long before I understood that was the best way to be."

"Really?"

"I know Matvey turns on to women too," Radoš said, his voice thin. "Maybe more than men. But he loves me and I can turn him on quite satisfactorily."

"I'm glad."

"You should be!"

"The young woman in Emils—I don't know whether Deror told her he loved her. Perhaps if he had.... She killed herself. It damaged him. He finished out his year and a half building ships and came home. He was damaged. Do you understand? There was nothing I could do for him." Jannicke's breath felt hard in her throat. For three years Deror had acted the dutiful son, learning the family business while his siblings, far away, established their own separate lives and businesses—for three years his mother had watched over him, unable to help. "His father would say, *He'll find somebody new.*" She glared across the strait at Olives. "He meant, of course, that I had found someone, him, after Llora's dad was killed." It was true. Ignominious but true.

"I'm sorry," Radoš said. "I'm not thinking." He sat again beside her. "It's just as hard for you as for Matvey. More? And he's not done just reacting— you're *thinking*. I'm sorry, Jannicke."

Moved, she swallowed hard. "Thank you for that," she said at last. "He won't forgive me, you know, your husband."

He took her hand gently, kindly, but made no attempt to persuade her otherwise. "We live in a sad, unkind, unfair world," he muttered. "Was it our boys, do you think?"

"I think...." She had tried not to think. "I don't think Deror begrudged you and Matvey your babies. But I think he couldn't— *wouldn't*—imagine himself fathering children except in the...traditional way."

"So in a way, yes: Matvey and I demonstrated a reality he wouldn't accept. Another sign the world wasn't going to change back."

Jannicke took her hand back, chilled.

"There's nothing traditional about it, you know, Jannicke, on this world of ours. Your generation was only the second to be made in somebody's bed. Your grandparents came out of bottles just like Sten and Kamen. And unlike my boys, they had no families to love and care for them—how sad that must have been, when they understood their mothers and fathers were dust, cent-uries dead, light years distant...."

It was Jannicke who stood up then, stepped away from the bench.

"They couldn't even know whether mother and father had been acquainted on that other world, let alone committed to each other, to the birth of their child. The seedship's AI made all the decisions as to which sperm would fertilize which ovum."

She had misjudged him, after all. He frightened her. "Radoš," she said, refusing to look at the darkness where he sat. "I'm going back to the house. Tomorrow won't be any easier than today." She took a step, reconsidered. "My son won't want me to know his sons."

"I will," he said simply.

Despite Radoš's promise, Jannicke saw little of Sten and Kamen, Steny and Meny, until after the divorce, by which time they were walking, talk-ing—Meny so resembled her memory of Matvey and Deror as children it could make her weep—had assumed their own personalities. Radoš brought them for long visits; when they were older and his life more complicated, he sent them by themselves to Citron-island every school vacation. Adolescent Kamen (no longer answering to *Meny*) met and seduced Zé in Olives one of those vacations.

Matvey in his bitterness had demanded sole custody of Meny, a claim that so perturbed the arbiter she revoked his parental rights utterly, permitting only such privileges as Radoš approved. Those Matvey refused to request. He left Praia Dourada, the lovely little island in Haven-archipelago where Radoš's family had lived almost since the foundation, severed contact with that family and his own. The boys had not seen or spoken to Matvey in nearly as long as his mother. Every now and then, twice a year at first, then at wider and wider intervals, Jannicke would remember to confirm her son was alive: he set up checks and safeguards that made it troublesome to determine more than the bare fact. When Kamen completed his global service and received the franchise, considered himself properly grown up, a man, he had braved Matvey's safeguards and checks, found him, faced him down—came home (*home* was Olives by now). "Your son is alive and well," Kamen told his grandie—"as you know already. He appears to be as content as his nature allows. He has no interest in being my father."

OLIVES-TOWN, AWAY: YC 181 ZIZDY 53

"Radoš," Jannicke said. She had sent Goffredo away with their empty lemonade glasses, claiming little boy and old woman both needed naps. She watched wisps of steam lift from the island outside the bay—from the fumaroles up the hill from *her* house—and dissolve into the west.

It was nearly thirty years since he'd been her son *in law*, but Radoš replied within scarcely a hundredth, his voice pleasant and pleasing in her ear as if he stood at her shoulder: "Was I meant to wish you a happy equinox, Jannicke? I'm sorry. Here on the equator we don't so much mark the seasons."

"Charmer," she said, unwilling. "Are you in the middle of anything? I should like to have a conversation."

"Lovely. I'll just sit down, then. Are you well?"

"About as well as a brittle, irritable, very old lady can be, yes, thank you." Jannicke was already seated: she steered through the pleasantries as quickly as she could without being impolite. "Radoš, do you remember a special toy when you were small?"

"I had plenty of toys. How do you mean, *special?*"

"It would have seemed more than a toy—a companion when you were lonely, a comfort when you were scared. A toy that, in your imagination, was almost alive." Jannicke glared at Pruta, sprawled on the arm of the bench, boneless and filthy and much loved. "Listen. You wouldn't really know about pets, the last of them would have died before you were ready to pay attention.

When I was very, very young, my father had a kitten. A baby cat. I wanted very badly to play with Dada's cat, hug him, cuddle him, but he had too much sense to have anything to do with a grabby, selfish baby who wouldn't understand how not to annoy him and would lash out if he defended himself. So Dada made me a cat, a soft squishy toy I could squeeze as hard as I needed to and that didn't have claws or teeth. Most of the time I knew she wasn't a real animal, but that meant she could be anything—anybody—at all. Whatever or whoever I needed her to be at that moment." She ran out of breath, running headlong into memory.

"Nothing like that," Radoš said, crisp, matter of fact, not unkind.

"Why not?" She took a breath. "Matvey had a cuddly puppy but I don't remember him being as attached to it as I was to my cat. I can't ask him, obviously."

"What could a puppy mean to him, Jannicke? Or me? I mean...I know what you're talking about. I've seen and read about stuffed toy animals in the library—it was bears mostly, wasn't it, *teddy bears?*"

"There were bears in Away's Spine when I was young," said Jannicke, dispirited. "The founders made sure there were gametes on the seedship. I never actually saw one."

"I don't suppose real bears were terribly cuddly. But you'd interacted with cats, dogs, other mammals. You could extrapolate. We don't have the context anymore, the only mammals we know about experientially are other people. Do you remember, years ago, telling me I was too young to remember meat from a slaughtered animal? It's true. The only meat I understand comes from a factory tank. If I stop to think about dinner's ultimate origin—" Radoš's shudder seemed to propagate across the aether, twelve thousand kilometers from Praia Dourada, troubling the phone on Jannicke's jaw—"all I can imagine is eating the flesh of another man. So I *don't* think about it."

"You're telling me, if I made a kitten or a puppy or a teddy bear for Goffredo, he wouldn't understand it well enough to form an attachment unless he thought about it very hard, and then it would revolt or frighten him."

"That's what this is about, is it?"

Jannicke levered herself off the bench, bones and muscles protesting. Grasping the porch railing, she looked out again across the bay to the island, her island. "The only thing he has to cuddle at night is his pillow! You can't talk to a pillow, imagine it having a personality."

"Why should he need to? My grandson seems quite self sufficient to me, a happy little boy."

"Radoš." She saw no way to avoid offending him. "Your son Kamen is a lovely man. He married a husband exactly like you. I might also point out your own very strong resemblance to my husband Jacenty."

It seemed to her Radoš was silent too long. Then abruptly he laughed— the first peal too loud, like a bell, but then the phone compensated, damped the piercing high tones. "Because—" he sputtered as hilarity ran its course. "... My first husband and my son married their fathers because they lacked cuddly toys as children?"

Annoyed, Jannicke bit her lip and tightened her grip on the rail.

"Also," Radoš continued, calmer, "Matvey wasn't much like my dad at all."

"What about Iefan?"

After another moment, thoughtful, Radoš admitted, "You might have a point there." He'd married Iefan four years after Jannicke's son divorced him. "But I'm not seeing how never having a teddy bear to cuddle adds up."

"I'm...not sure myself. It's probably nothing." Her hands hurt. Releasing the rail, she worked them against each other, massaging the bony knuckles. "It made me sad that Fredo had only his pillow, that he couldn't seem to understand what the cat my dada made had meant to me when I was his age. She—Radoš, I somehow think she helped me think about, imagine, people who weren't my family, who didn't live on Citron raising lemons."

"Sympathy, empathy, imagination?"

"You see—you're cleverer than I am."

"You're lonely, Jannicke. Who do you ever see besides Fredo and his dads? Are there any other women left in Olives?"

Strangely offended, Jannicke straightened her back, turned away from the island outside the bay and her past. "We weren't talking about me. I'm concerned about my great-grandson."

Radoš didn't relent. "Jannicke, I don't remember why I looked it up but I looked it up: there are fewer than ten thousand women still alive in the world—less than one percent of the global population. Every day I talk to men who've never met a woman, don't truly believe women still exist...if they—you—ever really did."

"I'm a cat, you're saying." She was angry. "A walking, talking myth. Something to frighten little children."

"Who don't have teddy bears to comfort them."

Releasing her breath in a thin whistle, Jannicke wasn't angry. "You frighten me, Radoš."

"I'm frightened," he said, serious, "when I allow myself to think it through. Without women, are we still men? Will men still be people? Whoever did this to us—" No geneticist or theorist disagreed that the gene that had wound itself into the X-chromosome and rendered XX-embryos unviable was anything but artificial, but where it had come from or how it had permeated the gene pools of every mammalian species on the planet remained still undetermined, nearly sixty years after the event. "—they meant everybody to die out, not just one gender, and sometimes I'm not convinced we shouldn't have resigned ourselves to that. What kind of world will my grandsons and great-grandsons inhabit?"

Jannicke exhaled again. "It was a team of women who worked out the method of making babies from two dads' sperm, Radoš."

"While the men failed and keep failing to...*disinfect* the gene pool. My point."

"No, mine: we don't, women don't, *I* don't want humanity to die out on this world. It's not acceptable."

"Jannicke, you obstinate old woman, I don't think you understand how precious you are to me. You should come visit."

She felt the smile stretch at her cheeks. "I'm far too old to travel so far, my dear, and it's too warm where you are. You come here."

"I will."

"Before I die."

"You're too stubborn to die."

"Perhaps I am—and the world you fear will never entirely come to pass."

Radoš laughed for her, again, but she heard the catch in it. Her own tears trickled freely, comforting. "You're very precious to me, too," she muttered, disengaged the phone before he could reply.

OLIVES-TOWN, AWAY: YC 181 RABDY 54

She pulled the last stitch tight, cut the thread, laid scissors and needle aside. Pruta wasn't magically herself again: the mottled fading and wear of her velvet coat couldn't be repaired any more than Jannicke's own faded, mottled, worn and crêpey skin. Ageing was never an aesthetically rewarding process. But disembowelled and washed, skin and stuffing separately, dried on the salt breeze up from the bay, and with a fragrant handful of lavender blossoms mixed into the fibers that gave her shape and substance again, the toy no longer smelled bad, resembled a cat as much as she ever had—good for another eighty years.

Holding Pruta to her cheek, Jannicke lifted her eyes, gazed across the channel to Citron-island. Since speaking with Radoš she'd spent scarcely any time at all staring over the bay to her real home. It was good to be busy. Soon enough, if she kept up, the fragrance of lemons would be pleasant merely, not the occasion for regret or nostalgia. On the volcano's slopes, the lemons would be coming into blossom, but here it was olives (olive blossom had no scent she could distinguish over the clean, resiny smell of leaf and bark), while lavender greened up along the orchard paths and sent up tender, budding stems. A rose planted below the porch was meant to climb its supports and balusters—Zé promised its scent was good—but it was making a slow start in its first spring.

Setting Pruta aside again, Jannicke took up her journal. Her project's pigeonhole was marked: finding it took no time at all. The first sketches, which she had doodled on the tiny display of the journal itself, were crude, scale too small, implements too blunt. But then she had moved to the worktable in her bedroom, sitting on a hard chair for two or three intervals at a stretch, sitting until spine and hips locked up. With Kamen's uneasy blessing, she had instructed the house AI to bar Goffredo from her room unless he asked and received permission—Kamen and Zé wouldn't think of barging in—so she needn't worry about interruption. "I'm making something for him," she'd said, "for his birthday. I want it to be a surprise." One still said *birthday* though the word *birth* had fallen out of the vocabulary: Goffredo had been decanted in 176, would turn five on Teldy 63. She had nine and a half fivers, forty-seven days.

If a cat, a puppy, a teddy bear were incomprehensible and distressing, Jannicke reasoned, the only animal familiar enough to be stylized into a toy that would meet the value she wanted for it was a person. Reptiles, amphibians, fish, even birds were too alien, impossible to imagine cuddling.

First, simplifying as Dada had simplified the living kitten that had been Pruta's model, she sketched out the idea of *boy*. She didn't draw well but there were AIs she could access through the aether that did and she worked with them to improve her sketches. When the AIs transmuted the sketches into a 3D prototype hologram, suspended in the air above the worktable's glassy surface, she found it horrible: smirky, cunning, dead without ever having lived. It appeared boyness was a quality that didn't survive abstraction.

She started over. Working from an informal portrait of Goffredo, she abstracted the image only as the AIs insisted was necessary to meet the medium's limitations. That prototype disturbed her almost more than the first: stuffed firmly enough to keep its shape, it looked rigid, stern, unfriendly, but also as though the stuffing might burst its skin, like a sausage on the fire. If less or less firm stuffing were used, the toy became grotesque in another fashion, wizened and wrinkled, incapable of supporting its own weight. Unlike toy cats, boys weren't meant to be floppy. The face and hands were particularly unpleasant.

One of the AIs diffidently suggested using a molded rigid or semi-rigid membrane instead of cloth for at least the head and hands. Jannicke had to explain that the essential quality of the toy she envisioned was cuddliness, a concept the never-embodied cybernetic entities had difficulty grasping. At length, having assimilated her wishes and objections as best they could, a collaborative team of four AIs of differing expertise and interest presented her a new conceptual prototype.

Suspended in glowing air, the hologram appeared to stand on its own feet. Midway between portrait and caricature, it resembled Goffredo—or, more accurately, Jannicke felt, *evoked* her great-grandson—but was not distressingly lifelike, nor did it look dead. She couldn't mistake it for anything but an artefact: the seams that shaped facial and corporal features were clearly visible, the glossy filaments of black hair visibly rooted in the scalp, white sclera, molasses-brown iris, and black pupil unmistakably formed of molded resins behind glass cornea, disconcerting but not frightening. Ears were paraphrased as little more than flaps, well formed lips were sealed, nostrils apparently painted on. A magnified view revealed warp and weft of the fabric skin. As she watched, a disembodied arm clasped the figure about the waist, demonstrating both resilience and a certain softness. A disembodied hand interlaced its fingers with the figure's, which did not return the grasp but also did not look sausagey, each appearing to contain internal structure and jointing of some form.

"How are these effects achieved?" Jannicke asked.

Seams split and the fabric skin peeled back as if the figure were being flayed. The effect might be grotesque but Jannicke found it somehow fascinating. Under the fabric lay a webbing of soft, springy fiber nearly the color of blood, slightly iridescent. *This layer serves the same purpose, aesthetically, as a human's subcutaneous fat,* the spokesAI said. *The skin adheres to it with a weak bond that allows flexibility and some slippage.* The red fibers began to break up and unravel.

Beneath, she saw not the simple stuffing she expected but woven or braided cables that made up a schematic of the human muscular system. *The muscles and tendons are elastic,* said the AI, demonstrating how *biceps* bunched up and *triceps* stretched when one of the figure's arms was flexed. *They also organize the body's structure so that the limbs, for example, do not resemble, as you said, sausages.*

"That's very clever." Jannicke wished she could touch the figure, close her fingers around a wrist or the upper arm, prove how it felt. "Show me more."

Muscles whipped away in a flailing tangle that obscured what was left of the figure for an instant. The fluffy fiber stuffing she expected puffed out a little when muscular tension was released, but neither fiber nor muscles provided all the figure's structure: stuffing puffed out around and between the translucent members of the figure's skeleton. Jannicke knew enough anatomy to understand how drastically that armature was simplified.

"I see," she said, and the AIs began to reconstruct the toy. When she protested mildly that the design, pleasing as it was, appeared too complex for her to craft by herself, they showed her the rejected prototypes again. The qualities she wished for the toy, they told her, could not be achieved with no more than fabric and stuffing. (She chose to read regret into the passionless characters on the worktable's display.) Skeleton and muscular system would be manufactured and assembled for her, but she might sew the skin and complete the toy.

Gazing at the prototype, Jannicke made it revolve slowly. In its way, it was beautiful. More beautiful than Pruta had ever been—she didn't believe this judgment disloyal to the effort Dada had put into making Pruta: her expectations for the two toys were different, they were separate genres. The AIs' execution of her concept pleased her and she felt she could do her part, could complete it in time for Goffredo's birthday. But now the concept troubled her. Her shoulders and lower back ached. The worktable's time display told her she hadn't moved from her chair for more than three intervals, had missed lunch for the second day running.

"Keep it," she said. "Encrypt it, please, for my access only. I'll decide tomorrow."

It was *tomorrow* now. She was still troubled. She regarded the tiny image of the toy on her journal's display. Apparently floating in thin air, it lacked context. "Will it stand on its own?" she asked the AIs, and they told her *no*, though modifications could of course be made.

"No. Let it fall."

The figure dropped an apparent half meter (in the AIs' minds, it seemed, it had been floating in midair) to sprawl on a featureless surface, one leg bent, arms thrown wide. As much as something that had never lived could appear asleep, it looked as if it were sleeping.

"Put it in Fredo's bedroom."

The room rose around it in an instant: now the toy lay on the carpet by Goffredo's bed, as if the boy had tossed it out in restless sleep. That was context: the room was cluttered, though the display was too small and the light too dim for her to make out many items within the clutter. A broad patch of light from the window broke across the bed and fell to illuminate the figure's legs and its tight, immature genitals. In thin shadow, the single visible eye glinted. For an instant, when Jannicke blinked, she thought the head had moved.

"I want to see it with Fredo. Remain in his room."

The bedroom door slapped silently open and Goffredo darted through. Without her prompting, he crouched at the toy's side, pushed his arm under its shoulders, and lifted it upright. Side by side, they displayed themselves for Jannicke, clothed boy no less expressionless than naked toy. Supported, the toy almost appeared to stand of its own volition, weight on the leg pressed to Goffredo's leg. They were of a size. The journal's screen was too small for Jannicke to make out adequate detail.

"Hold that for my worktable—I can't see it well enough now."

She had slept well enough, had performed her strength and flexibility exercises on arising, had soaked for a quarter in a hot bath. She had eaten a satisfying breakfast. Still, she felt aged, sore and stiff. It took several hundredths to establish sufficient resolve to stand.

Just inside the door of her bedroom, the holographic image of Goffredo's room stood on her worktable. For an instant she might almost have fooled herself that both standing figures were boys, embracing like brothers. Twins, nearly.

Jannicke had borne and raised identical twin brothers. Goffredo's father Kamen and his brother, Sten, though they had no more in common genetically than any two random people, were twins. She sat down as comfortably as she could, peered at the two boys for some hundredths more.

"The toy's too young," she said. "It shouldn't be Fredo's age. Make it grow up, please—make it eleven and a half or twelve, an adolescent."

Still standing though the image of Goffredo couldn't support it properly, the toy grew smoothly taller. Its belly slimmed down and face grew more angular and defined while the trunk broadened and limbs lengthened. The fine hair on its scalp coarsened, waved, and new hair bloomed on its belly and around the maturing genitals. It stood all but twice Goffredo's height, gangly, gawky.

"Will Fredo really grow that tall?"

His profile suggests he will be significantly taller than either father. We project 2.05 meters at full growth.

"Let the boy hold it up."

The toy's knees buckled and the image of Goffredo caught it up under the arms. Boy embraced toy as if he were the elder, stronger, wiser — as of course he was, or would be if both weren't figments of coherent light. Nose to nose (apparently Goffredo's nose could be expected to grow more prominent), toy regarded boy with glassy, unblinking eyes. Then boy turned toy to face his great-grandmother, fabric knees dragging on the floor and nerveless feet bouncing and flopping.

Sitting back, Jannicke stretched her back and rocked her shoulders. "No, not yet. Older. Twenty-one, old enough to have completed global service."

These changes were more subtle. The toy grew several handsful of centimeters taller, though that was hard to gauge as it wasn't standing. Muscles lengthened, thickened, acquired more definition, shoulders and chest broadened. Expressionless face seemed to acquire more capacity for expression. A blue-grey shadow of beard thickened above the upper lip, on chin and cheeks and throat. Jannicke thought that was painted, like the rose tinting of lips, eyelids, nipples, foreskin and scrotum, although the hair that rooted up the crease between abdominal muscles and sparsely across the pectorals was knotted, hair by hair, into the skin.

"Have it stand on its own again."

The crown of Goffredo's head barely reached the toy's hip. Whimsical, the AIs had lifted its right hand to rest on the boy's head, as if it were about to lean down and confide a secret.

"That's good." She regarded the two figures a moment longer, then pushed her chair back and stood. "Show them to me at their actual size."

The maquette of Goffredo's bedroom dissolved. The images of the two figures expanded, standing firm and flat footed on the surface of Jannicke's worktable. She stepped farther back. The toy towered above her on its pedestal, benign but disinterested. Circling the table, she inspected it from all angles. "Make it smaller," she said at length. "Maintain the proportions but take it down...twenty-five percent."

As it shrank, the doll's right arm bent further to keep its hand on Goffredo's head, where shrinking fingers disturbed the boy's hair. Now it was scarcely twice Goffredo's height. "How much would it weigh at this size, in comparison to the boy?"

Approximately one fifth, the AIs replied. *We have specified very light materials.*

That was luggable—would become still more manageable as Goffredo grew. "Very good. Do it."

The hologram vanished. Jannicke blinked. *Fabric and thread sufficient for the skin will be delivered to you on Tanndy 54,* the AIs said. *Assembled armature and fiber stuffing on Rabdy 56. Charges have been deducted from your accounts.*

O L I V E S - T O W N , A W A Y : Y C 1 8 1 T E L D Y 6 3

The rapping on her bedroom's inside door was louder, sharper than she would expect from Goffredo—she heard it easily from her seat on the porch—and earlier: she had asked Zé to restrain his son till after the sixth interval, when he and his dads might join her before breakfast. Not that she wasn't ready for him. She had never intended sleeping in.

Patting Goffredo's toy on its (she almost thought *his*) thigh, Jannicke stood, called, "Coming!" The house AI wouldn't open the door without her direct intervention today. Before going in, she looked back at the toy, sprawled in the corner of Jacenty's bench. It—he—felt not at all like a person when touched, in adequate light and direct gaze could not be mistaken for a person, but that had not been her aim and it pleased her. Her work pleased her. There had been no work for her for too long.

Another tattoo on the inner door. Allowing herself to feel irritated, she called, "I said I was coming," but, hand on the door jamb, glanced back once more. The quick, backward glance was more disorienting: for an instant she saw a perfect three-quarter-size replica of a handsome young man, at ease in the corner of the bench, paying her no mind, but instinct with potential, ready in a moment to spring up and accomplish something.

Then it was merely a toy again. Any potential it contained was Goffredo's alone to discover. Going inside, she left it to itself and went to open the door.

"Radoš," she said, startled.

"You told me to visit. Here I am."

"Goffredo?"

"He'll be along. May we come in?"

Startled again, Jannicke saw Radoš's husband over his shoulder, their eighteen-year-old son. Withdrawing from Radoš's embrace, she stepped aside. She had not properly had visitors since moving into Zé and Kamen's house: it felt odd. Radoš bore past her without qualm, but her grandsons' stepfather appeared to appreciate the oddness—they had no particular relationship— and hesitated before embracing her. "Iefan," she said, recollecting herself, "it's been too long. Please come in. And Bieito—I heard you were on global service?"

"Just over the mountains this half-year," said the confident youth, taking her hands politely. "Growing oats and barley in the central valley. When dad reminded me of Fredo's birthday, I said I'd take leave to visit big brother and his family—"

"Whereupon I said it should be a proper family gathering." Radoš, behind her. "We expect Sten and his boys this afternoon. Childishly—" his breath warmed her nape, then he moved away again—"I wished to surprise you."

"There's coffee...." She waved them toward it. Radoš and Iefan were nearly the age she had been when Deror killed himself, Bieito just five years younger than her dead, ageless son, but cheerful, animated, self-possessed in a way she could not imagine of Deror. Perhaps growing up with his mother had deformed Deror's expectations of the world she had given him and his brother. It was two years after the last live birth of a girl that she'd found herself pregnant with twin boys.

"I liked your house on Citron better," said Iefan, settling with his coffee on the couch beside his husband, "but this is very pleasant."

"That was a pioneer house. My grandparents built it by themselves." Offended on Zé and Kamen's account—though they might agree—Jannicke took her own cup to sit at the worktable. "This one just hasn't been lived in long enough."

"*Was?* Have they torn it down already?"

"I believe they plan to transform it into a retreat for jaded urban islanders on holiday, but I don't expect the new house is ready for them to move in yet."

"I remember this from the old house," said Bieito, stroking the small bronze sculpture Jacenty had cast of his adolescent sons wrestling. Bieito knew well enough it was too heavy to lift easily. "Is this your *cat* Fredo told me about?"

Pruta was no burden to pick up. Like kneaded bread dough, she overflowed Bieito's cupped palms, front legs poking through his fingers, head lolling. Bieito's expression was curious: not alarmed, but moved in a way Jannicke didn't understand.

"Yes," Jannicke said.

"It doesn't look much like a cat." He smiled for her, bright, false, unconvincing. "I've seen pictures."

"What about the gift you were making Fredo?" Radoš leaned forward, holding his cup much as his son held Pruta. "Kamen said you've been tiresomely secretive about it."

"Outside. On the porch."

Radoš made no move, regarding her steadily, but Bieito set Pruta down and crossed to the door. Jannicke looked away at his inarticulate exclamation—not so far she didn't see him step through the door. Inhaling deeply, she shut her eyes.

"May I touch him?" Bieito called.

Jannicke had to cough. "Of course you may. Not—not breakable."

A moment later, Bieito stood in the open door, toy cradled gently against his chest as if it were a real boy who had stubbed his toe. "He's...*wonderful*, Jannicke. I'm so envious of Fredo." Shrugging the toy's head up, he rubbed his cheek against its nose.

Jannicke exhaled. The unsteady feeling of nausea deepened. Bieito's opinion didn't count: he was nearly grown up. Without her noticing, Iefan and Radoš had risen, gone to their son and his burden. Iefan ran his fingers through the toy's hair. "Remarkable," Radoš muttered.

"Take it back out." Jannicke's voice surprised her, a weak, discordant croak. "Fredo will show up any time."

Radoš went with Bieito, but Iefan remained in the doorway, dark against the light outside. "I had a doll," he said slowly, "when I was small, younger than Fredo. It looked almost like a real baby but I didn't like to touch it—hold it. It was hard, rigid, some kind of molded polymer. It frightened me for a long time and when I stopped being frightened I found it hateful."

Bieito's head appeared at Iefan's shoulder. "Would you make one for me, Jannicke?" As if regretful of having given up the toy, he wrapped his arms around his father, clasped his hands together on Iefan's belly, squeezing.

"That's too much to ask," Iefan protested.

"No," said Jannicke, startling herself again. "Yes, Bieito, dear, I'd like to do that for you. —If you're not just humoring an old lady."

Jostling his father, Bieito shook his head.

"Shall I make one that resembles you instead of Fredo?"

Beginning to grin, Bieito nodded. "Please."

"When do you complete this assignment and move on?"

"Just after new year's. I'll have a fiver's leave. I could come visit you again." Jannicke calculated. "That should be sufficient time."

There was another knock at the door. "Grandie, let me in!" Goffredo yelled, his voice muffled. "It's my birthday!"

Hopeful, Jannicke told the house AI to unlatch her door.

Olives-town, Away: Eve's Judgment 92 (YC 215) Melky 34

"Stubborn old woman," Goffredo muttered. "You waited so long, but you couldn't wait for me to get home." When his father called, Goffredo had purchased a berth on the first hydrofoil out of Zanji-Bar but it was a two-day voyage at best. Eight thousand kilometers of open sea still stretched before him when the second call came. "You were the last, you know." He shivered. The room was chill, but that wasn't why. "The last old woman in the world. And now there aren't any."

He stepped closer. She hadn't known, of course. Jannicke hadn't understood much of anything for nearly twenty years, all his adult life—had not recognized her own daughters' deaths. Kamen confessed it a sad relief when the municipality built the little hospice for their most famous citizen—not just the oldest woman but the oldest *person* in the world—and assumed her care, 'round the clock, 'round the calendar. They could never have expected her to hold on so much longer.

One hundred nineteen years in all. In the morning, the Presidium in Haven—who happened, this half-year about to end, to be Away's president, a man Goffredo had known, disliked, when both were schoolboys—had broadcast a eulogy: Goffredo listened on the hydrofoil's observation deck, watching the empty waves. Jannicke was the final link, Gjon said, sounding resentful (Goffredo recalled there were no women in Gjon's family), with the world the founders meant to create when they built the seedship so long ago, so far away, and sent it on its journey across the light years. She was older than the calendar...not that Jannicke had been lucid when the referendum passed, changing Goffredo's decantation year overnight from 176 to 53 and establishing *Eve's judgment* as the sanctioned term for the year women stopped being born. Earlier, a newsfeed commentator had pointed out that, since this planet's year was longer, on the world of humanity's origin Jannicke would have been one hundred twenty-five.

As the world's ceremonial head of state as well as president of Away's governing council, after delivering the eulogy Gjon had boarded a fast government aerofoil, would reach Olives that evening. The president of the Spice Islands—where Goffredo had lived for a decade and a half, managing a jungle resort on the northeast coast of Zanji-Bar and twice voting the man into office—was meant to assume the Presidium in four days, on the solstice. Already in Haven in advance of the investiture, he and the other archipelagic presidents travelled with Gjon. Goffredo wondered how much political theatre they would make of the funeral: if the first minister was also aboard the same government aerofoil, whether they would conduct the Presidial hand-over in Olives or rush back to Haven. His fathers would know. None of the politicians, not even Gjon, had ever said as many as two words to Goffredo's grandie when she could sensibly reply.

He took another step toward the bed. It was *her* bed, his dad had insisted, the ancient lemonwood bed she'd brought over from Citron. All the monitors and life-support devices that had surrounded it on his last visit had been removed. Her caregivers, he supposed, when they cleaned her and dressed her and laid her out, had meant her to look asleep, serene, peaceful. She looked dead.

Pruta lay on the sidetable by the bed. Long ago, Goffredo had asked his grandie why she'd named the toy after the tenth part of a sheqel. "Because she was as precious as money," Jannicke said, "but very small."

His toy, the toy she'd made for him and given him when he turned five, had remained nameless a long time. Disappointing her, he'd been afraid of it at first—he thought he remembered shrieking in terror when Grandie told him to go out on her porch and see who was waiting for him. Then his uncle Bieito had tried to comfort him, saying the *thing* would be his best friend, companion when he was happy, comfort when he was sad, and—wasn't it wonderful?—Grandie was going to make one for him, Bieito, too, though he was nearly grown up. Bieito's toy was ready for him when he visited again at new year's: Goffredo had watched Jannicke make it, though he refused to help and sat as far away as he could from the sofa where she stitched the horrible, empty, inside-out skin, his own vacuous, horrible toy reclining at her side. Bieito hugged the soft figure that looked like him as soon as he saw it (he never called it *it*, always *him*), named it *Benny*, an historical variation, he said, of his own name.

Then Bieito left again, taking Benny, off to his second global-service assignment. There was an unexpectedly severe quake late one night that autumn. Zé-daddy carried Goffredo out of the house to open ground. The world was still jouncing underfoot and Goffredo was screaming: Kam-daddy yelled from the open door of Grandie's room that he needed help. "You have to stay here, Fredo," Zé said, his worry frightening Goffredo even more. "Don't move!" Goffredo wailed. Zé abandoned him.

Grandie struggled against them when they dragged her out of the house, shrieking louder than Goffredo—an early outbreak, he assumed now, of the dementia that would claim her fully years later—yelling things he didn't understand about people he'd never met. His dads couldn't release her to comfort him. Grandie's hysteria scared him more than the no longer shaking ground. "Hox!" he yelled suddenly and darted into Grandie's room before either dad could stop him.

The cycling emergency lamp, *red! white! red!*, made it hard to see where things were, things that remained where they were supposed to be or things that had fallen. He stubbed his toe on the bronze sculpture of Kam-daddy's father and uncle. His phone, newly grafted to his jaw and still a novelty, kept shouting at him to come outside again *right now!* At last he found the toy: it had fallen behind Grandie's sofa. It was bigger than he but weighed almost nothing, but its long arms and legs kept getting caught.

Grandie was still screeching and flailing when he got the toy outside but Zé-daddy left her to his husband to come and shout at Goffredo: "You could have been injured, Fredo! It wasn't safe."

"You didn't rescue Hox."

"Hox?" Zé-daddy went down on his knees. "Is that his name?"

"Of course!"

"I'm glad you rescued him, Fredo, but it scared me when you went inside. That's why I shouted. I'm sorry. Can you and Hox take care of each other now, for a little while? I have to help Daddy with your grandie—she's upset."

By the time Olives Emergency Response came to check the house over and certify its safety, almost dawn, Grandie had exhausted herself into uneasy sleep. Kam-daddy dozed against Zé-daddy's shoulder. Goffredo lay half asleep in Hox's embrace—Hox didn't feel the chill of the ground so Goffredo lay atop him. The ER man admired Hox a great deal. "I wish I had something like that to give my own boy," he said.

"My grandie could make a Hox for him, if you ask her nicely."

"When she's herself again," said Kam-daddy hastily, "in a fiver or two."

Rare the night thereafter Hox wasn't at least nearby when Goffredo slept, if not in bed with him, under his arm. He was almost forty now but felt scarcely self-conscious at all lugging Hox onto the hydrofoil in Zanji-Bar or carrying him off and openly through the streets of Olives-town to Jannicke's hospice. In Olives, Hox was famous: the very first, the original Baby Daddy. (Bieito had trademarked the term.) It was odd Gjon hadn't mentioned the toys in his eulogy. He had known—enviously mocked—Hox in school. Nobody could claim Baby Daddies weren't a phenomenon of more cultural significance than anything Gjon could hope to achieve. Scarcely any boy in the world nowadays didn't have one—few men under thirty Goffredo had met hadn't grown up with one. Some dads made them themselves for their sons—the AIs that designed Hox for Jannicke were ready to help; some bought the outrageously costly, individually personalized, authentic hand-crafted Baby Daddies that had made Bieito's fortune, some the cheaper (not much less lovable) mass-produced knock-offs. Hox was the first, Benny the second, all the others came after, Jannicke's innumerable descendants.

He sat on the bed beside his great-grandmother's corpse, still holding Hox in the crook of his arm. Gently, he lifted Pruta from the sidetable, stroked her velvet head, gently settled her on Jannicke's unbreathing chest. He had brought Hox across half the world from Zanji-Bar intending to burn him with his grandie. An ungrateful impulse, perhaps.

He had not made much of his life in thirty-nine years. Jannicke was not to be blamed: she had loved him, as annoying child, as moody adolescent. Had *imagined* Hox for him and then made him, patiently waited for Goffredo to understand. Had never accused him of lacking ambition or complained (unlike his dads) about his never bringing home a husband or providing sons to be spoiled. If not for the dementia, he supposed, she might have done both.... He thought not. He knew the story of her son, his great-uncle Deror.

Goffredo was barely into puberty when he understood he was one of those many unfortunates whose erotic and affectional compass spun wild, uncontrollable, seeking a pole no longer to be found on this globe. He could never love another man the way his dads loved each other. Over two and a half decades, true, he had (more times than he cared to count—the resort was a conducive environment) had sex with other men. Love never entered into the transaction. He preferred not to sleep with them afterward. His own right hand satisfied him as well, often better.

He might have raised sons on his own. Many men did. (Bieito would surely have offered a discount on Baby Daddies for them, if not made a gift outright: Bieito was not an ungrateful or selfish man, was fond enough of his disappointing nephew.) He did not. He felt he could not love them as they would deserve to be loved. He feared they would be like him.

Goffredo sighed, dissatisfied, unhappy. The world was what it was, he was what he was. He stroked Pruta again, lightly touched one finger to Jannicke's chill lips. "I loved you, old woman," he said. "I miss you." Leaning down, he kissed her brow. His eyes were dry, painful. "Thank you, Grandie."

Standing, he gazed down on her one last time. The coverlet was wrinkled where he'd sat. He smoothed it out. Holding insensible Hox tight, he left the room to find his dads.

✦ ⊕ ✦

Liam and the Wild Fairy

Liam missed the school bus. Deliberately. From the far side of the rutted athletic field, he watched the yellow monster trundle away with its monstrous cargo and pulled out his phone. When he flipped it open, the animated carrousel of tiny *family-n-friends* photos-n-unassigned-ikons spun for a second before it settled on his dad grinning up at him. Dad #1. They'd been fighting, but still. One kept up the forms or got grounded. Liam thumbed the *call* key and lifted the phone to his ear.

It went to voicemail, probably not deliberate. Liam waited for the beep, then said with great fake cheer, "Hey, Dad. Missed the bus—" *again* would be taken as understood—"so I'm walking home. See you in forty-five or so. Love you."

Folding the phone shut again, he stuffed it back in his pocket and started walking. It was only about a mile and a half, rural roadsides until he reached the park, and he did like to walk. More than he liked trying to ignore Harry and Brandon and Tyler and the hurtful things they said that made the girls giggle meanly and put Joel's back up. Why the only kid in the freshman class who could make sophomore Harry back down should be bothered Liam didn't like to think about—he disliked feeling beholden and Joel's interference just made Harry and his pals more vindictive when he was out of sight.

❧ composed 2010, Pawtucket, Rhode Island ☙
❧ first published in Icarus #5, Summer 2010 ☙

There was always the worry Harry would get off at Liam's stop—Harry lived only two lots away—and try to start something. He'd done it before. Harry was a coward and his folks were Christians of the hateful sort who'd been piously gratified when Liam's dad #2 decided he didn't like being married or a dad anymore and ran away to California. Except Bryan, Dad #1, didn't then choose to remove the foul contagion of himself and his son from the Hogans' neighborhood—Bryan and his former husband had bought their house two years before Harry's family arrived. Would the Hogans have settled here if they'd known beforehand?

Liam's phone vibrated against his thigh. He pulled it out again, checked the little display on the outside of the clamshell. "Hey, Dad." Who else would it be?

"What was it this time, Liam?"

Liam shook his head. It wasn't like he could be grounded from school. "Just ran a little late."

"No baroque excuses to entertain your old man this time, huh? It's not especially convenient for me to come pick you up right now."

"Better not to spew more climate-change toxins into the air anyway." Liam shook his head again, determined to take the high road. "It's a nice walk. I could use the fresh air and I'll get home long before dark."

"You want fresh air, join the cross-country squad."

Liam had a hard-fought exemption from PE. His dad had done most of the fighting.

"Babe—" The ritual endearment sounded inflammatory. "You know Ms Abadi reports you every time you're not on her bus and I get a call from the principal the next day."

"What are they worried about?"

"They watch the news. The district's legally responsible for you till you get home."

Liam glanced around. Every house within town limits stood on at least an acre. A certain amount of quixotic family agriculture stretched out the distances even further. Visiting friends—if you had friends—you had no choice but to hike or bike (Liam didn't have a bike) or get your parents to drive you. "Sex criminals can't afford to live in this town, Dad," he said, trying to sound reasonable. "Like they'd be interested in me anyway."

"You might be surprised," his dad muttered, then more clearly, "I'm actually more concerned about the high-powered jerks who can afford high-powered cars, don't believe speed limits apply to them, and get distracted when their cell signal drops."

"You know I'm careful."

"I know *you're* careful. You're not driving an overclocked SUV."

"I've got eyes in the back of my head." Not literally, but Liam was fully aware of the three tons of steel coming up behind him even though he couldn't quite hear it yet. The driver was going slow, would see Liam's fire-engine-chartreuse backpack in plenty of time. In the far lane, in any case.

"Harry and his bastardy posse again, or was it somebody trying to make friends?"

"Hey, now. They're not bastards. *Their* parents were legally married when they spawned." Liam took a breath and watched where he put his next foot. No way he was going to address the other issue right now. "Look, nothing *happened.* I just had kind of a long day and didn't feel like dealing with anybody and it's a pleasant afternoon for a walk."

"Liam. It's high school. Some kids are going to be mean and stupid no matter what. If you had friends—"

"I don't *want* friends, Dad."

"Everybody—"

"I'm not everybody. You know it as well as I do."

The truck had sped up. Liam could hear the deep growl of its engine but didn't look back as it rounded the curve behind him. On the straight, it sped up faster, staying within the speed limit and its own lane. Incurious, he glanced over as it levelled with him, in time to recognize the older brother of one of Harry Hogan's friends at the wheel of the big black pickup. In time, if there'd been any real chance of it hitting him, to dodge the soda can that came flying out the open window. Liam didn't break stride. "Fairy!" the kid yelled—your hearing had to be as acute as Liam's to catch it over the engine noise. He watched the can bounce off tarmac onto the shoulder and roll into the ditch.

"What was that?" his dad asked, jumpy.

"Truck passing. Gave me plenty of room."

"Why don't you want friends, babe?"

Halted, Liam regarded the soda can glittering in half an inch of muddy water at the bottom of the ditch. "Dad—" He resolved to ride the bus every afternoon for the rest of the year, no matter what. His dad didn't understand about not rocking a half-sunken boat. He didn't want to get into it over the phone—didn't want to get into it at all but particularly not now. Maybe he was a little jumpy himself. "We can talk about it when I get home." Again.

"Liam—" Bryan swallowed whatever he meant to say. "We'll do that."

"I'll be there soon."

"You'd better be, son of mine."

It would be *that* conversation again, the one about driving him to and from school every day if the bus and the kids on the bus were so intolerable. Wouldn't that just improve Liam's image among his peers. Then the subject of private school would come up. As if his grades were good enough to get him into one. As if prep-school kids were magically less small minded and hateful than other adolescents—as if Liam would magically become a different boy himself, ready and eager to join in. And then, if Liam didn't nip it right in the bud, there'd be sad musings about sending him to live with Dad #2 and his new boyfriend because surely high-school students in San Francisco were more enlightened. "Their parents voted to repeal gay marriage," Liam would say (had said), and Bryan would say, "Not San Francisco parents," and Liam would have to say, "Ricky and his guy don't *want* me." Which was so true it didn't even hurt anymore but it wasn't supposed to be spoken aloud. Besides, the prospect of living in a city terrified him.

Liam kicked at grass sprouting at the road's edge where asphalt crumbled into dirt. Recovering, he noticed the soda can in the ditch again. Feeling virtuous (soda cans were aluminum, safe to touch), he clambered down to pull it out. There were no sidewalk trash cans around—no sidewalks—let alone recycling bins, but he was almost to the park.

Reaching it, he detoured off his regular route to find the bin marked CANS ONLY by the little kids' playground. When he got there, though, he discovered the battered plastic receptacle had been replaced by one of those high-tech solar-powered compressor bins. The handle you had to pull down to deposit your can had the look of brushed stainless steel. He hesitated a moment before reaching for it. The sting of incipient burn bloomed in his fingertips before they got within three inches and he snatched his hand back. "Dammit," he said, blowing on his fingers. "Try to be a good citizen...." It wasn't worth the effort to go digging through his backpack for gloves. Easier just to carry the grotty soda can the rest of the way and drop it in the recycling at home.

Liam started walking again, not really paying attention, holding the can away from himself in case it dripped. He hated the smell of every soda he'd ever encountered—he was pretty much allergic to high-fructose corn syrup and aspartame was worse. The dirt path away from the playground led him under tall trees alive with new leaves. He inhaled the fresh greenness gratefully. Leaves and pollen and damp earth mingled and murmured and calmed him. *This* was one reason not to ride the bus. The fug of growing boys and girls and their rampaging hormones, the horrible industrial fragrances they felt honor bound to steep themselves in, the horrible foods they ate and the odors the foods caused them to exude...it was difficult enough to withstand in large classrooms with climate control. Concentrated within the vibrating, painfully metallic capsule of the bus, it became unendurable. By the time he got home, always, always, he would be queasy and nearly high.

He suspected it was hormones made big, tough Joel so stupidly protective and friendly. Just today, Joel had barged up to the table in the cafeteria where Liam was eating his home-made lunch to ask about the book he was reading. Liam had to insult him hard to make him go away, and then Joel looked so sad and hurt Liam felt kind of bad. Not bad enough to go after him and apologize, until it was too late to carry through without raising Joel's expectations. Whatever Liam's own freaky hormones were doing to him, it didn't involve irresistible urges to get close to people or find them sexy—whatever that meant. Joel'd been wearing a tight t-shirt, too short so that when he stretched (deliberately, Liam thought) half his taut belly came into view, navel winking: a fool's errand if the display was meant to get a rise out of Liam.

His dad was naïve and solipsistic to believe all Liam's problems rose from Bryan's being gay, having been gay-married and now gay-divorced. Not that it didn't reflect badly on Liam, but he wouldn't be less...sensitive if he'd been adopted by a white-bread str8 couple who called him Bill. Actually, the white bread would probably have killed him long ago.

Walking along the path, thinking too freaking hard, he stripped a tender lime-green leaf off a low branch. Bruised by his fingers, it smelled so good that he raised it to his nose and crushed it and then, intoxicated, stuffed it into his mouth. The juices were clear and vivid, more alive than the brightest Florida orange or the pomegranates his dad bought him in the winter. Concentrating on the complex flavors, the textures of the leaf's fibers mashed and wadded by his teeth, he tripped.

The soda can flew from his hand, tinkling into the underbrush. Liam yelped, more surprise than pain, when one knee and then a palm struck the ground. The lump of masticated leaf had caught in his throat, as minorly distressing as a stone in his shoe. Lying still for a moment on soil that felt chillier than it really was, he became aware of tears starting from his eyes and grunted, "Clumsy."

"You are bleeding."

Liam yelped again, startled. The leaf came up, sweet, unexpected, as he imagined bubblegum might taste. He spat it away.

"Please. I can smell it."

Ready to flee, Liam rolled up to a crouch. The voice didn't sound human, clear and thin and edgy, like struck crystal.

"Please. I am unwell."

He hadn't tripped over his own feet but somebody else's. Somebody's long, slender, pale bare feet, protruding onto the path at the ends of skinny, bony bare legs. In mid-April, it was still too chilly to go bare legged, barefoot. The rest of the person, from the knees up, lay hidden by leaf and shadow.

"Who?"

"If I might...taste it. Please."

The copper and ionized silver that served his cardiovascular system as iron did his dad's made Liam's blood pale, greenish and iridescent, difficult to distinguish against his skin under the dirt on his palm. He hadn't even noticed the smart. "Please," the other fairy said again.

"Why?"

One bare foot trembled and then both withdrew. Leaves and shadows shivered. A long moment of near silence almost convinced Liam either to run away (he had never encountered another person like himself) or burrow into the bush.

Eyes. Eyes peering through rustling leaves, huge anime eyes with big black pupils that contracted almost to nothing as the face emerged further into light, irises of two distinct colors, crescents of pale gold framing ellipses of silvery green. They were disproportionate to the rest of the face, if you were used to human features, and didn't blink for the longest time. A pointed tongue licked thin lips. The fairy said, "Only a taste. Please?"

"Who are you?"

"I became lost, disoriented. Now I believe I am ill. This terrible, terrifying place!" The fairy's chin moved side to side, a wag so rapid it was over before Liam registered it. The skin around his eyes looked bruised, tinted with green and lavender shadows that stylish girls at Liam's school would emulate if they could. "I sensed you before you fell, before the...blood. Please."

At the bridge of the fairy's nose, the inside ends of his thick sable brows, two long filaments trembled like a butterfly's antennae or cat's whiskers, seeking, searching. Frightened and excited, Liam moved closer, and they swivelled toward him, still shivering. First his dads and then Liam himself had always trimmed the errant hairs of his own eyebrows—he hadn't realized how long they would grow nor that at each tip would sprout a tiny gem like a lustrous pearl. "It's dirty," he said, offering his open palm.

The fairy grasped his wrist, the fingers with their extra set of knuckles going all the way around. Liam couldn't tell whether the strength of the grip was innate or desperation. Eyes widened until they appeared to take up a third of the triangular face, then narrowed as the fairy used Liam's arm to pull himself out of the bush. Like miniature javelins, his antennae went stiff, straight. Light glimmered within the pointy little pearls. "Thank you," the fairy murmured, but it sounded like a threat and the small teeth behind his narrow lips looked jagged and very sharp. Scared, Liam tried to pull free but the fairy had him. The thin, pointed, whitish tongue lapped at the dirt and blood on his palm.

It wasn't like a cat's tongue, prickly and grating but comforting. Liam didn't think it was like a dog's but he didn't know for sure—Ricky's dog had been afraid of him, resentful, never volunteered any sort of affection. He felt it wasn't like a human's tongue either, which always appeared sloppy with saliva and meaty. He supposed it was like his own—they were the same species—neat and pointed and merely damp rather than moist.

Gradually, the fairy rose to his full height, drawing Liam up with him. He was much taller, taller than Joel or Liam's dad. Liam didn't notice when he noticed the fairy was nude, something that possibly meant fairy nudity wasn't anomalous the way human nudity surely was: Liam had never seen a naked woman, unless she was art, the only fleshly naked man his father, accidental glimpses that seemed to unsettle his dad more than him. The fairy hardly resembled Bryan, who looked human, grown up, but Liam almost saw a resemblance to Joel and other lithe, lanky adolescents always taking their shirts off for no reason at all. But Joel's body hair looked animal, the fairy's ornamental; Joel's muscles decorative, the fairy's feral.

The likeness of the fairy's body to his own Liam wasn't ready to consider.

"You said," he struggled to say, "just a taste."

He felt a little pang in his palm as if, out of surprise or pique, the fairy had grazed tender flesh with those savage teeth, but a final lap of the tongue soothed it. "Apologies," the fairy said, sounding cruel, knowing, again. "It was greatly refreshing." He appeared healthier, the celadon glaze of his skin now opaque. His grip on Liam's wrist never slackened. "Now we shall go."

Flinching, Liam attempted again to reclaim his hand. "Go? I don't know you—I'm not going anywhere with you." Liam was inhumanly strong (something he never let the school bullies discover) but the adult fairy stronger: he felt the bones of his wrist rub together in the fairy's grasp. "Let me go!"

"You do not belong here. It is unwholesome for you." The fairy seemed to be smiling though his eyes had turned away, his gaze turned inward. "Come, it's not far to the door. We will take you home."

Liam knew stories about fairyland. He flashed on Harry Hogan and his pals leering at him—on Joel's big puppy-dog eyes and eager smile—on how much of the world he'd grown up in made him ill, how much he didn't fit. On his dad's face, disappointed and angry and hurt. "Let go of me! This is my home." Too distracted to think of raising his free hand, he twisted and pulled at the other with all his strength.

"Did you believe yourself a man, poor little fellow?" The fairy did something peculiar with the fingers holding Liam's wrist and abruptly there was no pain—no feeling at all in the limb. "Come now. Mother wishes to welcome you home."

He had been scared and ambivalent. The word *mother* enraged Liam. Without conscious intervention, the fist that still worked came up to sock the fairy's delicate jaw and then his pretty nose, solid, furious blows saved up for years as if the fairy were Harry taking his taunts one step too far. "I don't have a mother," Liam was yelling. "I never had a mother. She abandoned me like I was trash—like shit! Like the sorriest piece of shit on earth!"

It seemed the fairy had never learned to defend himself, nor to fight. Releasing Liam's useless arm, he quailed back without being able to escape the fist that functioned, although Liam had never learned to fight either. His punches and slaps flew wild, some not hitting at all, but the fairy staggered away, making sad whines and chirps of protest. Iridescent blue-green blood spilled from his broken nose. With the enormous eyes clenched shut, his face looked pinched and incomplete. One antenna had broken, its pearly tip swinging wildly as the fairy stumbled.

Pursuing him, Liam stumbled, too, thrown off by the dead weight of his left arm. The next blow to land, a savage slap to the fairy's lovely whorled and pointed ear, nearly overbalanced him, while the fairy swivelled and ducked, sobbing hoarsely, wordlessly, turning up his shoulder to deflect another punch. Liam saw the fairy's wings.

He'd never properly seen his own. It required mirrors, or his dad taking photos, a pastime Liam wasn't morbid enough to encourage. Anyway, Liam's wings were barely better than vestigial—he had no control over them, useless stumpy appendages of chitin, cartilage, and glassy membrane that chose embarrassing moments to flex. The scholar Bryan occasionally permitted to examine his son opined that they were immature, they would grow and he would grow into them, but nobody knew much about the fairy life cycle and it seemed just as likely inappropriate diet and childhood environment had stunted Liam's wings.

Folded down his back like quivers of glass arrows, the fairy's wings extended nearly to his knees, glistening. Even as he wanted to break the fairy's face or run away, Liam wished to see the wings spread up and out and lift: to see the fairy fly.

But apparently he was too disoriented to think of it, of how easily he might flee Liam's punishing fist. As he staggered blindly away, the wings bounced and rattled on his back, sounding like distant rain.

Liam lurched after him, panting with fury—too furious to encompass his anger, own it. It had felt good to hit the fairy, good in a despicable way to damage such beauty and cause it pain. It was all mixed up. He'd always believed himself strange, grotesque, ugly—he resembled neither of his handsome dads at all—but he knew the fairy to have been beautiful before Liam broke his nose, knew they looked as like as son and father. He'd often pined to know who he was, how he came to be, but the records of his true parentage were sealed, as far as he knew, and it would hurt his dad, his *real* dad, if he went digging. Nobody, not even his dad's professor friend, could tell him (he felt it was *could*, not *would*) what it meant to be himself, raised in the human world, a wonder and a freak. All he had was stories, fairy tales.

At the center of the park rose a round hill like an overturned mixing bowl. Its peak stood higher than the crowns of all but the tallest trees so the obelisk honoring the town's war dead was visible throughout the valley. Over the years, many had believed it to be artificial, remnant of some unknown pre-Columbian culture, but excavation yielded no evidence. The lunatic fringe insisted it was a locus of supernatural influence, a site of magical power. Liam had never noticed anything particularly special about the hill, beyond its oddity. Now they were climbing it, Liam trailing behind the sobbing fairy.

It was not a difficult haul but the fairy was broken and Liam's dead arm had commenced shooting pings of sensation from wrist to shoulder. He teetered every time they hit and fell behind. In a way, he feared reaching the crown of the hill: there were sure to be people there—admiring the monument, admiring the view—neighbors and tourists. They would see the naked, wounded fairy, see Liam.... He lagged farther behind.

But the fairy halted, scarcely a third of the way up. Unsteady, he merely stood for a moment, but then he looked back over his shoulder, eyes vast, and saw Liam still toiling after. The fairy shuddered. The long wings trail-

ing between his shoulder blades jittered as muscles jumped, then snapped
open. Liam caught his breath. Late-afternoon light trapped in the crystal cells
within the venous structure of the upper vanes turned them to liquid gold.
Around the outer margins clung scales of dense, textured color like scraps
of velvet that held the light and made it their own. Below, the blade-shaped
hindwings were all translucent, filmy veils of watery blue and green captured
for only an instant within branching and rebranching jade veins.

Turning, the fairy faced Liam, looming above him, facing him down.
Sunlight made him solid, intimidating, despite the damage to his nose and
the liquid stains of blood on chin and chest. He exposed his teeth, not a smile,
and his long fingers flexed.

Liam raised his foot, took another step up the slope. The fairy flinched.
Behind him, where a moment before had been only grassy hillside, a door
stood up from a slab of silvery, polished granite, its frame carpentered into the
air. The fairy's wings cast powdery stained-glass shadows on planed planks
fastened together by intricately carved bracing.

Liam ventured another step. The fairy moaned and shut his eyes for an instant. As the door began slowly to open behind him, he fluttered forward and
down, horror implicit in every tentative step, head half turned as he watched
to ensure the door didn't catch wings or heels.

Liam grunted, a hard sound in his throat. He had to—what? Punish the
fairy more? Prevent his escape? Follow him?

The door stood wide. Frozen like prey, eyes as wide and deep as eternity,
the fairy gave Liam a last stricken glance. "You might—" the fairy bleated.
His wings beat hard—a noise like approaching thunder and a gale of turbu-
lence bearing scents that made Liam's heart contract—and whatever else the
fairy said was lost as slender toes scrabbled to maintain his balance even as
they lifted from the grass.

Liam rushed the last few yards but the fairy was already aloft, suspended
from glistening wings like a slaughtered lamb from the cruel iron hook between its shoulders. Leaping, Liam swatted at the sky. Beating wings drunken-
ly swooped the fairy higher, farther, away. His limbs dangled like a mosquito's,
paddling the air. A drop of cooling fairy blood splatted on Liam's cheek.
Clumsy in the air, the fairy made a slow half circle out over the leafy park,
high above Liam sprawled weeping on the stone sill of the magical door, and
then half closed his upper wings and darted, a stooping hawkmoth, over Liam
and under the lintel.

Staring at endless blue sky through veils of tears, Liam hyperventilated. The wind through the door, brushing coolly over his face, smelled—tasted—like no air he had ever breathed. He had never before been offered fresh air to breathe. Whimpering, he hauled himself to his knees, grabbed the frame of the door to drag himself upright. Shivering against feelings he couldn't name, he peered through the portal.

A twilight that never ended. White and amethyst and garnet stars sequinned the indigo horizons. It seemed there must be a full moon somewhere but Liam couldn't find it. Below him fell the spreading skirts of an everlasting antique mountain velveted with forest and meadow every deep shade of green and purple.

Something like a hawk or dragonfly or immense firefly fleeted up a shallow crevasse toward the door, toward Liam, trailing flickering sparks as if the air were so thick with oxygen and vitality that it ignited at the strike of wings. Liam wondered if it was the fairy, his fairy, but then he saw there were many more, flitting or swooping or fluttering above the landscape and high in the sky, each with its comet-tail of sparks. Breath filled his lungs with immeasurable silence and sorrow and he felt the stumps of his own wings fidget, struggling against the weight of shirt, jacket, backpack.

Unthinking, he shrugged the pack off, unhearing, heard it thud to the grass behind him and tumble a way down the hill. Still he stared. His vision was sharpening. He believed he saw a great river wind across a broad plain and a strange obsidian city or palace erupt where river purled into unlimited ocean. He believed he saw a mountain sculpted in the likeness of a sitting leopard, snarling silently at the fairies that circled its head, spritely and unconcerned. He saw a rocky bluff upon which stood the disembodied stone heads of a hundred titanic kings and queens, their blind eyes weeping. His lungs were so full of the air of fairyland he could no longer breathe.

Flexing, writhing, his wings tore through the fabric of shirt and jacket. They vibrated with such intensity that he moaned. If he chose to step across the threshold, he might take nothing of the world he knew with him. Frantic, he ripped the noisome rags from his shoulders and arms. A shred of t-shirt drifted through the door and burst into blue flame before it touched ground. He reached for the brass buckle of his belt.

Unfastening it, his hand brushed the oblong lump of the phone in his pocket. If he were to set a single foot on the soil of fairyland, only for an instant, when he turned back the world he knew would have changed. He would no longer know it. Climate and weather patterns would have shifted in ways no scientist could predict. The sea would have risen to make an island of the distant, enchanted city where his dad #2 had settled, if not drowned it utterly. People, human people, would be half machine. Harry and Brandon and Tyler, even Joel, would be old, bitter old men if they lived at all. Liam's dad, Dad #1, the only person in the universe who truly cared about him, would be long dead.

Liam sobbed aloud and inhaled another draft of the intoxicating wind. His wings fluttered with contained longing. The closing door nudged his heel.

Clenching his eyes against further sight of the land that called him, he tumbled out of the door's way, into sun-warm grass that smelled of sour rags and iron rust and plastic. He coughed and coughed and wept until all that marvellous air had dissipated from his system and all that remained was all he had ever known.

The phone vibrated against his thigh. Flailing, he pulled it out. He was weeping too hard to read the name on the display, couldn't take in sufficient of the foul air to speak when he opened the phone and lifted it to his ear.

"Liam?" The worry in his dad's voice would have saddened Liam if he could become any sadder. "Liam, are you there? It's been almost two hours."

Liam uttered a croak that was meant to be *Dad.*

"Liam! What's wrong? What happened?"

Liam coughed. "Daddy."

"Babe, what is it? What can I do?"

"Daddy, please. I need you. Please come get me."

"Where are you, Liam? Are you hurt?"

Everything hurt. "I'm all right. But I just need you so much right now, please. I'm in the park, on the west side of the hill. I love you so much, Daddy."

"I'll be there in five minutes. Liam, babe, I was so worried. I love you more than anything ever."

Liam coughed his voice clear again. "Backatcha, Daddio," he said, and closed the phone. "So very much."

Slipping the phone back into his pocket, Liam shivered at the cooling air on his bare torso and felt an unfamiliar tug and pull in the center of his back. Craning to look over his shoulder, he saw the jewelled edges of his open wings, straining to catch a vanished wind.

✦ ✦ ✦

Ban's Dream of the Sea

Some time after the fierce, out of season tempest had passed, Ban woke to hammering at the door. He started and lifted his head, perplexed to discover himself slumped over the desk rather than in bed. A thin whine of wind pierced through intervals in the banging. A loose shutter rattled, wanting to break its latch. Wiping the drool from his lips, he called, "What?"

"Ban!" came his brother-in-law's voice, hardly muffled by the door and thick walls. "Banto!"

On the surface of the desk, Ban's candle had guttered down to a puddle of cold, hard wax in its chipped saucer, wick twisted and bloated with black carbon. A sliver of daylight made the water-filled glass globes and polished steel mirrors positioned around the candle shine dully. He had fallen asleep reading.

"What?" he called again. "I'm coming."

Stiff and chilled, he pushed the chair back and levered himself to his feet. The storm had got into his bones and tendons. Pulling the robe tighter over his chest, he crossed the room, fumbled at the overcomplicated Akkatese lock. The city's original builders had not bothered themselves with locks—or doors. All their portals were always open, if not welcoming, until people from the far side of the world came to block them up.

 composed 2011-2012, Pawtucket, Rhode Island
 first published in The Touch of the Sea, edited by Steve Berman (Lethe Press, 2012)

Keron gave him no time to speak, hammering the door inward immediately the tumblers fell. The lower edge struck Ban's slippered foot. "Your sister!" Keron yelled over Ban's yelp, storming in wild eyed and windblown. "Is she here?"

Biting back irritation and the pain in his toes, Ban said, "Of course not. She disapproves of me, where I live. Why would she climb my stairs?"

Keron was out of breath from climbing those stairs himself: Ban rented rooms at the top of one of the ancient towers, cheap because of the laborious climb. "She's gone," Keron gasped. Mottles of red and pink mapped unknown archipelagos on his cheeks above the patchy, greying beard. "Into the night—into the storm. We quarrelled."

"Sit down," said Ban. "You woke me—I'll make chocolate."

Keron knew as well as Ban there was no comfortable seat. Agitated, he pulled the brocade cap from his head and passed it from hand to hand. "Banto," he began but went no further. The brocade was threaded with silver. His drab black casaque was likely of more value than his brother-in-law's entire wardrobe.

"I disappoint my sister," Ban said, his tone light for he was no fonder of her. "Etkass sees little use in me and resents the small demands I place on Father's estate. I'm the last comfort she'd seek after a quarrel." Turning to the battered iron brazier in the corner, he stirred the coals under the kettle, coaxed up a flame. "Doubtless she has confidantes...."

"I do not know them."

Shaving chocolate into the jug, Ban half saw Keron reach toward him. Curtailed, the motion looked clumsy and shy. "I disappoint you," Keron mumbled.

It was an old plaint of which both were weary. "Don't speak nonsense, my dear," said Ban, scrupling to look up and embarrass Keron. "Tell me about this quarrel."

Keron paced. "She woke me. I was dreaming. The dream had made me amorous and she took it as for her."

"Keron...."

"No, Ban. You know full well I don't favor your sister, any woman, but my father will have grandsons so I do my best. I *did* my best, once I understood it was Etkass, not my dream, but it was neither enough to satisfy her nor to make sons. So we quarrelled before she slept. Her dreams too were amorous. When she woke, she asked why it was I could not pleasure her as the man of her dream did. Bitter, I said it was possibly the same man in both our dreams."

"Keron," Ban said, aware of a heat in his cheeks. The water had nearly reached its boil. "Do you have these dreams often? Does she?"

"Etkass? I wouldn't know. Myself? Not of such...intensity, no, not often."

"Was it a man? Truly?"

For an instant Keron's expression was offended, before he became thoughtful. "For my purposes, in my amorous delirium, surely he was, but...perhaps. It's difficult to recall. Until your sister woke me, he gave me such pleasure as I have not known for some years."

Ban lowered his eyes from the accusation of his brother-in-law's regret, poured steaming water over spiced chocolate in the jug. They had agreed—Ban had bullied Keron into agreeing—it would not be fair to continue carrying on as they had while boys once Keron wed Etkass.

"He had no hair, none at all, on his head, on his body, no beard, no eyebrows. His skin was oddly cool, oddly...thick. Resilient, rather like rubber. So somehow not human, perhaps you're right. But a man, equipped as a man, that he was."

"I...." Peering into the jug as he whisked the chocolate, Ban watched foam form and break, froth up again. "I have had such dreams. Recently. Not last night, but the night before, I think. On earlier occasions as well. He is a very great lover, yes, that creature, but not a man. Did you notice, were you in your own bed?"

"Of course not! How should I take a man into your sister's bed? I was—"

"Under the sea? Were there bones, human bones, strewn about the sands below as you...cavorted, suspended in deep waters?"

"Banto?"

"Did my sister say she meant to find him, the *man* of her—of your, of our—dreams? I fear you are widowed, Keron."

"You—" Keron paused. "You are saying things I don't understand."

Without speaking, Ban rose to fetch cups. He poured out the chocolate, handed a cup to his anxious brother-in-law. The bitter fragrance from his own unsettled him: chocolate was a drug Akkatese had not known before they discovered the New World.

"People disappear often, have you noticed, from our city."

"How could I not notice my own brother?" Keron demanded. "Stupid boy—the promenade's no place to stroll in a storm."

Ban had forgotten the fate of Keron's brother. That was long ago. "Not always the promenade. Not always a storm. Often after a peculiarly vivid dream, the records suggest. The admiral was the first." Sipping, calmer but not calm, he moved toward his desk. "Perhaps you didn't know that."

"The admiral?"

The book Ban had fallen asleep over was old but not terribly precious, with multiple editions since the work had been discovered in the viceroy's archive half a century before: *A Narrative of Admiral Saro, His Voyages of Discovery.* Intended for the common reader, this twenty-year-old edition boasted no scholarly apparatus beyond its preface and was illustrated with fanciful engravings. Ban had it nearly by heart for the moment—merely glancing at the open page he recalled the passage he had read as sleep overcame him:

> *We came upon this marvel from the east, late in the afternoon when the sun dazzled upon the sea beyond so we believed it no more than a rocky island spired and chimneyed in natural stone. Wary of submerged rocks and reefs off an unknown coast, the admiral chose to drop anchor until morning. Happening to wake in the night when the great moon was high and full, I peered across the waters toward the undiscovered island some furlongs distant.*
>
> *"It appears a mighty castle or city, alone in the sea," said the sleepless admiral, joining me at the gunwale.*

On the following page, a fine engraving depicted that vision of admiral and chronicler: the city rising sheer and high from moonlit waters, the admiral's *Pearl of Akkat* and the two smaller ships of his flotilla, the *Ruby* and the *Sapphire,* becalmed at a distance along the moon's path. Although Ban knew well his own ancestors had built the Admiral's Spire more than a hundred years later, steepling above the builders' halls and towers, he felt the engraving's effect was not spoiled by its depiction outside its own time. The artist had drawn the admiral's vessel as a modern galleon rather than a carrack of the era.

Closing the book, Ban ran his fingers along the top edge where cloth had frayed against the board. The same anachronistic galleon was blind stamped at the center of the cover. Turning to his brother-in-law, he said, "The admiral spoke to his secretary the night before he vanished, complaining of dreams in which a devilish woman attempted to seduce him. There was no storm. No women had yet come from Akkat—it was only men, a tiresome thing for those who preferred women. The admiral was not the last of his men to disappear before the queen's viceroy brought wives, maidens, whores across the ocean. Afterward...not so many vanishings, two or three a decade in the records for three hundred years. But the number has been increasing lately, the last half or quarter century. Ten years ago it might have been two or three a year. These days—" Ban shook his head. "Not people you would notice for the most part, two or three each great month."

"What?"

Ban walked away, toward the shuttered window that faced north, toward the distant mainland. "As I said, not people you would notice. Young people, sons and daughters of fisherfolk, ferry tenders, small merchants and traders, laborers, clerks. I began to look into it some time ago, after my first dream. Did you not feel a powerful urge to join your lover?"

"A...wistfulness. I knew it was a dream, he was not real. I knew I could not survive beneath the waves with him."

"You were awakened early, untimely." Slipping the shutters' latches, Ban pulled the heavy wooden wings wide. Fresh, clean air boomed in, instantly banishing the human smells of chocolate, spices, ink, coal smoke—fresh, invigorating, heavy with salt over the faint, probably imagined fragrance of pine from the mainland's forests. Ban simply breathed for a moment before looking down. "The causeway is gone," he said, faintly shocked.

"Broken in the storm. It often happens."

"Not broken. Gone. Vanished, like your wife."

"That cannot be." Keron's voice was sharp, his hand falling heavy on Ban's shoulder. "You're imagining things, Banto."

Turning toward the door, Ban did not look through the window again, paused only when his brother-in-law implored him not to appear on the public street uncombed, awry, in stained house robe and slippers. On another day, Ban would have joked his fairest attire was not much more presentable, his reputation as tattered as his slippers. Throwing aside the robe, he dressed hastily, mindful only after, when he glimpsed the longing in Keron's eyes, how long it had been since he allowed himself to appear so defenseless, so intimate, in his brother-in-law's presence.

The fact of it, the lapse in the fiction between them, irritated him, so that he pulled the door open with unnecessary force. The hinges protested, the wooden jamb shuddered and creaked against the ancient stone to which it was clumsily fastened. "Come," he said brusquely, not looking back as he ducked under the lintel.

The stairs were also wood, steep and creaky, jigsawed onto the builders' spiral ramp, which men of the admiral's time had found treacherous to climb or descend in that age's high-heeled boots. Over his own footfalls, Ban heard

Keron drag the door closed and jostle the latch but did not pause. Without the key, Keron could not lock the door but Ban possessed little that would tempt a burglar. There was no particular market for thirdhand volumes of dubious scholarship, outdated maps. A thief who required Ban's aimless manuscripts to kindle a sad fire was, in the end, welcome to them.

The odors of old cooking rose to meet Ban from his neighbors' kitchens on lower floors, the myriad stenches of the city at the bottom of his stairs. Soles clattering, he plunged down, one hand trailing the stone of the ancient builders' walls.

When the sun rose behind the Pearl *in the morning, we saw the admiral's night vision had been true. A mighty, fantastical city rose from the waste of waves as if some deity had plucked up one of the great towns of Akkat or the old empire or another of the countries about the Home Sea and dropped it here, well offshore of these new lands half the world away.*

There were cries of anger, of amazement, among our men. The few peoples we had encountered on this side of the ocean were rude savages who spoke no civilized tongue nor recognized the true gods, built no great structures, whether of stone or wood. They boasted no architects or engineers. Nomads, they packed their dwellings of leather and withe on the backs of strange hairy camels as they moved from one hunting or foraging ground to the next. Their canoes and rafts were scarce seaworthy, so that only a madman would trust them to bear him across the wide, treacherous strait from mainland to this islanded city. In any event, as we voyaged west from our first landfall, we had met no people at all since the last waxing of the great moon. The men at the final slapdash encampment shouted at us from the shore, as if in warning, when we turned the Pearl *to follow the sun, and the fellow we had taken aboard in hope of teaching him to speak intelligibly and guide us became agitated, broke his bonds, and threw himself into the sea.*

Immediately the master at arms saw the city across the waters, he called his marines to order. The guns were rolled into place, creaking across the deck, matches lit. Men grown lax in all this time checked their powder was dry, the bores of their calivers clear. Yet the admiral on the foredeck said, gently but firmly, "I see no threat."

Indeed, no banners flew from the city's tall towers. The sharpest spyglass could pick out not a single person on the wide esplanade that circled the town instead of defensive walls, not a face at any of the myriad open windows. In the grand harbor rested no ships or smaller vessels. More astonishing

than its being a city in the sea far from civilized shores, then, it appeared
to be deserted.

Once they emerged onto the Queen's High Street from the tangle of dim,
narrow alleyways that made up Ban's sestiere, he paced faster where pavements
were swept clean and refuse hidden away. It seemed to him he noticed aspects
of his city that had never seemed important before. Was it peculiar to see so
many images of women and men? More, it almost seemed, than living persons.
In Ban's neighborhood, the night lanterns were simple white-glass globes or
guttering open naphtha flames where globes had broken. On the high street,
gem-colored blown-glass busts of grandees stood on plinths down the center
of the avenue. Caryatides and atlantes upheld the wooden porticos attached to
quite unimportant establishments. Frescoes of dubious quality encrusted the
unwindowed lower floors of buildings now warehouses or manufactories with
garlands of brightly attired dancers or processions of heroes.

Ban set too hard a pace. By the time they reached the waterfront and its
stenches of spoiled fish and produce and humanity, Keron was lagging, as
breathless as if he'd climbed the tower stairs all over again. His call for Ban to
wait was nearly a whimper.

Distrustful crowds milled about the piazzetta. Ban had to edge between
agitated grocers and wholesalers, scholars, marines, sailors. Luminously pale
bondsmen and freedmen of mainland heritage formed troubled groups, speaking their own barbarous languages in low voices. A cabal of grandees had accu-
mulated around the toll station. Rumor had it two centuries of tolls had long
since paid for New Akkat's greatest feat of engineering, though the holders of
the concession (Keron's father among them) never hesitated to impose new
levies for extraordinary repairs.

The brothers-in-law had nearly reached the colossal pylons that had anchored the final link of the causeway between island city and distant mainland, where crops were grown and cattle raised, metals and coal mined, stone
quarried, lumber cut and sawn. Between the massive shoulders of a pair of
stevedores, Ban saw that the pylons had changed. He stopped dead, grabbing
Keron's hand to halt him as well.

Keron looked back, eyes wide. "What is it?"

No longer plainly utilitarian piers of brick-faced concrete, the pylons had
become monumental statues, each seemingly sculpted from a single outcrop
of native stone, one hunkered into a crouch, the other kneeling. They were...
not men but masculine, figures as like as brothers, one to the other and each

to the lover of Ban's dreams. Barnacles like pox and tumors of coral marred stoney skin, garlands of blue-grey mussels and small pink-grey clams clung to the fissures where muscle folded into rocky muscle, skeins of iridescent rotting seaweeds draped tensed limbs as the statues attempted to lift the sea into the city.

Between one blink and the next, Ban discovered himself to be alone with Keron on the desolate piazzetta, though the agitated echoes of the crowd's voices lingered for moments and the stenches and fragrances of their commerce seemed still to overwhelm the clean scent of the sea. He uttered a sound, a moan. Releasing Keron's hand, he turned about. The city looming was recognizably the same but no longer New Akkat, for it was flensed of four centuries' alien accretions. The Admiral's Spire did not steeple above older towers. Lower Akkatese buildings, brick or stone or wood, had likewise vanished. The builders' stark walls were stripped of foreign ornament, whether carved wood, molded plaster, or simple paint. Doorways and windows gaped darkly without the wooden and glass barriers bracketed on by folk who valued privacy and distrusted weather. No people at all marred the ancient architecture.

"I—" Ban felt heat rush back to the surface of his skin when he blinked a third time and saw his familiar, resplendent mongrel city once more. The Spire bisected the sky as it had all his lifetime.

"What, Banto? You look frightened. What is it?"

Over Keron's shoulder, Ban recognized the brick pylons, sturdy, eternal. "I.... Nothing. I felt faint for a moment." Pushing past his brother-in-law and the arguing stevedores, he reached the piazzetta's ruled edge, where bollards and iron chains presented no real barrier to one who wished to risk the rocks and reefs and treacherous waters below.

The pylons remained, but their great cables dangled limp as if they had never supported the causeway's first segment. In the open waters beyond, a few of the huge, roughly squared logs that had formed the roadbed bobbed on rough seas between waterfront and the artificial islet to which that segment had led. The gate that was half garrisoned fort stood up from its foundations in the submerged reef, banners flying, though storm had tattered the banners and no bridge now reached the great arched gate ten feet above the waves. Under the arch stood soldiers of the garrison, who seemed not terribly concerned, and below a party of marines was hauling a small barge from the sturdy boat house.

"Broken," murmured Ban, "merely broken, not vanished."

Moving closer, Keron studied him. "You haven't eaten. Knowing you, you didn't eat last night."

Ban shook his head. "I don't recall." Could hunger cause such visions? He blinked again, squeezing his eyelids tight for a moment, but the fort remained.

"Come." Keron had decided. "Back to my house. Perhaps Etkass has found her way home from her wander. At any rate, there will be food."

—⚜—

Within ten days of our landfall in the deserted city, most of us had come to take the place for granted. The admiral had raised our flag on the waterfront of its fine, deep, sheltered harbor and claimed the island in the name of our distant, indifferent queen and the merchant-adventurers' company which had financed the expedition. The rough, gross prelate who accompanied us at our sponsors' insistence performed a rite meant to cleanse the place of native demons and ghosts; as the admiral would not countenance sacrifice of our last hog or laying hens, priest and gods must needs be satisfied with one of the hairy camels intended for the queen's menagerie. We had already determined the beasts were not good eating, less wholesome than horse even.

I do not know who among us first called the place New Akkat. Not the admiral, I believe.

Etkass had not returned. Her bondswoman, a mainlander in Ban's family's service longer than he could remember, extending the term of her bond again and again to buy freedom for one child after another, only cringed and muttered in her own language when asked of her mistress. She prepared a small collation for Keron and her mistress's scholar brother, which Ban could not recall eating after it was gone.

Then—imported from the Old World, more precious than silver—coffee instead of chocolate. Ban savored the rare bitterness of the drink and permitted himself not to think: of his vanished sister, of the broken causeway, of his inexplicable visions. Across the parlor, Keron had laid aside his own cup and drawn up his feet, leaning back into the settee's corner, contemplating nothingness with his chin up and eyes downcast.

Ban regarded his brother-in-law for some moments. Keron had never been handsome, the beard he had allowed to grow in the last year did not flatter plump cheeks and thick neck, but he was comfortable and...dear. Ban had been appalled when his boyhood friend (*lover* was not a term either ever used) first paid suit to Etkass—not because Ban loved his sister so much but for the suit's cynicism. Not a trait he had previously ascribed to Keron.

"You truly believe she is dead?" Keron asked, speaking to the high back of the settee. "My wife?"

Ban shook himself. He set down the coffee cup. "I believe she won't return."

"I treated her unfairly."

"I feel you did. But she was no kinder to you."

Liquid glimmered in the margins of Keron's eyes. "It was you I loved."

"No."

"Yes."

"No. We pleased each other, for a time."

"We must leave. If you're right about the dreams." Turning tragic eyes on Ban, Keron set his feet on the floor. "We should go far away. I can't lose you too, Banto."

Ban hardened his heart. "You chose to marry."

"I had no choice! My brother...."

"Where would you go, Keron? Your name means nothing in Akkat. Nowhere in the Old World. You haven't enough fortune of your own to make a new name."

"I—" Keron wept openly now. "I'm frightened. What you tell me—I cannot think about it."

Reaching again for his coffee, Ban declined the invitation to comfort his friend. "Then don't. Forget it. Wait a suitable period, then find another girl. Sire sons and raise them."

"How can you—"

"Or follow your dream lover into the sea."

"Banto!"

Ban rose to his feet. "Thank you for the coffee, my dear. I must go. If my sister should return after all, please send word."

❧◦❧

After some weeks, the prelate demanded to see the admiral. Two men-at-arms and I stood attendance, for nobody—the admiral least of all—trusted the priest or his distant, luxurious masters. As the admiral's amanuensis, I sat to one side with my ink and pens, while the soldiers stood behind and to either side of his chair. The priest was displeased to see us but endeavored not to reveal his displeasure. "My lord admiral," he said without hesitation, "this is an evil place."

"In what way evil?" inquired the calm admiral.

The elder man-at-arms, a person one had not known to be pious or righteous, muttered, "The men are forever buggering one another."

The admiral dismissed his concern. "As they will on any long voyage or campaign, deprived of women. Unfortunate, perhaps. Not evil." He turned his hard eyes again to the priest.

"It knows not the gods and the gods decline to know it. We must destroy it, crumble it into the sea, and depart."

The admiral smiled coolly. "But, sir, one might say the same of all the lands we have discovered on this side of the great ocean. None of the people we met on the mainland recognized the gods. Indeed, the same might be said of our own home. Was not the great temple in Akkat first built for worship of the old empire's false god?"

"The great temple and all of Akkat were cleansed of that taint long ago."

"As you cleansed this place the day we made landfall, no? Here there are no men or women to know the gods or not. It is, it would seem to me, a blank page on which we may write a new history to the glory of the gods and our queen."

"You persist in misunderstanding, my lord," the prelate said, anger mottling his face. "The builders of the great temple, the men of the old empire, mistaken into evil though they were, were men. This place was raised by demons. It is unholy and cannot be cleansed except by destruction. It must be thrown into the sea."

"Demons?" It was apparent the admiral, an educated and well travelled man, did not credit their existence. "An intriguing theory. It is true we have not met men on this side of the ocean who appear capable of such architecture." Pondering, he leaned back in his chair and regarded the high vault of the audience chamber.

Understanding he was being toyed with, the prelate became more angry. "You have no standing, my lord," he said, "to quarrel with the gods' commands."

Irritated himself now, the admiral sat forward, peering into the priest's small, piggy eyes. "Sir," he replied in measured tones, "I will answer to the gods when that time comes. Until then, I answer to the queen. This place, this readymade port and fortress, answers very well to the queen's needs. I will not abandon it, still less destroy it, on the suspect demand of a minor prelate who has been hounded out of every temple he served and who fetched up on my ship because his influential relations preferred he—you,

*sir—cease embarrassing them at home in Akkat." He gestured over his
shoulder to the younger man-at-arms. "Please, escort this gentleman into
confinement. He will speak to nobody without my permission. I believe he
has been fomenting treason."*

Across the avenue from the door of Keron's house stood the sole remaining
temple in New Akkat of the old Akkatese gods, who had not prospered in the
New World. Built of brick and stone to traditional design, it appeared somehow more out of place than even the Admiral's Spire. Ban could not recall ever
seeing woman or man climb those steps between wolf-headed warrior gods
to step under the lintel carved in high relief with other gods, owl and stork
and bear and spider headed, feasting in their palace atop the cloud-wreathed
volcano far across the ocean. Once he had known their names—the names
of the greater seventy-seven, at any rate—but more compelling knowledge
had long ago crowded them out of his head. Now and then he glimpsed the
middle-aged priest or his elderly acolyte sidling about the town in their robes
more threadbare than his own. Both, he knew, were unwilling exiles of the
Old World, inspiring as little confidence as the first prelate in New Akkat.

As he studied the temple's statuary, Ban recalled later passages of the
Narrative. That prelate had been permitted to poison himself rather than en-
dure the excruciation and execution due a traitor. Before that, he had dictated
a screed on the unholiness of New Akkat—it did not survive but the admiral's secretary provided an epitome largely unintelligible to one not familiar
with the histories and heresies of the old faith. The point Ban remembered,
the prelate's damning proof, was the deserted city's lack of images. Demons,
he claimed, were incapable of creating art.

"Ban."

It was only a few moments, surely, he had lingered on the steps across from
the temple.

"Please. I'm sorry. Please don't abandon me. I shall try not to be foolish."

Ban didn't turn. "I meant to go to the watch, to inform them of Etkass's
disappearance."

"I'll send the bondswoman. It's not your place to deal with the watch."
Keron's hands grasped Ban's hips as he laid his cheek against his brother-in-
law's shoulder. "Please stay with me. Don't be angry."

Knowing he would give in, Ban waited another moment. "Have you," he
asked, "ever visited the temple?"

"Why would I?" Keron sounded perplexed, his breath tickling Ban's neck. "Does anybody? It's all nonsense."

"Like inhuman lovers that call to you from beneath the sea?" Turning in Keron's embrace, Ban kissed him roughly. He felt Keron's prick harden up, pressed to his thigh. "Come, bring me indoors."

Keron scrupled to take his wife's brother into his wife's bed. After sending the bondswoman out to the watch, he led Ban to the study where he managed the few accounts his father allowed him. There, the door locked, he stripped his old friend, exclaiming that Ban had not changed at all, unless for the better, in the three years since last one saw the other nude. "But I have grown flabby," he admitted sadly, "in body and mind."

In turn, Ban removed Keron's garments and laid him down on the narrow couch. Keron was eager, too eager, reaching his climax early, before he was ready. Ban was self conscious, regretful, clumsy. He hurt Keron, who cried out, spoiling it for Ban, which caused Keron to weep again.

"No," murmured Ban, petting him, soothing him. "It's nothing. We'll try again later, learn the way of it all over."

❧❦

I had seldom seen the admiral troubled. When one great month's sailing into the wastes of the ocean had not brought our flotilla to the new lands he had predicted, he was merely disappointed, then irritated he must persuade the captains of Sapphire *and* Ruby *to continue on. In the event, it was merely another five days before we sighted land.*

But when he woke me that night nearly half a year after dispatching the Sapphire *back across the wide ocean to Akkat with news of the queen's new dominions, I knew at once he was not himself. "Old friend," the admiral said after I dressed and he pressed on me a cup of wine from nearly the last cask. "Old friend. Perhaps that man was right."*

"That man?" I did not understand whom he meant.

The admiral sighed. "The traitor prelate. Or perhaps I have simply been away from my wife too long." He glanced at me with a sardonic glimmer of his usual temper. "It would not do, of course, for the admiral to bugger a common sailor, and one's hand becomes tiresome."

I believed I knew what he was saying. Though the prospect revolted, terrified, perversely excited me, I was ready to offer.

"No, old friend," the admiral said gently. "I would not ask it of you. I value too well our friendship—as well as my marriage vows, of course." He sighed again.

"How was the prelate right?" I ventured, at once relieved and disappointed.

"In the nights——" the admiral began. "In the nights, I am visited. Nights, you understand, my hand has not done its job. By a...woman who wishes me to give her the delights of the flesh. A kind of woman. I feel they are not dreams, these visitations, for I have often, away from her, dreamt of my wife and other women I have known, though those dreams ceased when we landed here. It is unlike those dreams and she is strange, this person. She seems more a creature of the sea, where I meet her, than of the land, and when I am with her I too can breathe beneath the waves. And yet, too, I know somehow she belongs to this strange city, or the city to her. And so I wonder if the priest was correct that this place was not built by men like ourselves but these seductive, terrifying sea dwellers. As a lure or trap, perhaps. Is she a demon? I know not what else to call her. Have——" The admiral hesitated. "Have you been visited? Or heard of peculiar dreams from any of our men?"

I had not. I nearly wished I had.

"Well, after all, it must be a dream. I have been too long from my wife, as I said." Rising from his seat, the admiral bade me goodnight and left me with troubled thoughts.

In the morning, Admiral Saro was not to be found. In the night, I was myself visited by a strange sea-dwelling person, a kind of man who wished me to act upon desires I had always feared. Two days later, the Sapphire returned from Akkat across the ocean, accompanied by more ships bearing more cargo than the admiral had requested, and I must inform the admiral's wife she was widowed.

The lover in the sea was far more able and less clumsy than Keron, and it seemed that Ban's own stamina and powers of recuperation were magnified beneath the waves. Their lovemaking went on and on, unwearying, ever changing. When they were restful or nearly, Ban gazed upon his lover and marvelled that he had ever found men—fragile spindly men like himself, like Keron—beautiful. Then he worried his lover would soon tire of him, imperfect man of the world of air, until he saw the reflection in his lover's great mirrored eyes and saw that he, too, Ban himself, was a magnificent creature of the sea, handsome as a seal, mighty as a whale. And they fell to pleasuring one another again.

He was far from weary when his lover took his hand and together they swam over coral gardens, through kelp forests, among shoals of brilliant fish, for a very long time. At last they came to a place that appeared somehow familiar. The stone colossi on the promenade had succeeded in pulling the sea into the city that had briefly been New Akkat, or drawing the city into the sea.

Familiar but strange. Strange. Of course the Akkatese additions that had spoiled the city's peculiar symmetry were gone, but it was more than that. Ban found himself able to understand the buildings' odd proportions now, for the sea people were considerably larger than the vanished usurpers, more apt to swim than stride upright. Every bracket or cornice that had appeared incomplete now was intricately carved, every empty niche or pedestal filled, every breadth of naked wall mosaicked. Everywhere he turned were images, statues, depictions of the people of the sea.

Everywhere he turned were the people of the sea themselves, calmly going about their day-to-day business. He glimpsed a monumentally beautiful woman sorting kelps in the market whom he believed to be his sister Etkass. Two great men passed overhead, swimming in the wake of the school of tunny they tended, and Ban felt certain the stranger who saluted him was Keron.

His lover urged him beneath the open arch of one of the city's towers. In dim undersea light, they followed the long spiral like the interior of a conch shell that had once, briefly, been deformed by the land dwellers' stairs. Up and up they rose, through turn after turn, until—still within the tower's nacreous walls—their heads broke through the ocean's comforting grasp.

For an instant Ban could not breathe, until he followed his companion's example and painfully coughed life-giving water from his lungs. The air that replaced it was thin, burning like acid, and he must take great, fast gulps of it to sustain himself.

Clumsy as seals out of their natural element, Ban and his lover clambered onto the damp floor of the tower's topmost chamber. Rolling from belly to back and back to belly, Ban peered about, his eyesight strangely dimmed and altered. Though all the possessions of his former, land-bound life were gone, the walls encrusted with barnacles and mussels and wizened anemones awaiting the tide's return, he recognized the place.

Flopping like a landed fish with the hook still in his mouth, he rolled into his lover's arms, who gazed long and wisely into his eyes, then propelled them both off the landing, back into the embrace of the sea.

Gasping, coughing, unable to breathe, Ban woke thrashing, alone, falling from the damp velvet of the narrow couch to a slick of wet, a puddle, on the hard stone floor of his brother-in-law's study. He smelled salt, nothing but salt, felt salt brim in his eyes.

✦ ✤ ✦

Tattooed Love Boys

TO CHARLOTTE BRONTË AND LUCY SNOWE

The second week, Emma discovered a tattoo parlor down an alley off the main square. The young man behind the counter took one look at her and said, in careful English, "You are too young for a tattoo."

"I don't want a tattoo. I don't think I do. My brother does."

The guy (his name sounded like *Raf*) asked how old Theo was—seventeen—and suggested she bring him in. Raf looked only a few years older than Theo. Emma liked the little blue-black glyph inked on the concave bone of his left temple between hairline and eyebrow. She thought it was meant to evoke a bird's wing. But then Raf turned to change the CD and the tattoos on his shoulder and back, what wasn't covered by his wifebeater, disappointed her. Koi fish, lotus blossoms, a whiskered Asian dragon—boring. As cliché as the horned skulls and flames and roses Theo dreamed about.

But when Raf returned his attention to her Emma decided he was good looking so she asked how he'd known to speak English. "You speak it very well," she added. She wanted a moment to contemplate the image that had just come to her of Raf kissing her big brother, caressing Theo's shoulder and

composed 2009, Pawtucket, Rhode Island

first published online at GigaNotoSaurus.org, March 2012

arm. Raf's long fingers left strokes of color on Theo's skin, fire-breathing skulls, schools of glistening koi.

"You have the American look," Raf said.

Emma didn't believe he meant to sound condescending.

They'd come on vacation, Emma, Theo, Mom, Dad, but it promised to be a dreary sort of vacation because Mom and Dad had responsibilities—for them it was a working vacation. Every morning they took a train to the bigger town thirty kilometers away to do research in the university library, leaving their children to entertain themselves.

Theo wasn't much entertainment even back home. In a foreign country where he didn't know the language, he spent hours hunched over his laptop (he had terrible posture). Complaining to friends on Facebook, playing World of Warcraft, piecing together angsty doom-metal loops on GarageBand though he never seemed to paste the loops together into actual songs. Now and then he took a break to reach for his sketchbook, struck by another vision for the sleeve of tattoos he intended for his left arm as soon as he turned eighteen. If he wasn't on the internet, he was usually in the home gym at the top of the house.

They'd traded houses with a professional couple, a dentist and a professor, who were abnormally fit for men in their forties: there were photos of them without shirts on all over the house. Theo made fake gross-out noises over the photos but he attacked their exercise machines with fervor and learned the metric system right away so he could keep track. When he didn't smell of sweat, he smelled of the rank bodyspray TV commercials back home had told him would attract girls. Not if they had functioning olfactory organs, Emma often almost told him. Emma thought her older brother might be more interesting if he were gay. Emma thought she'd make a better boy than Theo.

She had the guts to go out with her phrasebook and wander the town. Village—it was barely a town, surrounded by fields and pastures. Her guidebook to the country said the village had once been known for its livestock fair, but now the market ground had become a park and the abattoir municipal offices. She didn't carry the guidebook with her because the village rated only half a page.

Emma walked through the park, noting the public pool for a future occasion, but she saw a cluster of girls her age who she could tell thought themselves too pretty to get wet. She had exactly as much use for girls like that as they would for her.

Walking the towpath beside the canal east of town, she imagined boarding a barge that would carry her upstream to the university or downstream a
hundred twenty-five kilometers to the capital and the sea. On the far side of
the water, a fence prevented golden-brown cattle from blundering into the
deep canal. Approaching the fourteenth-century bridge, she startled a gang
of teenage boys. They scuttled down the bank into the water. She saw several
white butts before brown water hid them, before she noticed heaps of clothing
by the towpath. Crouching in the shallows, the boys glowered up at her, and
she wondered whether she found the notion of skinnydipping with a bunch
of girlfriends appealing.

Not really. She couldn't imagine any of the girls she knew being up for it.
She wasn't certain she would be. Public nudity was different for boys, she
thought, though she still couldn't imagine any of the boys she knew, American
boys, willingly hanging out bareass with other bareass boys (certainly never
Theo). But the image was oddly attractive. If she'd known these boys she
might have gathered up their clothes and run off with them.

She didn't know anybody in town yet. Raf at the tattoo shop wasn't the
only person to speak to her in English but he was the only one who knew
right off his native language wouldn't serve.

Walking on, leaving the boys to their fun, she recalled the dream she used
to have of waking one morning to find herself a boy. Emma had read about
gender dysphoria—she knew she didn't suffer that. She had never felt any
conviction that really she was a boy trapped in the wrong body, but if she
played World of Warcraft she would choose a male avatar. All the best adventure stories, the heroes were boys who got to slay dragons or be apprenticed to
wizards, embark on voyages of discovery or quests to rescue magical talismans
(or tiresome princesses). Girls *were* tiresome, generally, the ones she knew.
Although it was entirely likely, if she could penetrate the secret world of boys,
incognita, she'd find they were also tiresome, consumed by trivial concerns she
wouldn't even comprehend because she lacked the context.

Theo was tiresome in just about every way—he smelled bad—but she had
to admit he was pretty to look at when he forgot to look sullen. It was easy to
place her brother's face on the untried heroes of fantasy adventure novels, to
populate the sweet fumblings of slash fanfic with Theo's lithe body.

It would revolt him utterly to know that about her, the uses her imagination
put him to.

Besides, Raf at the tattoo parlor was prettier, really, though she didn't usually find blonds appealing. He didn't give her that look, that startled, hungry,

boy look, as if he'd just noticed you weren't hideous and were a girl, so she thought probably he was gay.

The second time she visited the tattoo shop, she asked Raf if he'd like a soda or coffee from the café on the square. "You didn't bring your brother," he said.

Emma was used to boys being disappointed. She hadn't even told Theo about Raf and the shop. "He's afraid—" she thought he was—"to get inked while he still lives at home. Mom and Dad might get angry."

"It's not their affair, surely, what he does to his own body."

Emma saw the hole. "Then it shouldn't be anybody's affair if *I* wanted a tattoo. I'm only two years younger than Theo."

"But you don't want one." Cheery, Raf grinned. "I don't even know why you're here."

"To talk to somebody friendly. To fetch you a cup of coffee or a Coca-Cola from the café."

Raf went wide eyed in a charming, fake way. He glanced around the empty shop. The stop-start buzzing of an electric needle came from somewhere in back, behind the life-sized ventral and dorsal photos of a Japanese man vividly inked over every square centimeter of skin below the neck. "As you can see," Raf said, "I have no customers presently clamoring for my artistry. I will walk with you to the café."

When he turned to call in his own language to the invisible co-worker, Emma saw his ventral tattoos weren't what she remembered. Glossy black spikes and blades pierced his pale skin and showed through the thin fabric of his shirt, looking like the crazy weapons of *Star Trek* Klingons, clashing. *Tribal,* she thought the aesthetic was called, just as clichéd as the dragon and fishes she must have imagined. She was relieved, when he came around the counter, that the wing glyph at his temple hadn't changed, and startled by how short he was. The floor behind the counter must be raised. Theo would be a full head taller.

"Shall we?" Raf asked. "We'll bring our treats back here, if you don't mind. Better for Hender not to be interrupted."

He walked beside her, asking how she and her brother came to be visiting this tiny, unimportant town. He knew the professor and the dentist—the dentist was his dentist, he'd done some of the professor's ink. Emma found herself telling him more than she meant to, if she'd meant to tell him anything, on the short walk to the square. He was easy to talk to, dropping all the right hints to lead her on. Theo interested him but that was to be expected: Theo might be persuaded to drop a couple hundred euro on ink. If Raf was gay, he might find Theo attractive. Theo *was* attractive. Once again, the two boys were making out in the back of Emma's mind, beautiful, almost innocent, so she was surprised when Raf opened the café door for her. Going in, she noticed a porcelainized plaque fixed to the wall beside the door, Delft-blue letters spelling words she couldn't read.

Inside, it was noisy and cheerful, smelled of coffee, warm milk—spices and baking bread, hot sugar, mustard, salted meats. The odors were comforting, though Emma imagined they could also be nauseating as she realized she'd forgotten lunch. "Are you hungry?" she asked Raf.

"Are you?"

"Famished. I only noticed now."

He smiled in a way she liked for a moment, then didn't like so much as he walked right to the counter and spoke to the man behind it too fast for Emma to have any chance of understanding. She stepped up beside him. He was barely taller than she, still smiling, but the fellow behind the counter was taller than Theo and quite nice looking. "Perhaps ten minutes," Raf said.

"I'm paying."

"Not this time. You may dislike what I chose for you."

"What?"

"A traditional hot sandwich and our traditional way of serving coffee. Hot milk and a taste of bitter chocolate."

Coffee Guy (so she christened him) blinked, encouraging.

"Yummy." Emma held out the ten-euro note in such a way that Coffee Guy would have to fold it back into her hand or take it. Raf made falsely remonstrative noises but Coffee Guy took the bill with a smile.

Moving aside, Emma asked, "What does the sign by the door say?"

"Hmm?" Raf was still pretending pique. "It notes that this is an historic building, dating to the early sixteenth century, and that it was built over the site of the witch's house. Excuse me." Returning to Coffee Guy, he accepted a white paper bag and a cardboard caddy carrying three tall paper cups with plastic sippy lids.

"Witch's house?"

Raf was leading her back to the door. Outside, he indicated two words on the plaque that Emma could now interpret—the languages were not so distantly related. "Another tradition," Raf said, "older than the coffee or the sandwich." He seemed in a hurry, brisk and brusque.

As he strode away and Emma hesitated, puzzled, it appeared to her the inky spikes and blades and flourishes on his back were writhing, contorting, blushing with blots of clear color, but when she blinked and looked again, hurrying after him, they had resolved into intricate flowers tangled in wreaths and garlands on his shoulder and upper arm. Scarlet poppies, indigo cornflowers, peonies, Japanese chrysanthemums—she didn't recognize half of them.

"I become anxious about Hender," Raf said when she caught up. "I'm sorry. He is not always good with people."

"Your tattoos—"

"Yes? I like the flowers better as well."

From across the street, through the plate-glass window of the shop Emma saw a customer waiting, back turned, peering at the display of photocopied flash as if each sheet were a painting on a museum's wall. "An American," said Raf.

"How can you tell?"

"I can tell. Perhaps your brother."

"Theo has long hair. Halfway down his back." She didn't have to see him close up to see the *American* customer had little more than the shadow of stubble on his skull.

Raf leapt the step to the door, pushed it open, and said in ringing English as the bell tinkled, "I'm sorry there was no-one here to welcome you."

"He said you'd be right back, the other—" Turning from the wall of skulls and dragons, magickal symbols and WWII pinups, Theo froze when he saw his sister behind Raf. "Emma?"

"What happened to your hair?"

Triumphant, Raf grinned.

"What are you doing here? You're too young for ink."

Startled into petulance, Emma blurted, "So are you!"

"My friend Emma bought me coffee," Raf said equably, placing cup caddy and sandwich bag on the counter. "That is why I wasn't here to greet you. Let me just give Hender his and then we can discuss your plans and wishes."

When he took one of the paper cups behind the curtain, Emma asked Theo again, "What happened to your hair?" It had been beautiful hair, wavy and lustrous—much prettier than hers.

"His *friend?*" Self conscious, Theo shifted his sketchpad from one hand to the other, then back. "Since when?"

First surprise passed, Emma imagined Theo was maybe even handsomer without long hair to distract from the fineness of his features, the shocking paleness of his eyes. A queasy-making thought to have about her brother when he stood in front of her big as life, so she turned away. Incomprehensible voices sounded behind Hender's curtain, three of them (she hadn't seen Hender yet), and the thrumming of his needle. "How'd you find the place?"

"Google," Theo said, but not as if she was stupid.

Distracted by annoyance, Emma didn't often remember how shy he was. She took her cup from the counter and sipped through the vent in the plastic lid. The coffee wasn't very sweet, not like cocoa—she tasted milk and coffee more than chocolate. "Why?"

"You know I want them."

"Why now?"

When she looked over her shoulder, Theo was sitting on the bench below the display of flash. Staring at his clasped hands, he looked miserable. For an instant she felt sorry for him. "Why now?" she asked again.

"Simon got one. Bragging about it on Facebook."

Simon and Theo were barely friends, back home. Simon had a guitar and people to jam with, not just GarageBand on his laptop. They were World of Warcraft rivals, though Emma didn't really understand how that worked.

"*Your friend got one* isn't a good excuse for a tattoo," Raf said, pushing through the curtain. He went straight for his coffee. "It's a permanent alteration to your body—" Emma wondered about his, Raf's, though—"you need to really want it."

Theo raised his head. "I do!" His face was tragic.

"What did Simon get?" asked Emma, mildly curious.

"Line of kanji down his spine. Really hurt, he said."

Emma snorted. "Bragged, you mean."

"Close to the bone hurts more," Raf said in the tone of a master craftsman imparting lessons to his apprentice. "I do not recommend it for your first experience. I won't do kanji, either, by the way. It's not my language—I don't like to trust the published interpretations or the designs themselves. They're often inaccurate."

"Simon's probably says *happiness puppies*," Emma said, uncomfortably sympathetic, "instead of what he wanted."

Theo looked down at his hands again. "*Fight fierce, fight strong*," he mumbled.

"That's possibly stupider than *happiness puppies*."

"Your sandwich, Emma." Somehow Raf had got it out of the bag and wrappings without her noticing, arranged nicely in little wedges on a pretty plate.

Emma's hunger asserted itself. Ravenous, she stuffed a wedge into her mouth. It was still hot. Crunchy and buttery toasted bread enfolded molten cheese and shavings of something like prosciutto. Feeling guilty after bolting two, she looked up to offer a taste to Raf and Theo.

They sat side by side on the bench, knees nearly touching, Theo's sketchbook between them. "Any of these might be executed to fine effect," Raf said, flipping through the pages again. "But you can't decide, am I correct?"

Emma edged closer. The uppermost page showed a disembodied arm (thicker, brawnier than Theo's) encrusted with patterned lozenges like Turkish tiles, but Raf flipped it and the next arm was decorated with a menagerie of vivid zoo animals.

"I keep changing my mind," Theo admitted, his voice mournful.

"Then I'm sorry to say you are not ready."

Theo lifted his eyes, stared into Raf's for a long moment. He looked ready to cry before he moved his gaze to Raf's upper arm and shoulder. "Yours are..." he began.

Beautiful, Emma thought he meant to say, but beauty wasn't a quality Theo could ascribe to another man. They were beautiful, Raf's garlands of inked flowers. Theo raised one hand as if to caress them, another gesture halted as he abruptly rose to his feet. The sketchbook clattered to the floor. Raf looked up mildly.

"You're right." Theo crouched to retrieve his drawings. "I need to decide what I really want." Without another word, he bolted out of the shop. The bell over the door tinkled gaily. Emma sat beside Raf and they shared the rest of her sandwich, except one sliver saved for Hender.

After the first bitter bite, Emma didn't mind the needle chewing at her skin. She'd had to assume an awkward position on the settee to give Raf access to the fleshy inner surface of her upper arm, and the moment of removing her shirt had been disorienting. She'd never done it for a boy who wasn't interested in what was inside her bra.

She had determined Raf wasn't. He was interested in what was in her brother's undershorts, but not in any urgent way—when Emma confessed her fantasy of Raf and Theo necking, Raf just laughed, delighted, and wondered aloud why it was so many women loved those images. When she decided, quite abruptly, she *did* want a tattoo, just a small one in an inconspicuous place, he wasn't difficult to argue around after she told him what she wanted. He sketched the symbol for her, fast and decisive in colored inks, and Emma became even more determined to have it. He ushered her behind the curtain at the back of the shop. She got only a glimpse into one small room where a man in a white undershirt like Raf's leaned over the serpent on the back of another man, before Raf waved her into the second. He gave her a moment to settle herself, ducking into the other room to give Hender his wodge of sandwich.

It didn't actually take much time for Raf to inscribe the design on Emma's arm three inches below where she shaved. She liked his hands on her, swabbing the skin with alcohol, then transferring the design, finally going to work, though she wished it was skin to skin uninhibited by his latex gloves. After a while, the rhythm of the stinging needle and regular pauses to wipe off blood and ink relaxed her into a kind of trance that blundered into memory.

Unfamiliar memory. Half-familiar memories. They were old, well worn, blurred around the edges as they bubbled up from among quite different memories she knew to be hers but that faded even as she reached after them. When her little brother Theo was small he couldn't get his mouth around the four syllables of his big brother's name. *Emma*, he called her, and had to be taught that Emma was a girl's name. Theo's brother's name was Emmanuel, which didn't admit of a convenient shortening like Theo for Theodore. (Theo had been *Teddy* until he turned ten.) What had their parents been thinking?

She remembered throwing a football for Theo, who was miserable at catching it—she remembered wrestling with him when they were nearer the same size—she remembered helping him with his algebra homework, impatient when he didn't get it.

She remembered the first boy to kiss her (not the first she wanted to kiss), Steve, a nerdier nerd than her brother, who refused (at first) to suck her cock though he was extremely happy when she went to town on his. How old had she been? Fourteen. Almost nineteen now, lying still under Raf's calm hands and the sting of his electric needle, she felt her dick plump up a bit in her boxers at the memory, felt her balls shift around.

She remembered the expression Theo got when she told him his big brother was gay. Liked other boys instead of girls. Liked their muscles (some of the boys she liked didn't possess much muscle), their scratchy beards, their odor. Liked touching them, kissing them, sexing them up.

Theo didn't so much recoil as subtly withdraw, bending his head so dark hair obscured his transparent eyes. "I'm still your brother," Emma had said. "Nothing's changed, except that little bit of dishonesty between us. You want me to be honest with you, right?"

Now Raf set the silent needle aside and swabbed her arm again. The evaporating film of alcohol tingled, its fumes fizzy in her nostrils. Raf stood, stretched, clenching and flexing the fingers of his right hand, and gazed down at her, his expression neutral, thoughtful. She wasn't the type of boy he was attracted to.

Annoyed, Emma said, "Done?" The depth and richness of her voice distracted and pleased her.

"Yes. Do you wish to see?"

A big mirror hung on the wall but Raf reached for a hand mirror and held it for her. First, momentarily disconcerted, she noticed the aggressive growth of hair in her armpit that thinned only a little where it fanned out to mesh with the hair on her chest. The kind of boy *she* was attracted to would never shave his body hair. Raf shifted the mirror a fraction.

It was reversed in the glass, the symbol incised on the pale flesh of her inner arm, arrowheads pointing off past eleven o'clock instead of one. Inflammation blurred the outlines, seeping blood obscured careful gradation of tint and shading. It was probably stupid, overly obvious, but she liked it: paired Mars glyphs, unbroken circles interlinked, arrowheads parallel. Within indigo outlining, the rings and arrows were tinted like anodized aluminum. She liked it.

"I like it," Emma said.

"Nice work, Raf," said a new voice, more heavily accented speaking English than Raf's.

Emma blinked away from the gleaming oval of the mirror as Raf said, "Hender—my new American friend Emmanuel, who bought your coffee."

"And my tasty bit of sandwich? Thank you, Emmanuel. They were much appreciated."

Hender appeared older than Raf, ten, fifteen years. Emmanuel didn't find him especially handsome or his ear and facial piercings enticing, but his eyes, a brown so pale it was nearly gold, were compelling. The glyph on his left temple was larger and more complex than Raf's, foliated, tendrils looping and extending into his hairline, onto his cheekbone, as if Raf's were merely a preliminary sign, incomplete. Both stepped back when Emmanuel sat up and swung her legs over the edge of the settee. Hender placed a proprietary hand on Raf's shoulder—his fingernails were unpleasantly long, lacquered black, and he wore too many gold rings—and smiled, exposing teeth that looked inhumanly sharp. Under his hand, the flowers on Raf's shoulder appeared to catch fire.

Emmanuel blinked. Flickering flames resolved into stylized scrolls, yellow, orange, red, like the decals on an ancient muscle car's fender, and she blinked again, disappointed.

"Show Emmanuel how to care for his new art while it heals," Hender said, squeezed Raf's shoulder again, and went away.

Before she allowed Raf to tend her wound, Emmanuel rose to her feet and regarded herself in the mirror, pleased by what she saw. Wide shoulders, expansive chest, trim, defined midsection, narrow hips. The logoed elastic of her boxers cut straight across her belly below the hips, cutting short the furry trail that led the gaze toward the meaty lump behind the fly of khaki shorts. It shifted, all by itself, buckling the fabric of the fly to reveal a flash of copper zipper, and Emmanuel grinned at her reflection.

Raf swabbed the tattoo with stinging alcohol again, smeared it with greasy antibiotic ointment—he gave her the tube, opened fresh, to slip in her pocket—taped over it a square of plastic film, explaining as he went along how to care for it so it would heal quickly and cleanly. Because she wanted him to, he kissed her, but it was an uninvolved, almost chilly kiss—he was more attracted to Theo—and he wouldn't go further even after she groped his crotch and found him stiff. She didn't have enough cash on her to pay the full price of the tattoo but he said it didn't matter, she could cover the rest next time she dropped by.

Emmanuel liked being a boy. A man, really. Her voice was deeper and she was taller than her dad, outweighed him by twenty or thirty pounds. Nor was her hair thinning, though she kept it short and butch. Now and then she caught him staring at her, bemused by his big gorilla son or almost (she didn't really think so) remembering his daughter.

She liked being a big brother. She half remembered watching out for Theo when he was a geeky high-school freshman with no friends and girly long hair—remembered intimidating the bullies who wanted to intimidate Theo. Those memories gradually became more vivid, washing out bleached memories of growing up a girl, Theo's little sister. She remembered encouraging him to work out, get bigger and stronger so the bullies wouldn't bother him. She had moved bench and free weights to the basement because she knew he was uncomfortable *invading* her bedroom to use them. What really made Theo uncomfortable in her room, she knew, was the home-made screensaver on her desktop monitor, endlessly cycling raw beefcake. The nerdling needed just to deal: his big brother—bigger in every way, not just a year and a half older—was gay and pretty happy about it.

Well, not so happy maybe about not having done much recently. She regretted not pushing harder with Raf. God, the blue balls when he finished with her and sent her home to the dentist's and professor's house. That night she'd had to beat off twice before she could sleep. The first *experienced* (she recalled earlier but it wasn't clear they'd really happened) boy orgasm almost disappointed her. She kind of remembered girl orgasms being more profound, less localized and fleeting, if more effort to achieve. But she liked spunk. Splooge. Cum. Even the names were fun. As a girl, she'd thought it gross without much acquaintance—as a boy, she licked it off her hand, savoring the slimy texture, the salty-bitter taste, and rubbed it gummily into the hair on her belly and chest.

When she woke, early, she was delighted by the morning wood in her boxer shorts but needed to piss so she left it alone. She stumbled to the bathroom and remembered she could do it standing up, lifted the seat, fumbled her dick out. Unused to pissing while half hard (or maybe she just didn't care), she made a mess. After brushing her teeth, washing hands and face, replacing the dressing under her arm, she went back to the bedroom and fired up the laptop. She pointed the browser to her favorite slashfic site. After only a few paragraphs she found the story insipid. The boys were insipid, dreamy and yearny, barely out of adolescence—big eyed and delicate like the figures in yaoi manga, for which she used to have more patience. When she was a girl. Without much trouble, she found a site more to her liking and, reading badly spelled, pedestrian porn, rubbed out another. She smeared the splooge over her abs, sucked the remnants off fingers and palm.

She pulled on a pair of b-ball shorts, stuffed her big feet into shoes, and climbed the stairs to the professor's and dentist's gym. She preferred free weights, which required more finesse and, by way of their instability, worked peripheral muscles as well as those directly involved, but the machines were all she had till they returned home.

She was benching, legs splayed wide while her arms pressed the bar up, when she heard her brother's feet on the steps. She finished the set before looking toward the door. Theo gaped at her. "What?" Her shorts were too long for anything to be hanging out in public and perturbing his masculinity.

"What did you do to your arm?"

"Got Raf to give me a tattoo." She sat up. "Wanna see it?"

"*Raf*? That's his name? He didn't talk you out of it?"

"It was a sudden thing but I only had one idea, one small design, not dozens."

"Just nine."

Emmanuel peered at her brother. He was unhappy. "I'm going back today, if you'd like to come with me. Didn't have enough cash to pay him yesterday."

Aimless, Theo turned away. Running his hand along the white plaster wall, he paced until the descent of the peaked attic roof prevented further progress. "There's no point if I can't decide what I want."

"I should have let you get yours first." But then she'd still be a girl, and younger than Theo. It seemed likely, anyway.

"For once," he agreed without turning, his voice thin with unsuppressed bitterness. It was hard for Theo, being younger, smaller, less. "Is he gay, Raf? Your summer-in-Europe boyfriend? He shouldn't ask you to pay."

"I'm not his type, as it turns out." *You are,* Emmanuel didn't say. "You should come with me anyway. Get out of the house. Maybe we'd meet a girl for you."

Theo still didn't turn. "Are you done? I want to work out."

"Fine." Irritated, Emmanuel got to her feet. She was done. Her brother smelled worse than usual, as if the bodyspray had rotted his skin overnight. "Have at it."

"Wait," Theo said when she was almost out the door. "When are you leaving?"

They walked along the towpath in hot sun, brother and brother. Strangely, after his shower Theo hadn't fragranced himself to hell and back: he smelled of boy, soon of sweat. He smelled good. Emmanuel wanted to rub his head where pale scalp gleamed through dark stubble but figured it wasn't a liberty she ought to take. She wanted to ask again why he'd cut it. Probably some fallout from his on-line rivalry with Simon, like the disappointing first visit to Raf's shop.

"When I came along this way yesterday," she said, "there was a bunch of kids skinnydipping in the canal."

"Girls and boys? Or just boys?"

"Just boys."

"Musta been a treat for you."

Startled, Emmanuel laughed. She liked the sound of her own laughter nearly as much as the evidence that her brother had a sense of humor. "Not much to see—they were in a hurry not to be seen. You ever done that?"

"Not really my thing."

Theo didn't like even just taking off his shirt in public. He was shy about it even with her, though she had her suspicions about that.

"You?" Theo asked, startling her again.

"Sure," she said, not really sure. "Not here. Yet."

"Wouldn't try it *here*," Theo muttered. "That water looks nasty."

"Wanna find out?"

Before he could react, Emmanuel had him in a mild chokehold, lifting him against her chest. The stubble on her cheek rasped on the stubble of his skull.

"Fuck!" Theo grunted—she hadn't cut off his air—grabbing at her arm with both hands. Somehow he twisted and heaved in her grasp. As she went off balance, unlikely pain ripped through her shoulder and then the ground came up and knocked the breath out of her lungs. In an instant, coughing, she was tumbling down the grassy bank. The water pounded her with a crash. She went under.

She came up spitting. When water cleared her eyes, she saw her brother down the bank, teetering on the verge. "Stupid!" he hollered. "You've got an open wound!"

"What—" The new tattoo.

When she struggled upright, the warm silty water only came to mid-thigh, dragging at her shorts as she floundered back to the bank. Theo wasn't going to plunge in and help but he stood waiting, looking worried. "Jesus, Emmanuel, don't surprise me like that."

Emmanuel couldn't help herself: she guffawed. "How'd you do that, anyway? Been sneaking out to some dojo, little bro, learning super-secret martial arts moves?"

"You surprised me." He shook his head, extended his hand for her. "Are you okay?"

"Sodden," she said, letting him help her onto the embankment. "Fine. Maybe more surprised than you. Who knew that was even possible? Let me sit for a minute."

When she sank down onto the grass and pulled off one bucket of a shoe, Theo crouched at her side. "I'm not the whiny kid who gets beaten up at school anymore, you know. Are you sure you're okay?"

She worked the other shoe off, turned them both upside down and set them aside. She didn't expect further explanation for Theo's mysterious superpowers. "Yeah, sure." Testing the rotation of her shoulder, she felt the twinge but it wasn't bad. "Prolly some bruises and a bit of stiffening up tomorrow."

"I'm sorry."

"Don't be. Glad to know you can defend yourself. And like you said, I shouldn't have surprised you—my own fault."

"Pick on someone your own size next time."

Astonished again, Emmanuel choked on a laugh. Recovering, she said, "Excuse me, Theo, when did you turn into a human being?"

Regarding her gravely, her brother said, "Occasionally one has lapses." Then he sat down properly by her side. "At the moment I'm worried about your tattoo. You don't know what kind of bacteria were swimming in that water."

Reminded of it, she felt the clammy suction of the tape and plastic on her inner arm. Except for her shorts and what was in them, the rest of her, exposed to sun and air, was practically dry already. Peeling at the tape, wincing when it ripped hairs from their follicles, she said, "I doctored it up pretty thick with hi-test antibiotic stuff. It's greasy. Probably the germs couldn't even get through the grease."

"Still. I would be happier if you got it properly cleaned and tended. Soon."

Looking up, Emmanuel caught him staring at her fingers picking at the dressing, at her hairy underarm—her hairy chest. She didn't understand his expression.

"We're closer to your friend's shop than the house," Theo went on. "He'll know what to do. As soon as you're ready."

Raf was calm, undismayed—pleased to see them, Emmanuel thought. Pleased to see them both. With little fuss, he cleaned Emmanuel's tattoo—the alcohol stung, weirdly worse than the first times, fizzes and pinpricks more irritating than her memory of the needle—anointed it with a dose of antibiotic, dressed it anew. He advised her to keep a close eye on it as it healed although he had never heard that the canal bred flesh-eating microbes. Indifferent, he accepted the damp euro notes she pressed on him and rang them into the register. And then they were at a loss.

While Raf tended Emmanuel, Theo had been leafing through a thick album of photos of the shop's work, absorbed, intent—beautiful, really, as a studious child. He had failed to remark on Raf's transformed tattoos but now that Emmanuel noticed the cheap stylized flames were gone, the garlands of flowers returned. The same flowers? Possibly not but near enough. Had Raf changed them back on Theo's account?

He stepped away from Emmanuel to peer over Theo's shoulder and point something out. The smile her brother turned up at him made her heart contract and then thump uncomfortably. They were too pretty together—like manga boys, they looked too alike. Theo was quite a bit taller and their coloring was different but it was the difference between African-American Barbie and the standard model.

Her tastes had changed, it seemed, since she became a boy herself. The thought of them getting it on was still attractive (the inevitability of it, it almost looked like) but what she wanted for herself was a bigger man, a big, hairy, muscly guy. Like her.

"Anybody want coffee?" she said, loud. "I'll go get it."

Theo started but Raf only glanced at her, his expression mild. "That would be very pleasant, Emmanuel."

She half turned toward the door, then turned back. "Will somebody speak English?"

"Probably, but I'll write it down for you, shall I?" Raf did that, his printing precise and legible, and coached her through the pronunciation.

For some reason that reminded her and she asked, "What was that about the witch's house?"

"Witch?" asked Theo.

"Town legend," Raf said. He appeared slightly put out. "Perhaps *wizard* would be the better term, in English. A learned man back in the fourteen hundreds, more learned than he had need or right to be, not being in holy orders, lived in the house where the café stands now. There were suspicions about him, rumors, but they came to nothing until it was noticed there were strangers, foreigners, living in the house whom nobody recalled arriving. He called them nephews, or sometimes visitors from the Holy Land." Reciting, Raf's voice was thin, precise, almost pained. "The scholar was abruptly wealthier than he had been. Some claimed to have seen peculiar lights and other manifestations about the house in the depths of night. A child died raving, inexplicably. Another, older child murdered her father some days after being seen conversing with the scholar and the foreigners. A youth claimed one of the strangers had bespelled him to perform an unnatural act. Signs, portents—there were others: stillborn or deformed livestock, blights, comets. The mob chose him and his guests as their scapegoats but the guests had vanished. Under torture, he called them, the three of them, angels or sometimes devils whom Lucifer had sent to tempt and aid him. Naturally, he was killed, burned alive. His house was demolished, the soil under it sown with salt. The town's misfortunes eased. A hundred years later a new building was raised on the spot and eventually, say ten years ago, the café opened."

"Whoa," said Theo, fascinated. "We don't have history like that back home."

Raf regarded him soberly. "So you're privileged to think. The stories weren't written down, the storytellers died of smallpox and their languages disappeared, somebody built a Starbucks just like every other Starbucks on the salt-sown foundations of the forgotten wizard's house. Here we do too much remembering. You Americans are fortunate to live in the present as it happens." Turning away, he seemed to mutter, "I too prefer the now."

Emmanuel left them to argue that out—or not. At the café, Coffee Guy behind the counter didn't seem to recognize her (how could he?), but was charming, friendly, flirtatious, and spoke sufficient English that she didn't have to wrestle with Raf's language lesson. Taking her money, he touched her hand with his own in a way he didn't need to and looked into her eyes with great promise. When he turned to prepare her coffee, it seemed he fumbled his white shirt open two buttons more so she could be sure of the interesting knotted tattoo on his chest, just below the left clavicle, its flourishes glowing through curly brown hair. Flowers twined through the knots, poppies and cornflowers—she wondered if it was Raf's work. Surely it was, or Hender's. The town was too small to support more than one tattoo shop. Handing over the three tall coffees, he said, "See you around," as if he'd memorized the phrase but in a tone that made it both a question and a promise.

Walking back, Emmanuel pondered how to encounter him again without a counter and a transaction between them—how to discover his name. He was as tall as she, as substantial. She somehow didn't wish to ask Raf, who would probably know. Spend an afternoon at the public pool swimming and tanning—he had a nice tan, perhaps that was where he'd acquired it. Loiter around the café until he went off shift. Google for the places gay guys congregated. For a few steps they were making out in the back of her mind, Coffee Guy and Emmanuel, necking and groping—chest hair caught in her teeth when she nibbled his nipple—but then the vision became Theo and Raf again, similarly pleasing in a voyeuristic way but interestingly different.

They weren't necking when she stepped back into the shop, not that she'd really expected them to be. The front room was public space, windowed to the street. Theo was shy...wasn't gay.

They were, however, too preoccupied to acknowledge her entrance after making sure it was her. Raf leaned over a large sheet of paper, delicately maneuvering his pencil. Theo watched—watched Raf's hand but glanced up often at his face. Theo's expression was dopey with intent, and something else.

Emmanuel set a cup before each. Raf offered her a distracted nod but Theo nothing. The drawing taking shape was a spidery branch of cherry blossoms. Emmanuel could imagine it spiralling up somebody's arm, twining over biceps and triceps to spray blooms across the upper back, then up and over to deposit more on the round ball of the shoulder and a final profusion on the gentle swell of one pec. Raf paused, sketched in a butterfly alighting.

It was subtle, pretty. She wouldn't have expected *pretty* of Theo. The designs he'd drawn were aggressive, mannered. "I thought you wanted a full sleeve," she said, too loud and abrupt.

He glanced at her but didn't seem to see her. "So did I." He reached for his coffee.

"It's just an idea," murmured Raf, concentrating.

Emmanuel no longer had to imagine the tattoo: the spindly branch climbed Raf's arm, looped onto his shoulder and back, under the translucent white strap of his wifebeater onto his chest. Blossoms blushed rose over the paler pink of his skin. Faint blue shadows made them stand out. Unopened buds and baby leaves were tender spring green. The butterfly was black, blue, purple, with shards of clear, bright yellow. Bruise colors, except it was precise and fine within its outlines, not blurred and sore. She could never manage a seduction so well. She didn't have his talents.

She'd finished her coffee in fifteen, twenty minutes, and Theo and Raf hadn't become any more entertaining. "See you around," she said, echoing the object of her interest. Raf glanced up with a faint smile, Theo nodded absently. She left.

In the square, she waited a while on a bench across from the café, hoping Coffee Guy might emerge, but that would be too easy. Other people did come out. One of them she recognized as Hender. He recognized her as well, raised his paper cup in a salute, but didn't come over. She wondered if he was going back to the shop—if he would be annoyed or jealous at the sudden rapport between his protégé and her brother. She wondered if she'd ever see Coffee Guy again. She went into the café but he was no longer there. Disappointed, she blundered out again without buying anything.

The *Gay Guide to Labassecour* Google found for her directed Emmanuel to a pub that, while not strictly a gay bar, was the next closest thing in this small town. Another site suggested a grove in the park where sordid things might occur, and another told her to try the same café after midnight, when it was the only place still open. Overall, though, she'd be better off making a trip to the university town where her parents did their research. She filed all the information away for later.

It was Theo's night to make dinner, something he was usually pretty responsible (if resentful) about, but he didn't get home till twenty minutes before she expected their parents. He looked a little bruised around the eyes and—was she imagining it?—chafed around the lips. He looked halfway to exaltation and moved his left arm gingerly. "Did he do the whole thing in one go?" Emmanuel asked.

Theo grinned, open, delighted. "Just the outlines. Filling in and coloring later, couple of days." Then he winced and looked a little worried. "Don't tell the 'rents?"

"As if I would. They're going to wonder about long sleeves, though."

"Let them wonder."

"I want to see it but I won't ask you to get all unwrapped right now."

Theo shook his head. "After dinner, maybe. Oh, hey, help me make dinner? I'm kinda running late."

"You'll owe me."

He shook his head again. "Well, you know, I already owe you so what's a little more."

In the kitchen he got busy fast, pointing her at things he needed cleaned or peeled or chopped. It was going to be some kind of stir-fry, apparently. Slicing beef into thin strips, Theo ignored his brother, but when he had it marinating in soy sauce and the ginger she'd chopped he took a moment and just looked at her.

"What?"

"I'm, umm, going out after dinner. You want to come with so the parents don't freak?"

Emmanuel set her knife down. "Out? Out where? You never go out."

Looking away, he smiled. "Raf invited me to join him for a drink. He said you'd be welcome."

"You're underage."

"Not here. Civilized country. I'm not planning to get drunk or anything. I'll buy you a beer."

"Raf? Huh." Emmanuel snorted, keeping her delight to herself. "Am I to understand you're not as straight as I've always been led to believe? Or is this not a date?"

Startled, Theo squeaked, "Date? It's not—" He blushed, blinked a few times. "I guess maybe you could call it that. Hah. That's a shocker." Blush fading, he shook his head. "And I don't quite know what I am because I still think girls are all kinds of sexy but kissing him was hella sexy too."

"Well, good for you," said Emmanuel in jovial, big-brother tones. "Sure, I'll chaperone you, Teddy—" she hadn't called her brother Teddy since he was a little kid—"if you promise not to put on any of that noxious bodyspray."

"Lend me your big-boy cologne?" he suggested with a cock of his head both flirtatious and naïvely mocking.

After his shower, Teddy knocked on her door to show off his ink—get Emmanuel's help doctoring it. She was less surprised by the delicate tracery of branches and shoots and bruises on his arm and shoulder than the unprecedented act of his coming to her room wearing only a towel hitched around his hips. The temptation to make it fall, discover what he had in the downstairs department to offer Raf, tested her resolve. He smelled of her cologne (he'd used too much), which she really felt smelled better on her.

With a kind of brusque tenderness, she swabbed the twigs and branches and uncolored blossoms with a pad steeped in alcohol. The softness of Teddy's skin perturbed her. The hair on his forearms was translucent and there was none on his chest, just a faint glowy fuzz. Glancing at his legs, she noticed that shins and calves appeared only as downy as his arms. He noticed her noticing. "You got all the wild man of Borneo genes from Dad's side. I take after Mom's family. So I'll never go bald."

"Except on purpose." Emmanuel seemed to remember her little brother being more hirsute. Not like her, maybe, but not like a girl either. Under her hand, the muscles of his arm and shoulder felt different than as recently as the morning, when he tossed her in the canal. Not flabbier, but less purposeful than simply useful. Perhaps it was just that he was at rest. She smeared on the greasy ointment. When he stood up to have her apply the dressings, he looked willowy standing before her, not lean and wiry. "What's up?" he asked.

"Nothing." She went back to work, taping squares of plastic like patchwork to his skin.

When that was finished, she told him to go get dressed if they were going out. At the door, he turned back fast and had to grab for the slipping towel. "You didn't say what you think of your friend's work."

"It's—" Emmanuel hesitated. "It's not what I'd have expected for you. Not to say it isn't very nicely done. When Raf completes it and it's all healed up, it'll be...lovely."

Clutching the towel, Teddy frowned, but then he visibly let what he didn't want to hear go and opened the door. Fifteen minutes later he was back, dressed, black shirt severely buttoned and tucked into black jeans, buzzed head making him look an ikon of severity. It was momentarily impossible to imagine him necking with Raf. In her mind Emmanuel stripped off the shirt, finished off the tattoos, and then all was well. She followed him downstairs happily enough, out. She had dressed equally thoughtfully if with different calculation: tight t-shirt was meant to showboat her build, low-slung shorts make it evident she'd chosen to go commando. She hoped to meet Coffee Guy, though another guy might do almost as handily.

Teddy knew the way. He had memorized Google's map, she imagined. They walked through long summer twilight, bucolic suburb to mediaeval town alleys, not saying much until Teddy asked, "What's it like? What guys do with guys, after the kissing?" So he had taken note of her outfit.

She peered at him. He had his head down, looking away. "It's sex," she said. "It's big fun. I mean—" She turned her own head, not really embarrassed. "I mean, I've never done it with a girl so it's not like I can compare and contrast." She could, but not in a way that would be helpful.

"Me neither," Teddy muttered, voice small but defiant.

"Really?" It was almost not a surprise.

Teddy half stumbled, recovered. "Not all the way."

Brotherly, Emmanuel put her arm around his neck, holding him up. "It'll be okay, Teddy. You don't have to go through with it—you don't have to do anything you don't want to do. Say *no*, easy as that." Teddy was bigger than Raf.

"But I *do* want. I want to do everything. Will it hurt?"

Emmanuel released him, stepped away. "If you do that? For a moment or two, yeah. Not as much as tattoo needles."

Her brother hurried to catch up, passed her, remained a few steps ahead until they reached the pub, where he held the door open for her as if she were a girl. They saw Raf right away, pale as an exotic orchid in the gloom. Strangely, he was talking with Coffee Guy, who beamed when he saw Emmanuel. His name was Thijs—he spelled it for her. He wasn't wearing the collared white dress shirt and black slacks from the café but a dark green hoodie unzipped nearly to the waist so she could admire the furry expanse of his chest, his tattoo, the steel pin through his left nipple, and jeans worn so low she could make out his swimsuit tanline and be sure he, too, had foregone undershorts. It was all thrilling. By the time he'd bought her a beer that had so much flavor it astonished her she was entirely smitten and Raf and Teddy had vanished.

When the fact penetrated, she said, "Where'd they go? I have to look out for Teddy."

"See over there," said Thijs, soothing and calm. "Teddy is quite safe."

Looking where he indicated, Emmanuel saw a line of private booths and the backs of the two heads, one buzzed to blue shadow, the other blond. "I should—"

"Teddy is quite safe," Thijs said again. "Now and then Raf discovers an interest in women, *particular* women, an impulse that startles him so much he is extremely careful, gentle, easily dissuaded. Your sister will come to no harm."

"Teddy—" But Emmanuel knew her sister would be furious, if it was something he really wanted, if Emmanuel barged in like a clumsy knight in shining armor to protect the damsel's virtue. Still, she watched a moment longer, unsure, saw Raf's fine long fingers caress Teddy's skull and saw her sister turn his head for the kiss. He was beautiful, her little sister—the shorn scalp made his face at once stronger and more vulnerable. When he did it, their father, oddly pleased, said his daughter was prettier than Sinéad O'Connor and ran a Google Image search to show them how Teddy compared to the pop-star crush of his youth.

Thijs attracted her attention back to him by lifting her hand to his chest. One point of the steel pin, not quite sharp, poked her finger. Leaning to her ear, he said, "I also have a, what do you call it in English, a Prince Albert. Would you like to see?"

The sex was good. Not great. Perhaps they were nervous of each other, being so newly acquainted. Perhaps Thijs depended on the novelty of his PA in lieu of technique. She'd had a moment or two of wanting one for herself—he became inarticulate trying to express the sensations it gave him—but the desire passed. Rolling a condom over her own stiff dick, she'd felt a pang, thinking she ought to have said something to Teddy about the importance of birth control (she didn't know if he was on the pill) but Thijs distracted her before the pang could bloom into panic, and she didn't think of her sister again. Anyway, Thijs and Raf were housemates, it had turned out, sharing the big apartment two floors above the café on the square. Teddy was just down the hall. If he got scared, needed his big brother, he knew where she was.

But afterward, dozing on Thijs's bed with Thijs spooned up against her back (his chest hair tickled her when he breathed, the metal in his nipple scraped), Emmanuel had what felt like a dream. She remembered growing up with, not an annoying little tomboy sister, but a nerdy, differently tiresome little brother. Theo. Not Teddy. Then her breath strangled in her throat as she recalled that Theo was Emma's *big* brother and she, Emma, for almost sixteen years had been a girl.

She sat up abruptly. Thijs grumbled in his sleep. "Thirsty," Emmanuel said, though she didn't think he could hear her, and clambered off the bed. Still naked, she stumbled out of the room.

She thought she knew where she was going but ended up in the kitchen, where a low candle in a glass jar guttered on the breakfast table and somebody sat beyond it, face shadowed. "Thirsty," she said again because she didn't know who it was.

"Hard or soft?" The voice with its distinct accent was Hender's. He leaned forward and candlelight caught his stark features, gilded the piercings at eyebrow, ear, cheek, lower lip. The baroque ink at his temple looked purple, like wine in a glass.

"Water."

He stood. Emmanuel flinched back. "Sparkling or still?" Hender asked, stepping away from the table but not toward her. He was as nude as she. Thankfully, she couldn't make out details in uncertain, wavery light.

Unthinking, she took another step toward the table. "Just water."

"Sit, then. A moment."

She was afraid he'd turn on an electric light or just open the refrigerator and she would have to look at him, but he rummaged through the cabinet for a glass without hesitation, filled it at the sink. Emmanuel sat. The polished wooden seat felt unpleasantly slick and cool under her bare flesh. Hender set the glass before her, stepped back. "Thanks," she said. lifting it to her lips. As he turned to round the table, she caught a glint of heavy metal dangling below his crotch—another PA. Was Raf pierced down there as well?

"What did Raf do to my—to Theo?"

Hender sat down. "Raf wants an American wife." Then Hender grinned broadly. Flickering light gleamed unhealthily on his teeth. "Well, actually, of course, he would prefer an American husband but the laws in your country mostly do not recognize that relationship and a husband could not help him emigrate. You aren't concerned about what he did to you?"

"Why? Why not me? I was a girl...before."

"He likes to complicate matters. You were too young. He felt you would enjoy being a boy."

"I do!" The response came without thought but thinking only reinforced it. "I don't want to go back. But Theo never wanted to be a girl. Or a gay boy, any man's husband."

"Are you certain?"

She wasn't.

"It's true that Theo was more effort to...persuade." Leaning forward—now the fluttering light made the design at his temple resemble blood, drawn in intricate patterns like the henna on an Indian bride's hands—Hender shrugged. A billow in the shadow behind him made Emmanuel think of great black wings flexing with his shrug. "In any case, Raf's altruism is erratic. He wasn't attracted to you. To your brother, yes."

"What *are* you? The two of you?"

"Three."

"Thijs too?" she blurted, dismayed.

"We have been here so long," murmured Hender, leaning back again. "But Thijs and I are relatively content. Of course, Thijs has no imagination. He lives in the moment—the future is an impossible destination for him. It would not have occurred to Thijs to take advantage of your possibilities before Raf manifested them. Raf—discontent defines him. It always has, longer than you can imagine. You see, we may not leave this place without a sincere invitation."

"It wouldn't be sincere!"

"Are you certain?" Hender asked again. "Raf has gone away before, several times. When the invitation expires, he must return. Not to America however. America interests him. He will be disappointed, of course, for all the world is an outskirt of America in this era, but one can't reason with him. Come."

When Hender rose to his feet the shadowy wings rose with him, pinions glittering like black knives. Emmanuel shrank back but he reached for her hand. His touch was chill, not like ice, colder, and she found herself upright, enfolded in his arms, his dank, oppressive wings that smelled like incense. "You make a handsome boy," he murmured in her ear.

They stood in the doorway of Raf's bedroom. Raf and Teddy lay on white sheets. Emmanuel looked away from her naked sister, looked back. Raf's arm, crooked over Teddy's rib cage as he spooned the young woman, lifted the breasts on Teddy's chest, made them look larger, misshapen. Matched cherry-blossom tattoos seemed to grow together, one plant joining two bodies. Teddy began to stir and Raf, in sleep, tightened his grasp and pressed his lips to Teddy's nape.

"It is not the time, Raf," Hender said. The regret in his low, shuddering voice caused the world to flinch. "This is not the person."

Shrugging off Raf's arm with less effort than he'd taken to toss Emmanuel into the canal, Theo sat upright. He threw his legs over the side of the bed and planted his feet on the carpet, set wide. Emmanuel looked away again: her little brother's dick, at rest, was bigger than hers.

"You were right," Theo said, his voice foggy. "It hurt. But it was interesting."

Behind him, Raf made a noise like ice breaking. Indigo wings thick as snowdrifts clapped, disturbing the air, lifted him. For just an eyeblink, Teddy became a girl again.

"Not now," said Hender.

"Theo?"

Ignoring or unaware of angelic perturbation, Theo scratched sleepily at the flame-eyed skull inscribed on his left biceps. "Not really interesting enough, though. No offense, Emmanuel, but I think I really am straight." He yawned, shuddering.

"I...I don't need the competition."

"Hah." Theo blinked. "Where's my clothes? We should go home. 'Rents probably shitting themselves with worry. Grounded for life," he grumbled, blinked again, looked up at his brother and, as if properly comprehending her nakedness, glanced his eyes away. "Where's *your* clothes? Did you have fun with wotzisname?"

Raf made another noise, like air collapsing, and settled back onto the bed. Theo shifted his seat unconsciously as the mattress settled. Great blue-black wings cloaked crouching Raf, abstracting him from sight. A fierce itch flared under the skin inside Emmanuel's arm, but then was gone.

"But I *liked* Emmanuel!" protested Thijs.

So did I, Emma wanted to say. Her throat was frozen with disappointment and relief. She felt uncomfortable naked in a way she hadn't a moment before.

Thijs's wings were dull scarlet, not as impressive as Hender's or Raf's. His erection had been impressive but it wilted, dragged down by the weight of its metal, as he glared fiercely at the girl who had been Emmanuel. "He was handsome. And an excellent fuck."

Emma felt another intolerable itch, but this erupted between her legs and when she reached to scratch it, horribly, trivially embarrassed, Emmanuel discovered his own proper prick hanging where it should. He clutched it in his hand. The heavy surgical-steel Prince Albert was chill, but warmed against his fingers.

It wasn't nearly as late as they'd thought. Light hung in the west. As they walked the towpath back to the dentist's and professor's house, Theo asked, his voice merely curious, "Are you going to see him again?"

"Thijs?" Emmanuel shrugged, amused. "Probably. We're here another four weeks. Not a professional visit, though, it's not like I want him piercing anything else."

"Yikes."

Theo wanted not to sound appalled by his brother's adventure in body modification, Emmanuel thought without being fooled. He'd *offered* to show the pretty thing to Theo.

"What about you? Going back to Hender?"

"Of course!" Craning his neck, Theo tried to look at his own arm. His shirtsleeve hid the ink, though, and he stumbled. "It's not done yet! But *I'm* not interested in fooling around with him."

"He wouldn't mind, probably."

"No." Great sincerity thrummed in Theo's voice. "I mean, I've had moments of curiosity since...since you told me you were gay, but it's just not my thing."

Emmanuel scratched at his jaw. His stubble wasn't novel anymore but it still felt good. "Just as well," he said. "More boys for me."

"Seriously?" Theo was outraged. "You seriously think any guy wants into my shorts is going to be interested in a big hairy dude like you?" He threw a punch at his brother's arm that made basically no impression. "Manny, bro, even I know better than that."

Manny? As they scuffled, Emmanuel decided this new nickname was acceptable. "Fine, whatever." Grappling Theo around the neck, he knuckled his brother's bristly scalp.

"Besides, you've already got a summer fling goin' on. Now you need to help me find a girl. That's what gay big brothers are for, evolutionarily speaking."

Laughing, Manny pushed Theo away. "You're on." He relished a challenge.

A few minutes later, Theo said, "You know, I've been thinking. About how Simon wanted so much to impress me with his stupid kanji."

"*Happiness puppies.*"

Theo barked a laugh. "Of course, I wouldn't have got my act together to decide what I really wanted if Simon wasn't such a dick about the pain, the *horrifying pain,* and how brave he was. But it wasn't me he was really trying to impress."

"Don't say it," said Manny. He tried to remember what Simon looked like, if he was as tiresome as Theo.

Envoi

In late summer of 2009, I resolved to write a short story or die trying. This after nearly a decade in which I completed no fiction at all except by accident, and then a surprising year that produced a novella (since published as *The New People*) and related novelette ("Jannicke's Cat," reprinted here) but nothing, still, that wasn't intended as part of an ill fated larger project.

Inspiration and goad for that resolution was the estimable, capricious Mr Steve Berman, writer, editor, publisher, then a new friend. Who knew how far we would come together?

...Not that kind of together. Get your minds out of the gutter. I'm too old for Steve.

But not, as you have noticed, dead yet. I wrote that first story and, in the two-plus years since, quite a number more. Steve has been first reader for all, sensitive and demanding critic, cheerleader, and—all too often—comforter of the dejected. And now he insists on publishing a book of them.

Thanks, then, to Steve (who really ought to doff his publisher hat more often in favor of the writer hat) and his tutelary genius, Daulton.

My gratitude also to the editors who originally published some of these stories: Gordon Van Gelder (*F&SF*); Christopher Fletcher (*M-Brane SF*); Steve Berman again (*Icarus*, *Boys of Summer*, and *The Touch of the Sea*); Jameson Currier (*Chelsea Station*); Ann Leckie (*GigaNotoSaurus*). Thanks, as well, to patient early readers, including Kevin Borchers, Betty Harrington, Kevin Maskrey and Vincent Rhodes, Sandra McDonald, and Damon Shaw.

about the author

ALEX JEFFERS has published one full-length novel, *Safe as Houses*; two short novels, *Do You Remember Tulum?* and *The New People*; and a novel-length story sequence, *The Abode of Bliss*; as well as many works of short fiction in multiple genres. "Firooz and His Brother" was short-listed for the Gaylactic Spectrum Award and reprinted in *Wilde Stories 2009: The Year's Best Gay Speculative Fiction* (Steve Berman, ed) and *The Year's Best Science Fiction & Fantasy 2009* (Rich Horton, ed). "The Arab's Prayer" appears in *Wilde Stories 2012*.

When not writing or not-writing or attempting—with unseemly resentment and not much success—to earn an honest living, he designs, lays out, and occasionally proofreads books for Lethe Press and others. He is the editor of BrazenHead, an imprint of Lethe dedicated to publishing exceptional novellas of queer speculative fiction.

A recovering Californian, he lives in New England with two grumpy cats (Miss Jane Austen and Miss Charlotte Brontë) and thinks *often* about relocating to more salubrious climes.

sentenceandparagraph.com

CPSIA information can be obtained at www.ICGtesting.com
Printed in the USA
BVOW021434050712

294409BV00001B/51/P